Down By The Riverside

Down By The Riverside

ELLIS J. LAW

Library of Congress Cataloging–In–Publication Data

Name: Law, Ellis J., author.
Title: By The Riverside/Elllis J. Law

ISBN: 978-1-63960-040-3 **Paperback**
        978-1-63960-039-7 **Hardcover**
        978-1-63960-041-0 **eBook**

Published in the United States by Pen2Pad Ink Publishing.

Requests to publish work from this book or to contact the author should be sent to: ellisjlawbooks@gmail.com

Down By The Riverside

DEDICATION

To all the women who inspired me: your resilience, your smiles, your belief in a little black girl who was too smart and too black for her own good; your legacy lives in me.

To my pretty baby: I promised to make you proud. I hope that I have. With all the love in my heart, and for all the times we laughed together, cried together, and supported one another, with you still being my driving force, I do this for you. Your name will live forever, Kenidi La'Nay Scott. I love you.

PROLOGUE

"There she go," someone shouted from the porch. Whispers ripped through the crowd as hushed warnings passed from lip to lip.

A figure emerged in the distance, once the beacon of light in their community, now a mere shadow of her former self.

"Who?" questioned a young man, as he stood looking towards the field that separated their town from the body of water that lived at its edge.

"Charlette! She's coming down the hill now," came the worried reply.

"River's coming? Everyone, go inside," the young man's urgency echoed through the square, a sense of unease settling over the crowd.

With each step, her bare feet beat against the worn dirt road, a mournful cadence marking her approach to the town that once revered her. The once pristine white linen of her dress now clung to her form, weathered by time and hardship. Her long, thick, curls, once a crown of glory, now tangled and windswept, danced off the nape of her neck, sailing in the breeze.

"He leads me, He holds me, He guides me down the path of salvation. He stirs me towards the road of righteousness. It is through Him that I have my strength. It is by God that I have my power" she muttered. Her voice was low and firm. No one within four feet could make out what she was saying, but they knew she was praying. Everyone knew she was praying. "He leads me, He holds me, He guides me down the path of salvation..."

"She down 'nat hill now. She'll be home soon. Reverend Dex'll get her." Hop called out.

There was a time, not even two years ago, when the people of Freedman adored Charlette. She was the crown jewel of their small colored town–the epitome of beauty and grace with the kindest soul. She was one of those rare people who was genuinely loved by everyone. You knew her heart's intention the moment you met her, and her heart's intention was always shockingly and inspiringly pure.

Her parents named her Charlette, but everyone called her "River." That name seemed to suit her better because that's where you could find her most of the time outside of town, across the fields, through the trees, and sitting next to the New George River. It was her favorite place to be, a sanctuary where she found solace and safety. It was also where she felt closest to God. It was the sense of being enveloped in divine grace that captivated her heart most, it's what called her to the water.

This was her daily routine. It nourished her, it kept her fulfilled. From the time she was seven or eight years old, River would sit next to the New George and fiercely prayed by the water. She heard His voice — God's voice. As clearly as the day was long, River heard the voice of her maker. She heard Him just as well as she could hear her mother calling her name. When she saw even just the edge of the flowing, murky water, she heard the voice of the Divine.

"It's funny int'nit?" Hop stated.

"What?" Henry Stitts replied.

"How much the water's changed her."

CHAPTER 1

"River's blessed," Pastor Hendricks Johnson proclaimed. "She ain't out here foolin' around and following some silver-tongued devil, and she ain't out her singing on some godforsaken record. She has that voice and a heart of gold to match it. God's gonna use her, Cee Cee. The Lord has big plans for her, and she knows it."

River didn't know anything. She knew that the Pastor was sitting in her daddy's seat at their table, and he shouldn't be. As much as she loved and adored Pastor Johnson, he didn't add anything to their household, and didn't deserve to be sitting at the head of her daddy's kitchen table. In addition to that, River also knew that her mother's hospitality was just a shallow attempt at getting on the Pastor's good side, and she knew that at some point, Eddie Hendricks was going to come up. Cecilia, River's mother, smiled and blushed as she laid a full plate of food in front of Pastor Johnson. River's mouth fell open. Her mother shot her a short, but expressive look. Cecilia cooked like this every day, so it truly was no trouble, but she and River both knew that if her husband walked through the door, the wrath of God would fall upon them all.

It wasn't that Cleo, River's father, would be jealous of his wife cooking for another man, or that he didn't like sharing, but he was protective of his family. Part of his protectiveness was a sense of rationality and frugality. Work was hard to come by in their small town. He was lucky that the old railway needed renovation–it was the only reason he was able to find work so close to home. Otherwise, he'd have to pack up and find work in Savannah, or somewhere farther, to feed his family. The Montgomery family didn't have the luxury of being hospitable, or at least not his mind. But Cecilia was a proper Southern woman, and no Southern woman would allow her guest to leave her home hungry.

"Now, Cecilia, this is too much," the Pastor said. "Two fried eggs, ham, green tomatoes, and some biscuits with buttermilk? Girl, I'm a widowed man. Don't tempt me with your hand in marriage because I'll ask for it." He laughed as he leaned over the plate rubbinghis round stomach with anticipation. River could only imagine her father's rage if he saw this play out.

Pastor Johnson was the only colored Pastor for 10 miles on their side of Georgia. His father before him held the same title. There was no doubt his son, Edwin-Hendricks, would be a minister soon too. As far as anyone could tell, Johnson men had a calling on them. There would be a long line of clergymen in their lineage if the past or present were any indication of the future. The minister's father built their church when Pastor Johnson was still little Hendricks. The word of God was in his blood.

"Oh, Pastor, it's nothing. Cleo works nights down at the train station, so breakfast is our supper, in a way," she said with a nervous grin. "It was going to be made anyway."

Truth be told, Cecilia was nervous about Cleo coming home before the Pastor had the chance to make it at least half way through his breakfast, among other things. She looked over to her daughter and winked. She had hoped that the gesture could distract River from the inevitably of their conversation. Cecilia didn't know why she felt so skittish. They had this same conversation a hundred times, if not more, but something about this summer felt different. Something about this summer felt final.

"Call me Hendricks when we're outside of the church, Cee Cee, I been knowing you too long to allow formalities," he started. "But I have to be honest: I didn't come here to eat your husband and daughter's food. But I did come to ask you about Miss Charlette here."

"Charlette? Calling River by her real name sounds very formal to me," Cecilia expressed surprisingly. She tugged on her tightly closed robe and eased down into a chair. Her brows were furrowed, but her eyes were glowing–it was happening.

River's stomach knotted as she slouched down into her seat. She wanted to slide down the back of the chair and onto the floor because she knew exactly what he wanted to talk about. Edwin-Hendricks was just Eddie to her. He was her best friend, her brother even, but their parents had been urging them to date since they were fifteen years old.

"Mama, I don't feel too good. Can I be excused?" she asked. River covered her face with a heavy hand, extending her neck over the seat and her hair flopped backward. She felt as if she had rocks weighing her head down. It wasn't a lie because River didn't lie, but she was exaggerating. She *could* sit through breakfast and listen to her mother plan her wedding alongside Pastor Johnson, but she would have a headache from the discussion. The knots in her stomach pulled tighter as she peeked out of her fingers, locking eyes with her mother who clearly had no intentions of excusing her.

"Don't be rude, Charlette. Pastor Jonhson has something to ask you. I'm sure we all know what it is," Cecilia said, sitting high in her chair. Her back had straightened. Her nerves had subsided. This was it; Pastor Johnson was about to ask River to court Eddie this summer. He was about to ask for her, and Cleo's Blessing, to get the two of them together, it was going to work this summer. She could feel it.

Pastor Johnson opened his mouth to speak, but was interrupted. Everyone's mood changed as the sound of a rich, heavy voice filled the air, River smiled. She loved that heavy, blue-sounding voice. She loved its richness and the way it shook your soul.

"Sounds like Brother Cleo is coming. In perfect timing too—God's timing!" Pastor Johnson said as he pushed back in the chair to stand up beginning to button his coat. Cleo Montgomery was a beautiful man. Handsome wasn't enough to describe him. He was tall and wide with skin the color of molasses. He was intimidating to look at, but it was hard to pull your eyes away. There was a hardness to him that couldn't be ignored, but River softened even the toughest parts of him. Just the sight of her made him smile. The singing grew louder as he came closer. Everyone was on their feet and watching the door.

"Daddy!" River flew across the room landing in his big, bear arms. Cleo held her in one hand, his boots in another.

"What's going on here, family? Pastor" he asked. He glanced over the expressions of everyone in the room before fixating on his petite wife. It was happening. He knew it as soon as his eyes skimmed over Pastor Johnson. He was here to ask for his daughter's hand in marriage to the Pastor's siddity-ass son. Cecilia smiled nervously back at him. "Looks like breakfast started without me," he said, walking from their side door further into the kitchen.

"I came to speak to you and River, and Cee Cee too of course." Pastor Johnson explained.

"Her name's Cecilia, but gon' on." Cleo sat on the edge of the warm stove.

"Well, River, Charlette, I mean, is growing older by the year. More beautiful and somehow sweeter with age but older nonetheless." Pastor Johnson explained with a smile in River's direction.

"Alright. So you want her to go with your son, then, huh?" Cleo asked through a sly grin. He shot a wink at River while smirking at his wife. Cecilia's arms were crossed, her foot anxiously tapping. Already she could sense that her daughter and husband were about to undermine her well planned ploy to see her daughter married. Cleo and River were two peas in a painfully annoying pod. River was obedient to a fault, but she was a daddy's girl through and through. If Cleo said no, then it was a no; if Cecilia said no, then it was a no *until daddy* said otherwise. I'm just submitting to the head of the household, Mama. Please don't be mad at me.' River would say. 'She's just obeying her daddy, Cee Cee. She ain't doing nothin' wrong.' Cleo would ring in support.

"Well, yes," Pastor Johnson answered. "I think they'll be a fine pair. You know Edwin-Hendricks is in college and will be home for the summer soon. I reckon that's the perfect time for them to court and be married."

"Married? To Eddie?!" River shouted. Her face turned beet red under her warm brown skin. She felt as if she had all but melted into a puddle in her chair. She knew better than to talk out of turn when adults were speaking, but the thought of marrying Eddie was both funny and scary to her. How could she marry Eddie? How could she be a good wife to him? She wouldn't listen to a word he said, she could never obey him, she could never take him seriously. She'd seen him cry too many times; she'd seen him naked too many times. They laughed too hard together, argued too often. He was better off as a friend. The thought of him being more, well that was unsettling for River.

"She might as well be nineteen now, Cleo, this is the best way to make sure no simple man comes calling after her," Cecilia interjected. "Edwin's smart, he's polite, and we know he's God-fearing. He'll probably become a Pastor himself. Don't you want your daughter to marry a pastor?"

Her husband had moved from the stove to where she had just been sitting, and his playful grin was now a scowl. He hated these conversations. Every summer since River was about twelve years old, some boy or old man would come around to promise land or fortune for River's hand in marriage. It made him sick to his stomach: old men wanting to marry a child; young, stupid boys who hadn't even bought their own pair of drawers yet offering to take care of his baby girl. He hated it. The trails of raising a beautiful daughter. The burden of sheltering unadulterated beauty.

"It jus' make tha most sense, Brother Cleo," Pastor Johnson spoke to Cleo confidently but was cautious not to set him off. "Your River here has been one of God's greatest soldiers since she was knee high. I know grown ah-dults who don't have as much faith as this young girl. Imagine how blessed the entire township of Freedman would be if they had E.H. and River to turn to in times of need! We all seen tha things yo' baby girl is capable of, and with Eddie's education and knowledge of the word, they'd be a force! The two of 'em dere!"

Cleo had seen the things River could do. They all had. There was nothing like it. If it had not been for the realness of God, Cleo would be scared of his daughter. Her capabilities were beyond a normal believer's. River was just shy of being a miracle worker. Neither rootwork nor witchcraft could hold a candle to things his daughter could do. And Eddie was smart, respectable too. Who else in Freedman was good enough for his daughter? Who else would she marry?

"I'll say this: Charlette's fixin' to be nineteen this May. She ain't no young thing but she not a old maid neither. Let her live her life comfortably with her Pa and Ma until *she* decides who she want to marry. How dat sound?" Cleo asked.

Cecilia threw her arms up in defeat before fixing her husband a plate of food. She knew that the conversation was over as far as Cleo was concerned, and she knew River would have no contest to them closing the discussion. There was no winning. Their daughter would live and die as an unwed virgin if Cleo and River had their way. Cecilia always wanted more than that for River, but she was just an outsider. She was only the mother of the house. She had no real say in the going-ons of her daughter's life.

"She's a good girl. I trust that she'll lean in the way of the Lord's will," Pastor Johnson began. He grabbed a tomato and patted himself with his free hand. "I suspect I've worn my welcome, so I will bid you, Montgomery family, a farewell, and make my way to the church."

The tall, round man limped his way off their porch and up the road, heading toward his church on the edge of town. River was relieved to have made it to the other side of that conversation. She could finally make her way to the New George and have her daily conversation with God.

"You gets a rise out of embarrassin' me, don't cha?" Cecilia said. She dropped a large plate of food in front of her husband and began to walk away. She didn't even take a full step before her husband grabbed her wrist and pulled her into his lap.

"You makes it so easy to embarrass." Cleo leaned into her neck as she squirmed and blushed in his lap before continuing. "I only want to make the right decision for my family, and I believe that don't involve no outside word from a man who don't bring money into this house. Pastor or not."

"She's ruint, you know? Charlette ain't no good when you 'round. She's spoiled 'cause you spoils her."

Cleo laughed. He knew his wife was serious. She said it lightheartedly, but she truly believed that their Charlette was spoiled. She had raised her concerns to Cleo more than once in the past, but he always shut down the idea of their daughter being so used to getting her way that she was rude and disrespectful. River wasn't spoiled, she was supported. He supported her. And if River didn't want to run off and marry E.H. Johnson, then Cleo supported her decision not to jump the broom with him.

"Our daughter 'The Saint' is ruint and spoiled? Okay, Cee Cee," he declared as he lifted her out of his lap. He placed his hand on the small of her back and rested his head on her stomach. "I can be the bad guy who turned our precious girl into a wicked old witch with no man and no babies." Cleo laughed as his wife yanked away from him and started to clean their small kitchen.

He knew how much it meant to Cecilia that River lived better than they did. She wanted her to live in Atlanta and go to the girl's school they heard about, but they couldn't afford to send her. None of them had heard of a scholarship until Eddie had his, but by then it was too late. Cleo wanted the best for their daughter too, but he wanted her to maintain her happiness. He didn't want anyone to use her innocence against her. Her heart was pure and he didn't want anyone to manipulate that, not even her mother or their pastor. If River said she heard God, he believed her, and he wanted God's voice to be the only voice that guided her decisions.

"My angel. My saint. My pride and joy. Do you want to marry that Johnson boy?" Cleo asked River. She came around the corner fully dressed and ready to leave.

"I love him, Daddy, I do. But he's my friend. I don't love him that way. Don't reckon I ever will." She continued to braid her ponytail. "I just don't think the Lord made me to feel that way. I don't want it. I don't want no husband. I don't want children to run behind. Daddy I just don't want it." River leaned over her father's shoulder as he began to eat. She kissed the back of his head and rested her cheek against his rough hair. "You know Mama let him sit in yo' seat too, right?" River giggled.

"Charlette!" Cecilia jumped and turned around in one swing, while placing her fists on her hips. She swatted River's backside with a wooden spoon and pushed her towards the door.

"Gon' nie! Go talk to trees and pray to the grass. Pray yo' daddy don't break a pan over my head since ya wanna run ya fat mouth!" Cecilia shouted the words as she pushed her daughter towards their front door. The family erupted with laughter as River and her mother struggled through the door and off the porch. River turned and smiled at her mother before placing her arms around her neck in a loving embrace.

"You's a crazy woman, Mama. I love you as much I as I love the sun." She kissed her mother's cheek and began her trek to the New George River. On the other side of town, through the trees that were too bare to be called a proper 'woods' there sat her safe haven. A flowing stream of water that was no more than eight feet wide and 10 feet deep, at the deepest end.

River left that day with a smile on her face and a prayer in her heart. She skipped some and walked some, but the whole time she sang hymns in her silky voice. River always felt guilty when she thought of her local reputation. River: the girl who could turn sinner to saint with just her voice. The girl who never did any wrong. The pure-of-heart beauty queen who was not only humble but also gracious. Charlette 'River' Montgomery: God's Certified Favorite.

River never felt like she had a gift or a grand plan ordained by God. She didn't feel anything. She didn't want anything except to do what was right. She never felt any gold in her heart, and she never saw a sinner grow wings. She was just doing as she was told. She was just listening for God's voice.

CHAPTER 2

River made it to town and was ready to speak to everyone before going down to the New George. She smiled when she saw the general store because she knew old men were out back lying.

"Now int the Lord funny? River, whatchu doin' in here gal?" Pastor Johnson asked.

River gave him a weak smile and a side hug with it. "I'm on my way to the river and stopped in to see if Hop Wilson or Mr. Jenkins were in here." She answered politely.

He stretched his belly forward and tugged at his lapels. "Nie, River, you know those men are heathens, right? The Lord tells us to love thy neighbor, but some folk needs to be loved on from afar." River hung her head and played with the dirt under her boot as he spoke. Pastor Johnson took two fingers and lifted her chin. "I'd hate to see a girl as beautiful and holy as you be lowered by the likes of simple men."

His smile sent a chill down River's spine. If she didn't know any better, she would have thought someone had just slipped ice down her dress. She knew that smile. She had seen it so many times before, but never on Pastor Johnson. She tried to catch her breath and address the man before she could say more, but her attempts fell short of success.

"I promised Mitsy I would never remarry, but if I can't get you and Eddie to take up vows, I'll may make yo' daddy an offer he'd be a fool to refuse," the Pastor announced with a wink.

River jumped backward and landed on her heel. She stumbled a little and fell on a barrel of rice. She turned around and was greeted by the sight of Pastor's belly heaving up and down as he laughed at her clumsiness.

"Oh, girl I'm just foolin' witcha! I'm an old man. I can't handle no young gal. Mitsy was the only woman I vowed to love and that won't ever change. You's so pretty though. E.H. knows it, and he loves you. You knows it too, and I knows you love him. I just gotta get you two to realize that sometimes a husband and wife don't recognize each other as such until they're deep in the swing of marriage." He leaned over the glass counter at the register and called Mr. Brooks over with a nod. Mr. Brooks came to the register and spoke to Pastor Johnson. He smiled at River and nodded his head towards the back.

"Hop an' nem back dere, River. Gon' on and speak," Mr. Brooks said in an attempt to save River. He cut a piece of chewing tobacco for the Pastor then spoke to River again. "We know you gon' speak to everybody in the square 'for you go to the water. Make yo' rounds, baby." River smiled at him with gratefulness in her eyes.

She winked at the store keeper before skipping off to the back of the store. When she reached the back door, she heard men and women laughing together. She smiled at the sound. The sound of community and laughter sounded like God too. The sound of togetherness and love.

"YOU'S A LIE! YOU'S A LIE! YOU'S A DAMN LIE!" Mr. Jenkins yelled. He rose to his feet, nearly falling over. River almost went down with him, but she found her footing and saved them both the embarrassment. She lifted him to his feet and gave him a warm hug. Mr. Jenkins shook her from side to side as he laughed a big laugh in her ear.

"Girl you's a saint just like dey say." He released her from the hug and planted his hands on her shoulder. He smiled, took a deep breath, and admired her for her beauty and her grace. "My God, today. Cee Cee was a pretty little thing herself, but she couldn't hold no candle next to you girl." He gave her shoulders a small squeeze and another loving smile before he turned around and sat back on top of a wooden crate. He inched towards the edge and leaned over with his elbow on his knee.

Mr. Jenkins was a kind old man whose skin was like dark brown leather. Weathered and ashy and decorated with thick silver hair. He wasn't a smart man, but he was a good one. He didn't have a family anymore since his sons moved down to Florida. His wife died about fifteen years ago, and his sons left shortly after. Mr. Jenkins didn't leave with them because Freedman was the only home he knew outside of the plantation he was born on. He was only two years old when slavery ended. His father was one of the founding members of the township of Freedman, Georgia. That was his favorite story to tell and the only one nobody questioned. Mr. Jenkins lied about a lot of things but never about that or how much he loved his wife Robbie.

"Go on, nie, River. You done came in and saved this old man's life," Hop said. Hop Wilson was one of River's favorite people in the whole town of Freedman, Georgia. She loved him and she knew she shouldn't have. But she couldn't help it. He was funny. He drank more than he should have and he was known to keep the company of a woman–or two; River even heard he found a way to keep the company of three women at once after partying on the edge of Savannah, but she always figured that was the work of small-town boredom, though she wouldn't put it past him.

Hop was loved by most people except her father, who she knew secretly liked him too. Whether they realized it or not everyone had the same thoughts about him that they had about her. That he too was one who kept the town together. He was the voice of the people. His jossing and scoring and ability to make someone laugh was what people needed. In River's eyes, he was the town hero. She was just someone who knew how to pray.

"If you wasn't dere we'd probably be diggin' a hole and singing in celebration right nie," Hop continued. He struggled to hide a smile as he spoke but failed to disguise how humored he was by himself. The young woman in his lap slapped her hand across his chest and jokingly told him to hush. "Naw I won't neither. Dat damn Jenkins so old the fall woulda kilt him. Nigga woulda hit the flo' and seen God right den. My Lord, this is a old man. Nigga look like a damn mule. Ugly bastard."

River tried to hide her laugh, but her smile was so bright that it couldn't be covered with a bed quilt over her head.

"Okay, now, Hop. Be nice. You know how I feel about playing the dozens," River said as she leaned into a side hug from Mr. Jenkins. She rested her hip on his boney shoulder, and he curved his arm around her small waist. His balled fist rested squarely on her hip, waiting to swing if he or River were scorned enough. "I don't want to hear another word, here? Not about Mr. Jenkins." she demanded.

"That's why I tell you to gon' on. Nie git! Gon on from round here, girl. Go!" he shouted. The men and women all burst into laughter as River rose and threw her arms up in defeat.

"I only came to see you anyway Mr. Jenkins. I ain't studin' none of them," she said to her old friend before giving him a parting hug. She walked away with a switch of her hip and began to enter the store.

Shelly Hicks rose from Hop's lap and followed behind her. "River, baby, do me a favor and pray for my Ma. I'd do it myself, 'cept I'on think the Lord hears me anymore. He knows I give 'em every reason not to listen to me."

This happened to River often. People always stopped her and shared their prayer requests. She had a reputation of being what Mitsy Johnson would call "a waymaker." Every believer in Freedman knew it was true that He answered the prayers of those who were His children, but she was different. There was no waiting period after River's prayers. There were no seasons of silence. No need to fast or seek God's face. If she prayed for it, then it was in God's will. When your knees were bruised and weakened from all the time you spent praying with no answer. When the root didn't stick, when you were ready to give up and let go, River was the person you sought. It was as if she were God's interim when He was busy helping others. River hated this myth. She was just like everyone else. She told people all the time, but they never heard her. She explained that faith the size of a mustard seed was enough to will anything, but her words fell on deaf ears. People were more attracted to the thought of her being a biblical deity amongst them than were to believe that she was just a woman of radical faith.

Just as River broke a smile, she noticed Shelly wringing her hands and twisting her fingers as she spoke. People's embarrassment was the worst part. She wasn't a saint like they all claimed, and Shelly definitely wasn't unworthy of God's grace. There was no need to feel ashamed or embarrassed or guilty around River. But she knew saying that wouldn't do anything for Shelly. So, she outstretched her hand and grabbed Shelly's wrist. "Come tell me what's ailing your Ma. I'll send up a good one for her."

Shelly was just a year or two older than River. They used to be good friends until Shelly was caught with Mr. Jenkins' youngest son one night. It was the same summer Shelly turned thirteen. Ronald was seventeen years old and should have known better than to be friendly with girls who still wore pigtails and bloomers under their dresses. But he didn't.

Everyone knew about what happened between them. No one ever let Shelly forget either. Still, she loved Ronald and Ronald loved her too, or so he said. Shelly's father had left their family when she was still very young, but her mother did a wonderful job at playing both roles. When the whispers finally made their way to the Hicks' doorstep, Mrs. Hicks put an end to Ronald and Shelly.

They stopped seeing each other for a whole year until Ron snuck by Shelly's window one night and told her that he couldn't breathe without her. Ronald was almost nineteen and engaged to his brother's wife's sister. The sisters lived just outside of Savannah and had more money than anyone in Freedman could ever think of having. His fiancé was a bonafide yellow-bone too. That night by Shelly's window she asked him what he wanted out of her when he had a high yellow fiancé with silky hair. "She don't fuck like you do," he said candidly. The words rendered Shelly speechless. She sat there, laid there, left silent beneath her window, a word never spoken.

The whole time Ronald was with her, she replayed his words, mulling over everything each word meant. What every word implied. He didn't notice her unresponsive body. He didn't acknowledge the awkward silence that covered them like a blanket of shame. He got what he came for and married his yellow-bone wife the next week. Shelly became pregnant, and her fate was sealed. She would never be anything else for the rest of her life or at least as long as she stayed in Freedman. She was, and always would be, Shelly Hicks: the girl who fucks good.

Shelly squeezed both of River's hands. "My Ma is real sick, River, and nobody knows why. I've turned to everyone. Dr. Bailey said it's punishment for what happened to my baby. I asked Mrs. Gray to do some rootwork and give her somethin' that'll heal her, but she say my Ma's pass savin." Shelly started crying.

River wrapped her arms around the girl's waist and embraced her warmly. "River, I'm not ready to be without my Ma. I can't live without my Mama, I can't do it. I just can't." The two girls stood in the corner of the store and held each other. They didn't know who was using who for strength, but they stood that way until Shelly could speak again. "River, you know I didn't mean for my baby to die, right? God knows that, don't he?"

"He knows that."

Shelly's baby was born but he didn't live long. Not even a full month. Shelly did everything she could to take care of her baby, but he wouldn't latch. Mrs. Hicks tried to help her, Mitsy Johnson came over and prayed, but the baby would not, perhaps could not, consume a thing. Shelly named him Abel. It was biblical and Abel was a good, obedient child. I guess it never dawned on her how short a life Abel lived. Not until her son was twenty days old, blue mouthed, and cold. No one in Freedman had ever seen a coffin so small. No one in Freedman ever wanted to see one that small again. And just like before, rumors about Shelly spread, and she was the girl who had a baby so young she didn't even know how to take care of it.

Shelly accepted her fate after that. She embraced her reputation with open arms–and legs. That was who she was, all she'd ever be.

"Why don't he show me that he know it, den? Why I'm still sufferin'?" Shelly asked in defeat and frustration. River pulled the girl by her waist, bringing her closer. She looked at her squarely and spoke honestly.

"Shelly, you are grown. You have free will. You got to stop searching for Ronald in old men like Hop Wilson!" River was surprised by her own boldness. Shelly pulled away. She pressed her lips tightly, pointed her finger and started to step backwards from River.

"Don't do dat, River. Don't judge me. You better den dat River Montgomery, you are not like dat. You are not like dem!" Shelly's body touched the wall behind her, giving her the security to feel the tremor in her bones, the weakness in her knees. She slid down the wall, curling herself into a tight ball. She weeped quietly into her fists, shaking her head to rid it of her thoughts. River stomped towards Shelly and grabbed the girl's knees. She lifted Shelly's head.

"Looka here, nie. I would never cast judgment on someone when I have no authority to do so. I ain't got no heaven or hell to put you in. That's God." River explained with a shrug of her shoulders. "And it's God you have to talk to. It's God who gives you grace and shows you mercy. Nie, I ain't calling you no bad person and I ain't saying you need to be no different, but Shelly you can't keep doing this to yo' self. You can't keep putting ya self through this, you hear?"

River stood up and stretched her hand out to Shelly but the offer to help her up was swatted away. Shelly looked River in the eyes. She saw something fierce in River. Something powerful. It pierced her soul and shattered her ego. Her plan was to tell River that she was jealous because she had never been touched by a man. Despite being the prettiest colored girl in Georgia, River would never know the comfort laying in the arms of a man. She was going to tell her that she was so pure that she may as well have been damaged. No man would ever want to have the burden of being the one who defiled little miss Holy. Shelly's plans were to humiliate River. To make her feel as ashamed as she did, but when she looked into River's eyes she saw someone who was unshakable. Someone who could not be moved.

"River, are you gon' pray for my Ma or not?" she asked.

"I'mon pray for you both," River replied. With that, River walked out the store and through town while waving at everyone she passed. She let out a few "Heys" and "Goin' to the New George" every now and then, but the episode with Shelly left her not wanting to speak to anyone, not entirely. It left her thinking about herself too.

*"Why did I say that to her?... She needed to hear it. She needed someone to tell her that these old men ain't Ronald and she needed to realize that Ronald ain't no catch neither." River

thought to herself.

And the voice in her head made sense, but she still felt bad. It wasn't like her to be so blunt. Her words didn't feel like they were cruel, but they were harsh. They were unfiltered. They were brazened. Shelly came to her in need, and River responded from a place of frustration. That wasn't fair.

River tried not to think too hard about it. She was having a good day. There was no need to let a little spat with Shelly Hicks distract her. She'd gotten out of the "marry Eddie" conversation and that alone was enough to be grateful for. As she moved closer to the New George, she could hear the water crashing into itself as it folded over and hit rocks. She saw the tall grass that gathered at the bank and the reflection of the sun gleaming off of the water. River heard God loud and clear.

He was in the sound of the crickets, and in the croak of frogs. His voice could be heard in the cry of the locusts and in the buzz of horse flies. Sometimes, when she was down by the stream, she heard him in the flop of the fish that liked to jump up to feel the air every now and then. God spoke to her through nature. The sounds in the small things were a direct form of communication from Him. Every day she heard those sounds, she considered herself in His good graces. This was her absolute favorite place to be.

The grass is dry for it to be April, River thought. She searched for a place to sit near the water. Rarely did she ever actually slip into the New George. It was the presence of nature and the smell of the earth that she found comfort in, not necessarily the water itself–the tranquility and comeliness of creation is what she reveled in.

River crossed her legs and closed her eyes as she sat on tough, dry grass. She took a deep breath to let nature fill up her lungs. When she was ready to pray, she let out a deep sigh of reassurance. She turned her face towards the sky and felt the comforting sting of the sun on her perfect brown skin. Eddie told her once that her skin was like the color of thick honey in a jar after it had turned red from sitting in the sun. Ever since then, River always made sure to charge herself by letting the sun warm her honey-colored face.

She brought her head down to face the water before opening her eyes. When she looked up, she saw a little rabbit near the bank on the other side of the river. The rabbit's back was turned to the water. It kept looking between a wide tree with a hollow hole at its base, likely its home, and the riverbank. The small animal was fixated on the wet earth to its right, but River couldn't see what drew its attention. The rabbit hopped toward the tree, then stopped and turned around. It took two or three more tentative leaps toward home, then paused again, torn between the tree and the water.

River was curious about the game the little rabbit seemed to be playing and scanned the area for any other rabbits or bunnies that might be trailing behind. As she turned her head to the right, she spotted a water moccasin slithering from the water towards the rabbit. She jumped up, eyes wide, heart racing, watching the scene unfold. She wanted to yell at the little rabbit. Run! Go home! Get outta here! But no words came. Somehow, the rabbit must have sensed her desperate plea, for it suddenly snapped its head in her direction.

Run! Go! River whispered silently. It was as if they communicated telepathically, for just then, the rabbit bolted towards the tree. She had never seen a snake move so fast in her life; the water moccasin slithered after her new furry friend with terrifying speed.

River started towards the water but managed only two shaky steps. Run, little rabbit! Go! The rabbit paused and looked back, as if to acknowledge he heard her. Just as he prepared to leap forward, the snake struck, sinking its fangs into his neck. River collapsed to her knees.

"God bless the innocent and all whose souls' need You but

do not yet know it," she prayed. She opened her eyes and walked back to where she was before. Her heart was full, but she was not distracted from her work. She had prayers to make and requests to fulfill. She was late to her conversation with God. Death was inevitable, a tragic part of the story of life. Even with all the sorrow that surrounds it, death that it is, the earth still moves in the midst of it. As sad as she was, she knew life would go on, and just like the earth, she would not stop moving because Azrael had made a visit.

She sat again: legs crossed, eyes closed, and at the clearing near the water. She started off with her hands clapped in her lap, facing upwards like an antenna to the Lord.

"God…"

She spoke a prayer for her mother who worried too much, for her father who worked too hard, for those in need of love, and for those in need of strength. She kept her promise and prayed for Shelly and her mother. Then, she whispered another prayer for the rabbit too.

She felt an urge to feel the dirt and really connect with the earth. She stuck her hands in the ground and felt the grass between her fingers. The wind started to blow and the ground started to shake. The winds whipped around her forcefully grabbing the length of her hair, making it flow in the wind. The ground beneath her rumbled and quaked so intensely that she thought it would crumble under the palms of her hands. But she never stopped her prayer. She never let her imagination distract her from her work.

She prayed for the sinners of the world, the hypocrites who judged them in public but acted as the peers behind closed doors, for the children who died too young, and for this world that took them too soon. She turned her face back towards the sky and dug her fingers deep into the soil. Then for a second, just a second, she stopped praying.

Where is the ground? she wondered. Eyes still closed, she

shook her head, refocused her mind, and continued to pray once more. Her mind drifted further and further from the present and deeper into the words she said. She felt her body sway back and forward involuntarily as the Spirit moved within her. Her heart was pounding, her skin tingeled. She was being overcome by a wave of power she only felt when she had submitted her entire being to the Father, the Son, and the Holy Ghost. This was a possession; this was a capturing. She was no longer in control. River's heart fluttered with the joy being consumed by something bigger than she could ever imagine being. Her chest started to tighten, and her body became light, and she could feel the wind blowing beneath her.

Why do I feel the wind under me? River opened her eyes, and by God she was floating. Immediately she felt weak. Lightheaded from the realization. There was a heady mixture of exhilaration, fear, and disbelief that catapulted through her body, unconcerned for her physical wellbeing. This defied all the laws of nature, this defied everything that she knew. Her heart felt like it was being squeezed tighter and tighter, as if something wanted to deprive it of all its blood. Her eyes widened as felt her throat beginning to close. Frantically she searched for something, anything to save her from what was happening. Her eyes landed on the snake from earlier, recoiled and full. The undigested rabbit's body could be seen as a lump in the center of the scaly spiral the snake had made of itself. She wanted to cry, but River was using all the strength she had to try to force air into her lungs.

She closed her eyes and looked away. Her eyes shot open again, this time landing on a figure just beyond the trees, moving towards Freedman. It was at that moment, River remembered to pray. "The Lord is my shepherd; I shall not want…" she began. As the psalm flowed from the recesses of her mind, she floated slowly down to earth. It was the profession that even in the midst of death and darkness, she had nothing to fear that made her fill her lungs again. The acknowledgment that surely her soul would know the comfort of goodness and mercy, even when being confronted with the finality of death here on earth, that loosened the grip around her heart. "And I will dwell in the house of the Lord forever. Amen," she finished as her feet welcomed the heat of the dead grass beneath them.

River wasted no time heading back towards her home. She didn't stick around to ask questions, to ponder on what may have happened. She, quite literally, hit the ground running. Running towards town, running towards destiny unbeknownst to her.

"Have I lost my mind? Am I crazy? Oh my God. Did Shelly have Mrs. Gray put a root on me?" River thought to herself. That was it. That had to be the answer. Shelly done got someone to put her name in a jar. The realization sent River into a fit. A literal temper tantrum. As if she were three years old, River threw her hands up, stomped her feet and whined like a child right in the middle of the main road. Dead center in the center of town.

She kept this up until she felt arms wrapped around her. River's body stiffened from surprise, but melted from the comfort of the embrace. She looked up and saw the most beautiful man she had ever laid eyes on. More handsome than her father and more handsome than the men of the negro baseball team that stayed in Freedman last summer. He was beautiful. Simply beautiful. There was no other way to describe him.

"You okay dere, lil' missy? Look like something upsettin' ya, yeah?" He spoke through a side-lipped grin. River could only blink.

"I ain' mean to run into ya, nie. And I'on think either one of us was payin' attention," he said. He set River upright and placed her on her feet. He gave her a smile. It was lop-sided again, favoring the left side of his face. His teeth were big and white. He dressed like he had somewhere to be, like he was going to church or court or somewhere that called for a man to be in a tie and dress shoes on a Saturday afternoon.

"I'm – I'm alright, thank you kindly. I—I wasn't payin' attention, you're right. I—"

River stopped stuttering to look at the stranger again. Truth be told, she almost didn't think he was real. I mean, how could she trust her own senses after what just happened at the river. Was he real? The man smiled back at her, and all she could do was blush.

"Charlette?" A familiar voice caressed River's ear.

"Eddie?" River asked. Edwin-Hendricks stood on the porch of the store, dropping his bag when they locked eyes. He looked different. He was beautiful. But so was the stranger who still had his arms around her.

CHAPTER 3

Edwin-Hendricks Delroy Johnson. The son of a preacher and a future scholar. He was destined to be bigger than Freedman. According to his parents, it was prophesied that he would be the one to put this town on the map. To River, he was just little ol' Eddie. Eddie Johnson, her best friend. They knew each other all their lives. When they were very little, it wasn't uncommon for them to be bathed together. That's how well they knew each other. They sang in church beside one another every Sunday. They played outside together every evening. They both graduated highschool and got their diplomas together.

Mrs. Gray had an unmarried sister, Miss Tolbert, who was the town's elementary school teacher. Eddie and Charlette were her star pupils when they were children. Charlette was respectful and docile—always willing to listen and learn. E.H. was naturally smart and had a keen sense of curiosity, which allowed him to be very receptive to their lessons.

Before Pastor Johnson's father died and they moved into his home, the Johnson family lived relatively close to the Montgomery's. Cecilia and Mitsy would walk their children halfway to each other's houses and then send the pair of children up the main road to school. That daily pilgrimage to and from school nurtured Eddie's and River's friendship. They talked about what they learned in class and everything they witnessed when they were apart. They talked about Sunday School and why God wanted them to wear uncomfortable clothes to church. They talked about why they thought God made men of different races and complexions, why the cow says moo but the horse says neigh. They talked about any and everything that crossed their little minds, which forged a deep-found respect for one another.

They were always there for each other. When Rylo Evers pulled River's hair and spat in her face, for instance, Eddie was there to push him down and defend her honor. He got beat up for doing so, but he didn't care. River patched him up and walked him home as a thank you. And when River's daddy got angry at Mr. Brooks, then busted his lip, Eddie was in there in the store to hold her and cover her face, shielding her from the whole ordeal. River was always there for Eddie too. She was there when Pastor Johnson beat Eddie after catching him drinking hooch with the other boys, and she was there for him when his mother died of Pneumonia. River was even there after Eddie's first heartbreak when Eliza Hicks, Shelly's younger sister, rejected him.

"She don't want chu that way, Eddie, you wasting ya time," River explained to him as she followed him to the Hicks' home. Eddie had picked flowers from the road and marched up the dirt to the Hicks' family's house with his head held high.

"You just a silly, ol' girl, Charlette, you don't know nothin' bout no love!" he exclaimed proudly.

"Eliza's younger than me. She would know even less 'bout it than I do!" River was confused by Eddie's rationalization of the situation. She did not understand how his young mind worked. How had he determined that Eliza batting her lashes and smiling in his direction meant that she was ready for love.

"You didn't see the way she smiled at me."

"She smiled at you to sweet talk her way into a honey stick, and you fell for it."

He stomped his foot hard into the ground and turned to face his friend. "Letty, you workin' my nerves now, girl. Stop followin' me." They were about twelve years old at the time and River was taller than he was. Edwin-Hendricks was only three-months older than her, but she matured (and grew) faster than he did. He looked at the girl's perfect face and stared into her deep brown eyes. "Eliza is in love wit' me, and I'm askin' her if she wanna go with me to Miss Annie's house today. Whatchu got to do with me and some hoecakes, huh?" His eyes shot back and forward between each of hers. He was searching for something in her eyes, but he didn't know what it was that he was looking for exactly. River hung her head and started to play with one of her pigtails. She dug her bare toe into the dirt and swayed her body from left to right.

"We always go to Miss Annie's together, so I didn't think today was no different," she expressed shyly. Eddie walked over to her and put one hand on her shoulder.

"Letty, you know I wouldn't go to Miss Annie's or anywhere else without you. But there's some things a man has to do on his own. This here one of 'em, now. Gon' over there without me. Me and Eliza be there soon." He turned and walked away. He continued his march and left Charlette standing in the road tugging at her hair. River went to Miss Annie's where she would serve food and desserts in her backyard every second and fourth Saturday of the month. River sat on the porch leaning in Miss Annie's lap holding a glass of lemonade. She waited there for Eddie and Eliza to show up; serving tables, wiping chairs, all while waiting. Since River had longer hair than most people were used to seeing a little brown girl with, Miss Annie, like most women in Freedman, always wanted to comb it. By this age, River had gotten into enough trouble for letting other people play in her hair, so she asked Miss Annie to rub her scalp after everyone started to go home. Still, she waited.

"You sure it was here he said they was comin'?" Miss Annie asked as she stroked the front of the girl's head. River waited there for nearly three hours, and Miss Annie was only a 15-minute walk away. River watched Miss Annie serve about 50 people from this county and the next before the sun finally began to set. Finally, Eddie showed up puffy-eyed and alone.

"I know dat ain't E.H. Johnson showin' his face at sunset," Miss Annie began. "Had that pretty gal sittin' here all afternoon waitin' for you," Miss Annie proclaimed as the boy moped around the corner.

"Aw, Miss Annie, I ain't mean no harm. Can't you see I'm going through my first heartbreak?" Eddie said as he flopped on the wooden step at her back door. He looked at River with red, pleading eyes. He laid his head on her knee, and she cuffed the nape of his neck. He closed his eyes and covered his face while River sang some of their favorite hymns. Everyone who was left in the backyard slowly stopped chattering and started to listen or harmonize with the child. When River finished her last song, Miss Annie dismissed everyone and sent them home. "Charlette, you make sure dat boy get to his Ma and Pa alright, ya 'hear?" Miss Annie asked with a nod. Eddie was a short, thin boy back then.

Now, he stood on the steps of the Brooks' store as a beautiful, statuesque man. He wasn't the Eddie that left for Atlanta the year before. He had changed, and River saw it. She knew that he had been hurt by more than puppy love, but he became a stronger, more confident man because of it.

"Charlette? My, what a pretty name," the handsome man said to River as he rubbed his thumb over the exposed skin of her forearm. Although she tried to fight it with everything in her, all she could do was blush.

"I'm guessin' you don't know this man. You new around here?" Eddie said as he stepped down to the road where the couple stood.

"Why, yes I am, actually. Call me Dex. Dexter Alexander." The stranger outstretched his hand with a wink. Eddie looked at the man's hand and face. He took a wide swing and firmly grasped the man's hand while shaking it. Dex's handshake was firm and confident, just like his smile. Just like him. River took a step back and watched the two interact.

"What brings you to these parts, Mr. Alexander?"

"Same thing that bring any colored man from one town to another: work."

Eddie's eyes grazed over the man from toe to head. His eyes met Dex's. They were strange, like maybe one was bigger than the other, but he only noticed it because he was analyzing every detail of the man.

"What kinda work you do? I know everyone in the township of Freedman. I may be able to pull a few strings for ya," Eddie asked. He made a circle around Dexter.

"Well, I'm a carpenter by trade, but I always wanted to be a Reverend," Dexter answered following Eddie with a smile

"Eddie's a minister himself, right Eddie?" River interjected. E.H. snapped his head towards her and gave her a disapproving look. River lowered her head and took a step backward.

"Well, I'll be John Brown! You just the man I'm needin' to see, huh," Dex exclaimed. Eddie turned and stepped towards River. He kept his arms to his side, but his forearms were reaching for a hug. River smiled and walked briskly into his embrace. They held each other a moment, then Eddie grabbed her and spun her around. He placed her back on her feet and gazed in her eyes.

"Oh, I didn't mean to push up on ya ol' lady, Eddie, I—"

"Name's Edwin," Eddie interrupted. "Call me E.H. if you need."

Dex took two steps back and placed both hands over his heart. He half-bowed to the man and gave a wide smile. "My apologies, sir. I just wanted to let you know that you have a mighty fine wife, and I ain't mean no harm runnin' into her."

River let go of Eddie and brushed her skirt before tugging at the end of her braid. She put her head down and waited for

Eddie to announce that she wasn't his wife. When he didn't, she lifted her head, waiting to see what the two of them were doing. Eddie stared at Dexter, and Dexter smiled at Eddie.

"I'm not his wife, but we are good friends. The best of friends really." She nervously stepped between the two of them. Still tugging on her braid, River felt the need to ease this tension. She needed to speak to them individually, but she didn't know who to walk away with and who to send home. She turned her head to Dexter and smiled sheepishly.

"Edwin-Hen—Edwin is a scholar and minister, and he goes to school in Atlanta. He does know most people here in Freedman, being the son of the only colored Pastor for ten miles and all. So, it'd be smart to make his acquaintance." She was all but standing on his shoes and lifted her chin skyward to make her eyes meet his. Eddie relaxed his shoulder and folded his arms. Dexter did the same, but again, with a wide, charming smile that River couldn't help but copy.

Dexter stepped back. "Okay, Miss Charlette, I'll take yo' advice. You sho this ain't yo' ol' man doe? He look ready to turn me every way but loose. I ain't tryin' to cause no trouble, just want to make an honest living in a new place." Dexter spoke with a half smile and let a few chuckles slip out between his words. River giggled too and touched his folded arms while doing it. Eddie walked over to River and pulled her by her waist. He pushed her behind him and extended his hand as a gesture to start over.

"Been knowin' that girl since we were little. You can only imagine my surprise when I come home to a new man holding her, a man who don't even know her name at that," Eddie offered. Eddie and Dexter held each other's right hands and smiled at one another and turned their backs to River.

"You chew tobacco," Eddie asked.

"And drink hooch," Dex replied.

"Don't tell my daddy, but I do too. Hop Wilson make the best moonshine this side of the Mississippi." Eddie and Dexter disappeared inside the store. River watched silently.

That night, River laid restlessly in her bed. She looked out of her window and stared at the stars for a while. She felt the need to kneel at the head of her bed and stick her head out into the cool, blue air. She closed her eyes and listened to the cricket's chirp. She opened her eyes and saw lightning bugs dance across the yard.

CHAPTER 4

River kept her tradition of walking to and from the New George every day, except now she had escorts. Some days both men followed her, and sometimes one took her there and the other walked her home. Eddie was cordial with Dexter, and even laughed with him at times, but he never trusted him.

"I don't know, Letty. Something's off 'bout him," he suggested. They walked to the New George on a hot summer day. River's birthday was in a week, and she was in higher spirits than what she had been before Eddie was home. She knew that she missed him, but she didn't realize how much until he had come home. Eddie made her comfortable, he made her feel at peace. In his return, Charlette had realized that Eddie's friendship was transcendent. He was more than that, more than a brother even. He was her soulmate. His friendship was so much more valuable to her now that she had learned what life was like without it.

Eddie pressed on about how he thought Dexter was a fine man and fun to be around, but he couldn't trust him. River didn't respond to Eddie's remarks. Instead, she nodded here and there, giving the illusion that she was listening. Eddie stopped. River stopped a few steps ahead and turned around and smiled at him. Eddie stared at her looking for some sort of reaction, but River only smiled.

"Are you listening to me, Charlette," he asked in a frustrated tone.

"Not really," she replied honestly.

"That man ain't no good, Letty. I'm trying to tell ya," Eddie said as he and River continued toward the New George. He wasn't going to let the matter rest until she acknowledged what he was saying about Dexter. There was something about Dexter that E.H. found deceitful, but River couldn't see it. Eddie felt that he had to help her see it.

"Think he got a wife that he ran off on?" E.H. made the statement not even believing it himself, but he wanted to get River's attention, he wanted her to be wary of this handsome stranger.

Eddie started to say more but tripped over a rock he didn't see because he was swatting flies and spreading rumors. A grin came over River's face that was wide and unashamed. Eddie was hotter than a two-dollar pistol.

"You know what I'ma say, right," she laughed.

Eddie rolled his eyes and closed them. "River, if you say God don—"

"—like ugly, you sho right," River shouted. "That's exactly what I was finna say because he don't!" She grabbed his thick arm and pulled him from the ground. He dusted the straw-like grass off himself and stood up straight. He flexed his jaw, and grabbed his left suspender. He was being serious–he was trying to look serious.

"Now Charlette," he started.

"Oh, don't be embarrassed in front of me," she said as she started to walk away.

"Nah, I ain't embarrassed. I–," Eddie tried to share his piece, but River interrupted him.

"I don't want to hear about you not liking Dex neither." River waved her hand. She stomped off ahead of him and wiped her braid around her shoulder. She always tugged at her hair when she was nervous or thinking. She would even unbraid her hair sometimes just so she could braid it up again to soothe herself.

"I got something to say," Eddie announced. He grabbed her arm and spun her around. The two were standing so close to each other that their noses were almost touching. Neither of them said anything for a minute, they just searched for something in each other's expressions. Eddie took a deep breath and looked at River with disappointment. Her eyebrows furrowed as her concern grew. She snatched her arm out of his hand and took a step back. Her heart began to race in anticipation. Eddie always shot it straight with her, so his hesitation to speak worried her. They weren't the kind of people who held things back from one another. Eddie was the only person who would be his unfiltered self around her.

"Now what is it, Eddie, you got me sweatin' like a sinner in church. Come on nie," she demanded.

Eddie sighed. "I seen him coming from the back of the Brooks sto' with Shelly Hicks."

River was waiting for more but that was all he said. She waved her hands around to suggest that she was anticipating something else, but Eddie only copied her in a mimicking way. They both rolled their eyes, annoyed with one another.

"That's it! He goin with Shelly Hicks! That don't bother you," he shouted. Eddie didn't understand why River was unfazed by the news of Dexter and Shelly hooking up.

"That man don't go wit' no Shelly Hicks! He just friendly on women." River turned around and continued her journey to the New George. She knew what he was implying but Dexter was a good man. A God-fearing man. He wouldn't fool around with a loose woman — not that she thought Shelly was loose, but she couldn't imagine him wasting time chasing after a woman like her.

They made it to the water and River sighed. She stretched her neck and shoulders then turned her face to the sky. The sun kissed her with its rays and gave her a blessing of peace. She felt absolute serenity. She gave a wide smile. Eddie watched her from behind. Seeing her smile and unwind eased him. He smiled with her. He knew she liked to be there alone, but he couldn't turn away. He wanted to be there to see it happen. He wanted to see what she loved about this place. What was so special that even just being there brought her joy. He attempted to sit down as quietly as possible, but the grass was dry. She heard his every move. River looked over her shoulder. Eddie smiled nervously. He stayed frozen with one hand on the ground, one leg folded, and the other outstretched waiting to fold too. River turned to face him with a raised brow. Eddie stood up and began to campaign on why he should stay with her.

"Letty, I won't bother you. I'll place my hand on a Bible and swear it." River walked over and placed her hands on his chest. She was surprised by how big and strong he felt under her palms. She pushed him backward and tried to drown out the words he said by repeating "Goodbye, goodbye, goodbye, Edwin-Hendricks."

"But what about Shelly and Dex Alexander? Don't you want to hear more about it?" he asked.

"Ain't nothing to hear about, Eddie. Even if they are going together, it ain't no never mind to me," she responded unconvincingly. Eddie grabbed her hands and looked into her wide eyes.

"I know you sweet on 'em, Letty. I know he sweet on you too. You don't have to pretend that you not because of me," he said, consciously or subconsciously admitting that he would be hurt by Charlette taking a liking to someone other than him. River looked up at her handsome friend and parted her lips as if she had something to say. She wanted to say something, to acknowledge his feelings, but all words had escaped her at that moment. He brought her clasped hands to his face and rested his cheek on them. He brought her small knuckles to his lips and held them there before kissing the back of her left hand.

Something in River rushed to her legs. It felt like the warmth of hot liquid settling in your stomach on a cold day, but instead of staying there, it moved from her stomach down between her legs and all the way to her toes. She wanted to snatch her hands away but she couldn't. River realized that Eddie wasn't looking into her eyes anymore and was fixated on her mouth. He was leaning in and so was she. In all her eighteen years of living, River had never felt like this. She thought she was different from other women because she never cared to feel like this. She never even imagined what the touch of a man would feel like. The shortness of her breath startled her, the feeling of her heart fluttering in her throat caught her. River looked up to meet her friend's eyes.

Eddie paused and looked into her eyes again. His eyes were burning with desperation. They called out to her, inviting her to a moment that Eddie had been longing for since he was a teenaged boy. His eyes pierced through River so sharply that it almost frightened her. He wanted her. She could see that he wanted her, and seeing him want someone so badly, wanting her so badly, made River feel a heaviness within herself that she wanted to lighten as quickly as possible. She wanted to lean in. She wanted to go for it. She wanted it badly, just as badly as Eddie did.

She ached for her lips to be grazed. She longed for the feel of fingers on her skin. Just as their mouths were about to meet, she looked up and saw him. Really saw him. This was Eddie. This was *her* Eddie. She blushed when their eyes met. She turned her head so quickly that Eddie wasn't sure what had happened. River embraced him in a hug and rested her forehead on his chest. Eddie felt her head shake from side to side and saw her shoulders bounce up and down. He wrapped his arms around his friend and held her closely. His heart raced as he held her. He regretted everything he said and done in the last few minutes. It wasn't his intention to scare her. He knew that she was new to this kind of tension; he should have eased in more gently. He just wanted her to know that he loved her. He couldn't go another second pretending that he didn't. Not when there was a flashy, charming, shiny new stranger trying to woo her. River's whole body shook in his grasp. He tightened his grasp around her as tears began to form in how own eyes. He couldn't handle the fact that he had just made her cry. *She is so pure, so innocent that just the threat of a kiss brought her to tears,* he thought.

"Please let go of my head," River muffled from below. Eddie pushed her from himself and looked at her confused. River was grinning. She was laughing. He wasn't sure what to make of her laughter, but he felt embarrassed.

With her delicate hands, she gtabbed just on of his before resting her cheek on it. "I love you too, Eddie. But maybe not like that. Not yet at least." Eddie's shoulder dropped as she lowered his hand, still embraced by both of hers. He took the hint and nodded goodbye.

River sat with her feet in the water and her hair flowing down her back. She had already finished praying, but after everything with Eddie, she needed to sit with herself and think for a while. The ground was cold and wet under her, and she could feel it through her dress. The ends of her hair were dirty from sitting in the mud and water beneath her. But despite feeling cold and muddy, River felt safe. She felt soothed and untroubled being there in the cool New George River.

"God, You are so good. You gave us this earth with all the things we need on it. Plants for medicine. Vegetables for food. You gave us the chicken and the rabbit to eat. The cow and hog too." River's heart started to swell. "You gave us the calmness of nature to remind us to breathe and be still. You are so gracious and merciful. We are undeserving of your love, and yet you bless us with the gift of the earth every day. God, I thank You." She had been in deep thought, connecting with her surroundings, connecting with God, when suddenly she couldn't help but smile. God spoke to her. He told her that she had a choice to make. River knew that she was being assigned to minister to one of those two men. She felt that she was being called to marriage. She just needed to wait and watch Him work.

"I understand." She expressed through a grin.

Charlette couldn't sleep that night. She laid in bed for what felt to her like hours, in motionless determination. She tossed and turned anticipating a message from the divine. When she prayed at the river earlier that day, her heart felt a sudden calm that was followed by her Spirit telling her to be still and listen. So that's what she attempted to do, but to no avail, River could not sleep. As the moon shone on her face, kissing her delicate features with its glow, River couldn't help but think of E.H. She had to admit, to confess; she wanted Eddie to kiss her earlier that day. She remembered his touch and the intensity in his eyes, the fervor that hung finely between his lips and her own. She started to feel hot and sweaty from the unrelenting Georgia summer, or at least that's what she chalked up to. River tossed and turned, shaken by the phantom feeling of his lips on the back of her hand. She couldn't stand it. Charlette kicked the quilt off of her bed in an effort to cool the burning she felt within herself.

The heat on her skin became unbearable. She had to get out of there, she had to relieve herself from the torment of her own memory. She went into the kitchen and poured a glass of water. From the window she admired the stars that twinkled as silent witnesses of her struggle. She stepped outside and stood on the porch. Freedom was cloaked in a thick darkness that night. No one in their right mind would be anywhere but the safety of their bed, and yet River found herself walking away from her home and towards the road.

It was the dead of night, so late that even the crickets and possums had fallen silent and found security deep within the trees, but River couldn't stop walking. So badly did she want to turn around, get in her bed, and wait for a Prophetic word, but her body did not feel like her own. She walked and walked until she found herself on the banks of the New George River. She stopped just shy of the water. Still, her mind told her to run away and ask God for safety, but her legs were cemented.

With Charlette panicked and unable to move, the night stretched on. Her heart raced and so did her thoughts. She needed to go to God in prayer but she kept hearing her Spirit telling her to be still. Paralyzed by the terrors of her own mind– or perhaps by the wisdom of her Spirit–, River stood unmoving. Then she saw it. Right in front of her, she could see clear as day: her future.

In front of her, she saw a version of herself that had everything she wanted–everything she and her mother always spoke about. A life of honor and respect. She was a wife. Her husband was powerful, and well-respected. She saw herself as a healer and a mother. This woman had a command over people like something she had never seen before. This life was perfect. Except, when her husband was near, there was a cloud that hung over her. Gray and heavy. There was no love in their marriage, and her husband was a mean, cold man. No empathy in his heart towards her. She couldn't see who he was.

She watched herself reach out for this man, but he pulled away so forcefully, so violently, that she fell. River saw herself crying, mourning a marriage that had died before it was ever conceived. She wanted to call out to herself, to yell Get up, Charlette! You're better than this. But she saw another man approach her, his hand outstretched. When this version of herself grabbed his hand, the life she just saw faded away in a cloud of dust being carried by the wind.

In this new life, another version of herself, she saw a glow around her that almost blinded the Charlette that was standing frozen by the river. She was powerful. She was strong. She had been called to a purpose bigger than her wildest dream, but rarely did she see herself with her husband. He was there at first, and when they were together, River felt the heat of their passion all the way from the other side of the water. Then, just as suddenly as the man appeared, he disappeared, and the woman he left was formidable. River liked her. She wanted to be her, but she couldn't help but to wonder what the sudden absence of the man meant. Did he die? Was she a widow? Who was he? She couldn't make out his features either.

River wanted to watch this strong woman all night. She wanted to admire her, study her, for as long as she could. Then her knees went weak. Charlette fell to the ground and couldn't not get back up. Fatigue hit her in an overpowering wave. She tried to stand up and walk back home but she couldn't. Her arms felt like they had been weighed down by bags of wet sand. Her feet may as well have been cinderblocks. River gave up. She laid down by the water, holding herself tightly in a fetal position.

Behind her eyelids she could see something move, something coming toward her. She wanted to wake up and get away, but sleep had finally remembered her and was making a sudden visit. The man–the person–the thing–moved closer to her, nearly in arms reach. "No," River said softly. "Get away," she said in a weak command. "Get away from me," she said with more fight. It touched her. River's heart sank. "I said no!" She shouted, waking herself. River was back in her bed, in her room. She raised up and looked around. Her dress was unstained and her feet were clean. It was as if she had never left the safety of the four walls that were currently around her. There was no indication that she had ever moved throughout the night. Except, her quilt was on the floor and there was a bruise on her wrist where it had grabbed her.

Later that morning, River made her way to the New George. She felt strange after last night. The dream had taken more out of her than she wanted to admit, so she left home without waking or speaking to anyone. It was the first thing she did that morning.

Her mind chased her in the wind and the mud from her

dress was slapping her thighs. She was floating again. She did this a few other times since it first happened. Each time was less and less alarming.

"Thank you, God, for this gift," she announced quietly. She knew her mind was going to drift soon as it always does when she was in the air. Levitating was almost a sign of activation. Her prayers were no longer something she would be conscious of, but a powerful movement from within her instead. She started to hum. It helped her connect with herself and make the drift away less frightening.

Before she knew it, River's mind had drifted to a place beyond her conscious reach. She tried to focus on her own humming, but her prayers had become so intimate with God that even she no longer held the privilege to speak them.

Gradually, River's mind began to regain control after what felt like hours to her body. She tried to calm herself and begin her descent from this ethereal state, but she couldn't move. Though her thoughts were once again her own, her body remained under the control of another force.

River's heart pounded rapidly, echoing her nervousness. She could hear herself singing, yet all she could do was desperately yearn for the ability to reclaim her own body.

"Gonna lay down my burden
Down by the riverside
Down by the riverside…"

Her heart raced. Accelerating with every second, she remained frozen. *Gonna lay down my burdens,* she heard herself sing. Though she was unable to move, the sting of hot tears streaming down her face gave her hope. She could feel again. Her heart began to beat harder, more forcibly, as if it were going to leap from her chest and be swept away by the river beneath her. The kiss of a gentle breeze touched the tip of her index finger, jolting her out of the paralysis–she realized that her senses had come back. She could feel mud hardening as it tightened the skin under her thigh, and the itch that followed. She heard the sound of the water beneath her becoming louder in her ears, louder than the sound of her diminishing voice. Her finger twitched. She was coming back, slowly, and less petrified–still floating in the air. How long had she been there? Could other people hear her? Her thoughts raced as she returned to herself. Desperate, River tried to yell, to swing her arms and kick her legs. Nothing moved.

"Gonna study war no more…"

River had only been scared that way one other time before; the first time she found herself floating. Twice now, River found herself afraid of something that she assumed was a gift from God. But was it?

What did I do wrong? Are You still using me? She began to question God. She started hoping this was all a dream. She wanted her mother to shake her awake. She wanted her father to snatch her back to the ground and embrace her in a hug. She wanted to be held. She wanted to feel safe.

Before abandoning all sense of hope, she tried to speak again. The tiniest sound of breath escaped her throat. Like fresh air, the sound of her small sigh soothed her.

Before long, she felt the bottom of her dress soaked and clinging to her skin. She was standing barefoot in the river, but she was back. Back in control. She dropped to her knees and let the water flow around her. She fell again and caught herself with her hands. Her palms were flat on the ground with water rushing under them, wet, cold earth beneath them. Her tears fell and became an insignificant part of an infinite stream of water, salting the freshness of the river. She lifted her head and let out a wail. She started to sob and was struck with fear.

River tried to think, to understand what was happening. She was so afraid but could not put into words why. She forced herself to think, to confront the thing she was trying to hide in the recesses of her subconscious. She could not address the issue if she didn't *address* the issue. She didn't trust God. She no longer feared Him, but was afraid of Him. Was that the issue? Or had she somehow allowed herself to be seized by an entity other than God?

Just as she gained the strength to walk out of the water, Dexter Alexander appeared on the horizon. When he saw her soaking and weary, he ran to her aid.

"I know you likes the water so much they call you River, but I never thought I'd see you bathin' in it," he chuckled. River sensed his concern and knew that he was attempting to lighten the mood. He wrapped his arms under hers and put the weight of her body on his shoulder. River wanted to speak, but she didn't know what to say. She drew a breath of air to begin to speak, but the words choked in her throat, keeping her from being able to speak. She wanted to try again, but how would she tell him that she was just stuck in a trance, floating above the ground? She didn't even know how she made it off the ground in the first place. She didn't know how to explain what just happened because she didn't understand it herself.

As they walked, her knees weakened. Her head hung low. She let out a silent cry and covered her face. Dex lifted her off the ground. He carried her in his arms while looking straight ahead. River was in a vulnerable place and he knew not to pry. He knew that all he needed to do was just be there. Respect her honor, not acknowledging her soft whimpers, and just be there.

After putting quite a bit of distance between them and the water, River moved her hands from her face and rested her head on Dexter's chest. He squeezed her thigh acknowledging her comfort and encouraging her to steal a bit more from him if need be. They continued their walk in silence. When they approached the middle of town, Dexter made a left turn and avoided the square. River lifted her head and looked up at Dex, her arms dangling from his neck now while her head rested on his shoulder. As the Montgomery home came into view, River let out a deep sigh.

"Somethin' on ya mind," Dex asked. River patted his shoulder signaling that she wanted to be put down, and he obliged.

"I'm not ready to go home," she shared. She looked at the house and started to tear up. Dexter reached out to touch her face, but she turned away. River felt ashamed and confused. Her family, her community, and everyone she knew championed her as some kind of saint. They treated her as if she were an angel amongst them, but there she was: standing wet and afraid, questioning God. Dex took a step forward, wanting to hold her, but he saw her purity. He didn't know if it would be appropriate to touch her as intimately as he longed to.

"Charlie…" His hand meeting the small of her back, she raised her eyes and met his. Warm and inviting, they stared at one another. *Charlie.* This new nickname rang in her ear. She spun around to face him, and for the second time in her life, she was standing so close to a man that she could nearly hear his heartbeat. Still taking in one another, their foreheads touched. Their mouths met. They lingered in the moment before locking lips. River had never been kissed before, though many boys tried. They all attempted to woo her, and plenty of old men offered her money in exchange for a peck; but she never obliged. Dexter's hand engulfed her wet curls and his hips firmly pressed against hers. His other hand rested on her neck, being tickled by loose hair as her head turned from engaging in a passionate kiss.

River wondered who she was in that moment. She certainly wasn't herself. His lips released hers and moved to her ear then down her neck. His hands wandered up and down her back before resting comfortably on her backside. River rolled her eyes and bit her lip. She whispered the word stop when Dexter confidently grabbed her neck. He removed himself from her and stepped away. River followed him.

They walked until they were in the woods that fenced in

their small town. Dexter had grabbed her hand at some point, but let go of it to lay himself on the ground. As if it were second nature, River kicked her leg over his body and sat on top of him. The two of them rubbed and touched and kissed each other as if eternal life could be found somewhere between their bodies.

Dex placed his hand under her skirt and grabbed River's bare thighs. Her body tightened from nerves but quivered with excitement. He caressed her thighs up and down while subtly lifting her skirt. River felt the hairs on her arm and neck stand. She felt his eyes staring at her hot skin. She felt the firmness of his grip and the tension between their bodies. As he worshiped her legs, she stared at him. What was just a second felt like an hour. She could see herself unbuttoning her shirt. Lifting his over his head. She saw herself laying on her back, scratching his, gripping his glistening muscles. Imagining the sound of their moans echoing in the vastness of the trees captured River's breath in a way that startled her.

She knew she shouldn't. She never realized how bad she wanted to, but she knew she shouldn't. She pushed his hands down to her knees and lifted herself. His eyes met hers as they began a silent conversation. She looked down at him, lying beneath her, dressed in a bright, lopsided smile, and a shirt with no sleeves. She looked at his arms folded behind his head. They looked like high-peaking mountains covered in rich, dark, brown skin. She looked into his eyes and imagined all the things she just robbed herself of experiencing. She took a regretful breath through her nose. River stood up and reached down to pull him off the ground. Now standing, hovering over the petite girl, he pulled her in by her waist, and they bumped each other with their hips. Then, they put their arms around each other's shoulder and walked back towards her home smiling, laughing, and admiring the sunset.

"What happened back dere," he asked while looking forward. River lifted her head and looked at his profile. She admired the wideness of his nose and the way his lips protruded off his face. She took her arm from around his waist and started to braid one side of her hair.

"I don't know. It was a mistake though. I— I've never done that with anyone else, not even..." She stopped. She hung her head and dug her chin into her chest. She felt herself starting to cry before turning her head in shame. Eddie. Her first kiss was supposed to be with Eddie. How could she forget about him?

She looked at her feet as they hit the ground, watching them fade away under the blur of tears that began to form in her eyes. She looked into the blue night sky and watched the navy trees grow as they approached them. She remembered that Dexter was with her and tried to hide her shame, but he could read her. Dex grabbed her chin and kissed her nose. River blushed.

"He'll understand," Dex reassured. River's heart skipped a beat. How did he know she was thinking about Eddie? River Looked at him again, searching for something within Dexter, searching for an explanation for him knowing exactly what she was thinking. As she stared at him, something about him felt familiar, but not like she had seen him before; it was like she had *felt* him. That thought ended abruptly, interrupted by the notion that Dexter was saying that *He* would understand.

Her eyes began to water again as she thought of how she had sinned. Her body gave way to lust, and there was no denying it. She kissed this man. She sat on top of him, and he put his hands under her skirt. Her breath shortened just reliving what had happened.

Would He understand? Will God forgive me? She contemplated.

"Eddie's a smart man. A good man too. And he loves you. You been something like a sister to 'em all his life, Charlie. I can't imagine dat changin' on account of me." It was the first 'he,' that Dexter was speaking of.

Dexter grabbed River's small hand and held it in his. Then he brought the back of her hand to his lips and kissed it before swinging their arms back and forth between them. They made it to the front steps of her home and River looked at the door. She left the house with her hair in one tamed, neat braid and returned home in two slopely braided, wet and muddy pigtails. She tugged on the ends of both of them before walking up two steps. She turned to face Dexter and flopped on the stair up under her.

"Where you get Charlie from and why you think you can just call me that all of a sudden," she asked. He put one foot on the front step and draped both hands over his bent knee.

"It's short for Charlette," he answered with a smile. The door swung open with Cecilia standing in the center of the frame. She looked at Dexter then down at River who was avoiding eye contact with her mother.

"My aren't you handsome. You must be Mr. Alexander. Heard a lot 'bout you," Cecilia greeted. She wiped her brow with the back of her hand and started to dust off her skirt. River was terrified that her mother would know what she had done in the woods. She was so afraid of her mother seeing lust beginning to bud all over her, that she didn't notice the flirtatious grin Cecilia had shared with Dexter–who smiled back confidently.

"And you must be the famous Cee Cee Montgomery. I see where your Charlette here gets her beauty." He shook Cecilia's tiny hand and peered into her eyes as he kissed her wrist. Cecilia blushed and gave a girlish wave. Cecilia looked to her daughter and then back to this handsome man.

"You da reason she home after dark," she asked.

"I must admit. I kept ha out longer than she wanted. Blame it on my count of being new to this lovely town," Dexter responded. Cecilia waited for River to interject, but her daughter was speechless.

"She grown. Ain't no reason in keeping her home all da time. Although, I would like to meet the man courtin' my daughter 'for he start to court her doe. How 'bout you come 'round here for breakfast in tha mornin'? Meet'a Pa and get to know us properly," Cecilia invited.

"I think I can 'range dat, ma'am," he said with a smile at River. "What should I bring?"

CHAPTER 5

Dex was standing outside of Hop Wilson's house when he saw E.H. walking home with his tail between his legs. He knew Eddie was coming from the New George where he inevitably left River.

"Looka dere. The boy look damn pitiful," Hop announced.

"Is dat school dat do it to 'em," Henry Stitts replied.

"Nah, da boy jus' soft. School changed 'em doe. Put some hair on his chess. Is dat girl dat got him lookin' like a los' puppy," Hop countered. He leaned back in his old chair before spitting out the snuff he was chewing. Then, he turned back to Henry and Dex. "Got some hooch in'neh if y'all wantin' sum."

Dex excused himself and started up the road as the other men went into Hop's small, shack house. Hop was kind enough to let Dexter stay there after he was put out of Miss Annie's house by her husband, Fred. Miss Annie and Fred had a large four-bedroom home that they opened to the colored people passing through or to anyone who was in need of a place to stay. Like Cleo, Fred worked for the railroad to earn his living, but Miss Annie had a good job. She would follow the train tracks into downtown Savannah and work as a seamstress for a well-known designer. She made good money working behind closed doors in Savannah, and she kept her employer's clients happy. Mary Claire, the designer, was grateful for Miss Annie, so she'd tip her an extra $2 dollars at the end of the week. With Miss Annie being so rich, she figured she would feed her community on some Saturdays and let the colored people who were passing through town to stay in her home. Fred charged the tenants $1 a week for food and house cleaning, which also contributed to their ability to serve the community. Dex paid them $5 upfront in exchange for two months of housing. Fred all but asked for Dexter's ring size when he gave them the money in their parlor that day. To express his gratitude, Fredworked hard to keep Dex comfortable too—that is until he came home to him and Miss Annie alone in their kitchen.

Fred walked with Cleo for breakfast and hooch at Henry Stitts' house, so he came in through the back door. He saw his wife standing in the middle of their kitchen with her thick salt and pepper hair jutting out like black and white twigs sprouting from a bare tree. She was still, her hands at sides, her neck turned upward. All he could see of her face were the tops of her bushy eyebrows and her forehead. A strained, harsh hum struggled to escape her throat. Fred stood by the backdoor with his hand on the knob, listening as the sound grew louder. At one point, he felt as if she were standing behind him, groaning in his ear. Fred wasn't a religious man, but in the moment, he felt compelled to pray. He sat his boots down and started towards his wife, but with each step in her direction the distance between them seemed to stretch farther and farther.

An unnerving darkness fell on the house. Fred no longer felt like he was running in place, but realized that his body had been petrified, suspended in a realm that existed between this world and the next. He looked around the room and saw nothing. Ahead, his wife floated still with her head turned upward and her hair crowning her head like a halo of chaos. Silence had enveloped the house. No crickets, no wind— nothing. Even his wife's pained moans were a secondary to the thunderous beat of his heart. His chest tightened from attempting to free itself by way of his throat. His pounding heart ramming against his ribcage echoed loudly to his head. THUD, THUD. The pulsating beat crashed against his skull. He grabbed his head and doubled over in pain. Then, out of sheer panic, Fred let out a distressed, desperate scream. And just as fast as it all happened, he was standing at his back door again, one hand clutching the knob behind him, and the other gripping his boots so tightly that his short nails were nearly piercing the leather. His climbing pulse continued as he began to regain full sight of his home. Everything was just as it was before, but his wife was standing next to the table with her hand over her heart and a look of confusion on her face. He watched as her chest fell up and down in the same rhythm as his.

"Now what da hell you doing all dat screaming fo', Fred?! Huh?" Miss Annie was absolutely bewildered. Fred's knees grew weak. Her hair was pinned back like normal. Her feet were planted on the ground. And it appeared that she had just been serving coffee to Dexter, who was staring at Fred with his one-sided smile, sipping his coffee.

"You alright dere, 'Red," he asked. "Look like you done seen the devil in here dancin' witcho wife," Dexter snickered. Fred Jones kicked Dexter out of their home the same night. When Hop Wilson found him sleeping on the porch between Brooks' General Store and Woods' Shoe Cobbling Company, he offered a small cot and pillow to Dex free of charge at his small shack.

As he walked away from Hop's house, Dexter decided to saunter leisurely in the direction of the river. He was familiar with the townsquare and Freedman's residential areas, having explored much of its whistle-stop charm with River, but he had never taken time to see Freedman for all it was beyond that. He met just about everyone and visited every establishment but Dr. Bailey's medical office. Freedman was just south of Savannah, hidden in the middle of nowhere. When slavery ended fifty years earlier, Mr. Jenkins' father and about fifteen other slaves from the Whitmore Plantation walked for five days before resting in a small clearing in the woods just off the river. They had been in the small clearing for two days, when a group of ten other former slave families walked on their makeshift camp. They got together and decided to settle where they were. Over time, more and more colored people found their way from North and South of Savannah to that small clearing in the woods. Dexter was drawn to Freedman. Something had called him there. He didn't know who or what yet, but it was his mission to find out.

On his journey to the New George, curiosity consumed Dexter. Instead of meeting River at the water, where she had no doubt immersed herself in worship, Dexter decided to explore. He continued across the pasture, then crossed over the narrow end of the water to the south side of the river. He never thought to cross the water before, but something was calling him. There was something about the vastness of the land on the south side that was pulling him to it.

"Yes, Lawd, dis where I need to be," he announced. He walked over fallen branches and through grass that grew past his knees. He picked up bugs and sniffed the dangling leaves. He walked a few yards into the woods before heading back towards the river. He didn't remember how to get to the narrow end of the water, but he could hear it rushing and knew to follow the sound until he could see the river. He pushed past a veil of trees hiding the New George and made it to the bank of the river. He stopped in his tracks and flashed a smile so big and bright that it could have blinded birds flying by. He saw her, River, on the other side.

"Well, I'll be…" Dexter's voice trailed off.

He pulled up his pants, took off his shirt, and sat in the muddy wet ground beneath him. He was amazed and impressed. He knew she was special and beautiful, but seeing her there in the air made him truly see her. Dexter felt his ears burn from excitement. His cheeks ached from smiling. He was enamored, spellbound, and bewitched. The voice that had been guiding him spoke.

"Dis is her. Dis is the one. But be careful, his inner voice warned. *She's a force. I don' know if you can get dis girl,"* the

voice warned.

"Oh, but yes I can," he countered through a smile.

"Dexter, she strong. Stick with the plan and gon bout yo way," the voice said in an attempt to caution Dexter.

"I'ma get her. She's just like me. We powerful. I got tuh gettah."

"She gon be mo' powerful den you, and you gon' regret the day you came to Freedman. You might want to try sumn else," the voice advised.

"I'ma get this girl. And I'ma make her my wife."

Dex smiled. He undressed, making himself look more homely, my rugged than usual. He liked a touch of flare, but he knew that River preferred the humble type. He abandoned his shirt and suspenders, and turned to walk north of the water to find the narrow path to cross over. He crossed the water and waited for River. He found a place just below the peak of the hill in the pasture to lay and wait for his queue. He closed his eyes and started to sing as he waited. With confidence surging through his veins, Dexter chuckled to himself before singing a familiar hymn.

Gonna lay down my burden…

The next morning, as soon as day broke, Dexter was at the Montgomery home with a basket of eggs and two pints of milk. Cee Cee was fully dressed and just starting to cook when he arrived. Although her hair was still pinned from sleeping, she had on a Sunday dress, white heels, and ruby red lipstick. Dexter had never realized how much the mother and daughter favored one another. He found it interesting how Cecilia had the same eyes as her daughter, but each pair told a completely different story. Cecilia's eyes were almond shaped and brown, but they weren't as sultry or inviting as Charlette's. They had a profound sense of confidence in them that was alluring, but

Charlette's eyes were intoxicating. Cecilia had small brown freckles around her eyes that paraded up her nose, where Charlette had one little speck that adorned her right cheek like a perfect brown jewel. Cecilia noticed Dexter studying her. She blushed.

"Charlette's up, but I told her to get pretty dis morning, so give'ah time," Cecilia explained. She offered him a cup of coffee. He touched her hand as he grabbed the mug, and she lingered before pulling away. Cecilia turned and chuckled into her hand as she seared the pork frying in her pan. She didn't know why, but something about Dexter made her feel young again, something about him made her wish that she was the teenage girl experiencing her first love. But she wasn't. She was the mother. Her role was to impress Dexter for her daughter's sake and not her own.

"I didn't know what you'd like, so I made a little of everythang. Hope it don't get my head knocked between da stove and da wall, but I'm making smothered pork and heating up some leftover ham. I have some biscuits in the oven. Got some buttermilk for it, if you likes dat kinda combination. Got some fresh made blackberry and peach jam. River made dat two days ago. I'mon get to the eggs once things are close to being finished, and I started on some hoe cakes, but I thought it might be too much" Cecilia paused and looked from her stove to the table then up to the smiling handsome man sitting there. "Am I missin' anythang at all?"

He grabbed her hand and kissed the back. "Just the opportunity to stop and breathe." They laughed, and she brushed his shoulder before walking away. She leaned on the doorframe and crossed her ankles. She smiled at him and thought about how lucky her daughter would be to have such a fine man. She looked down at her feet and twisted one on the ground. "What's that," Dexter asked.

"What?" Cee Cee replied.

"What's that you ponderin' on over dere?"

"Just thinkin' bout ol' E.H. and how I never had him over here chasin' after River," Cecilia said. She stood up and turned her head as her daughter entered her room. She was glowing. Charlette's curly hair danced down her back with some of the front twisted back with a part in the middle, exposing her soft features. She had on a floral white dress with pink and green flowers and some unworn white shoes she was waiting to wear on her birthday.

"Well," Cee Cee started. She clapped her hands and placed them under her chin. "Here she is: The Queen of England." Laughter erupted in the kitchen, coming boisterously from Cecilia and Dexter, and sheepishly from Charlette. She entered the kitchen, sat next to Dexter, and started playing with her hair.

"Don't tell me you done swallowed some butterflies," he asked before kissing her hand.

"Just ain't ever actually wanted someone to meet my daddy before is all. I don't know how he'll react to me introducin' a man that I actually want to be with," River confessed. Dex pulled her chair and brought it closer to himself. Charlette's mother walked away to style her hair. He put his chin on Charlette's shoulder before kissing it. She inched her chair farther away from Dexter than where it was before. He grabbed the chair and pulled it closer and let out a disapproving sigh. "Ion like you like dis, Charlie. What you got to worry fuh?" He wrapped his arm around her waist and studied her profile.

"It's just...I really have never cared for men. Ion really look at 'em like dat, and my daddy knows it. What if he knows?" She looked at Dexter with her big, brown eyes that were full of worry and wonder. She pulled his arm from her side to rest it on his leg.

"Knows what," Dexter asked.

She turned her body from facing him back to facing the table. She scooted her chair away from his and slid closer to the table. She put her face in her hands and shook her head.

"You actin' like we made love in dem woods, girl. Calm yo' self," he whispered through her hair. Dex closed his eyes and inhaled deeply, letting her scent fill his nostrils and seep into his lungs. It was an intoxicating blend of sweetness and earthiness that made him linger for just a second longer than he should have. It was a fleeting moment, unnoticed by any onlooker, but not so brief that River couldn't feel his silent appreciation. The sound of his breath, the way he seemed to drink her in, sent a rush of warmth cascading over River's entire body. In that instant, they existed in a world of their own, a private universe of shared desire. River felt affirmed, validated, desired, and profoundly grown. Dex's confidence in that moment was unwavering; she was the woman who had drawn him to Freedman, the very reason he had been sent there.

The door creaked open, and Cleo Montgomery stood in the doorway, a towering presence that seemed to suck the air out of the room. Cecilia's heart pounded in her chest as she rushed out of her room and into the kitchen, her mind racing. She knew he would be upset by all the food and the fact that a man was sitting next to his daughter. A knot tightened in her stomach as she started across the room towards him, but the hard set of Cleo's jaw and the fire in his eyes made her freeze mid-step. She quickly turned back towards the stove, resting one trembling hand on the edge of the kitchen table and shifting her weight to the side in a futile attempt to steady herself.

Cleo's silent, piercing gaze bore into each of them, a silent demand for an explanation hanging in the air. The tension was discernible, a thick fog of unease that rendered everyone motionless. They all stared at him, their breaths shallow and uneven, waiting for the storm to break. Finally, in the heavy silence, Dexter pushed his chair back with a scraping sound that seemed to echo through the room. He walked towards Cleo, his hand extended, but his movements were slow and deliberate, each step a cautious approach towards the inevitable confrontation.

"How ya doin' sir? My name's Dexter Alexander. Your wife invited me over last night after I walked Charlette home from the river. She said it'sa 'bout time I got to know da two of you."

Cleo looked Dexter up and down. He hated his flashy clothes. He hated his crooked smile. He hated, most of all, how nervous his daughter looked. River had unwavering faith and more confidence than anyone he knew. Seeing Charlette sitting there, looking like a ball of nerves meant that she cared about his opinion of this strange man. Cleo looked Dex in the eyes and tried to intimidate him, but he was unmoved. Cleo met many men in his lifetime. Since the age of twenty, he had a way of unnerving men who were even twice his size. But not Dexter Alexander. Cleo wasn't sure if he liked this or not. On the one hand, his daughter was smitten by a man of strength and grit, but on the other hand, Cleo wondered if he was a man with too much strength and grit—a man with no fear. They shook hands and sat at the table across from one another and stared. The two women started to serve the food in silence. Everyone in the room was waiting for something to happen, but none of them knew what it was they were expecting. Cecilia sat full plates of food first in front of her husband and then in front of Dexter. River was right behind her with cups of coffee. Cleo smiled at his daughter as she handed him his cup, then shot a glare at the man across from him.

"Thank you, Charlie," Dexter expressed to River when she sat a cup in front of him.

"Charlie? Who da hell is Charlie? My daughter's name is Charlette," Cleo declared with confusion and annoyance in his voice.

"Oh, I just started calling her dat yesterday…" Dex started.

"It come from Charlette. I just shortened it and got Charlie. I likes it." He smiled at River. She stood next to him blushing.

"How old are you?" Cleo asked.

"Twenty-three come September." Dex answered.

"You likes young girls?"

"Not particularly, but your Charlette here ain't much younger dan me, not by my math anyway."

"You plan on marryin' my daughter?"

"Someday."

Cecilia shifted her weight in her chair and Charlette choked on her coffee. The two men stared at each other. Charlette stood up again before settling behind Dexter. She placed her hands on his shoulder and faced her father. Cleo leaned back in his chair, crossed his arms and waited to hear her plea.

"Daddy, I know this is different and neither of us are used to this, but I like Dexter. You used to think Eddie was silly, that he was too smart for his own good, but look at y'all now. I love Eddie. I don't mean to hurt him, but if it's okay with you. I'd like to get to know Dexter more."

Cleo let out a sigh as he looked at his wife. Cecilia threw up her hands as she tilted her head. Cleo turned to her lifting his chin. Cecilia responded by crossing her arms and pressing her lips. They ended their unspoken conversation by looking at River and Dexter with both their arms crossed, leaning back in their chairs.

"I heard about you. Fred Jones, say he don't trust you. Say you was in his wife's mind one day and talkin' 'bout da devil," Cleo announced.

"Da Devil?!" Cecilia shouted. River took a step back. She looked at her father, then looked at Dexter. She knew he was kicked out of Miss Annie's and Fred's house, but he never told her why, and she just realized that she never cared to ask.

Dex looked at Cleo Montgomery. Mr. Montgomery looked at him. Their eyes locked, unblinking. The tension in the room was palpable, the air sharp and brittle like it was laced with shards of glass. Even a breath too deep or too loud seemed dangerous. River shifted her weight, lips parting to speak, but her mother's silent warning held her back. She glanced from Dexter to her father.

The tension grew unbearable. Cleo's face began to twitch, then, Dex started to laugh. The dam broke. Cleo and Dexter erupted into laughter, their laughter explosive and uncontrollable. They slapped their knees, hit the table, and nearly toppled from their chairs, caught in the hysterics sparked by the absurdity of the story Fred Jones had shared with Cleo and the other men of Freedman.

"Man, I tell ya, dat damn Fred Jones'll tell dat story to anyone who listen. He say you was playing tricks on him, man. Made 'em feel like he runnin' in place. He say his wife was in da kitchen, hair just as nappy as da day she was born, den you come round da corner and it's lookin' right again." The two men shared a full-bellied laugh, genuinely tickled by how silly–and serious–Fred Jones was about this story. Dexter grabbed his stomach and doubled over laughing.

"Say, say, say," Dex started, stretching his arm to touch Cleo's. "Look man, he woke me up out my sleep dat mornin' with a gun to my face talkin' 'bout 'I knows what you did to my wife, I knows you demon.' I say to myself 'now I know I ain't no demon and I knows I ain't did nothin' to Annie Jones.'" The house shook from the sound of the two men laughing. Charlette and Cecilia looked at each other. Cecilia picked up her coffee mug and winked at Charlette. They both knew that she had her father's blessing and that, if she wanted, she'd be Mrs. Dexter Alexander by the end of the summer.

After a couple of hours of talking and eating, Cleo excused himself from the breakfast table. He kissed his wife on the cheek then kissed his daughter's forehead. He shook Dexter's hand and walked to his bedroom. Cecilia walked River and Dex to the door and watched them walk up the road and into town. They walked with their elbows cuffed around one another and their heads practically touching. She smiled. Then, just out the corner of her eye she noticed a tall shadow leaning on a tree to the left of her. Turning her head to see who was near, she found Edwin-Hendricks standing there. He tipped his hat to her before making his way up the road. He didn't walk into town, but instead headed in the direction of his father's church. Cee Cee placed her hand over her heart, watching the boy as he left. She knew defeat when she saw it. It broke her heart to see Eddie in pain, but nothing made her happier than the thought of her daughter marrying such a fine, young man.

CHAPTER 6

Eddie walked away from the Montgomery house, not feeling defeated, but *disappointed*. He had loved River since he was fifteen years old, but he never found the right moment to tell her. When he left for college, he wanted so badly to run off the train and ask River to come with him. He wanted to get on one knee and ask her to give him the chance to prove how good of a husband he could be. He wanted to ask her to give him just one year to show her what he was capable of. One year to prove himself. But he knew his friend. He knew how her mind worked. She would have asked him where she would live because she obviously couldn't live on campus. She would want to know where he would work to support her, or if she needed to work too, and if so, where?

Eddie didn't have the answer to any of it, so he waved at her from the window. He stared at her as she stood beside his father. The sight of her standing on the platform of the train station trying to hide her sadness behind sincere pride and excitement was etched into his memory forever. He mourned the loss of seeing her face, hear her voice, or listening to her laugh. A solitary tear escaped as he realized that it would be nearly a year before he would be able to wrap his arms around her again. It was that day, leaving his home in their small corner of Georgia where the women he loved lived, that he decided Charlette Marie Montgomery would be his wife. The thought of their marriage consumed his thoughts the entire trip to Atlanta.

Eddie was determined to spend his first two semesters establishing himself. He was going to work hard, start a ministry, and lay down roots. He was going to come home, woo his friend, make her his wife, then take her back to Atlanta where he was a well-respected man. But when Eddie came home, he learned that telling God your plans was a joke that He enjoyed loudly.

The possibility of coming home to River being held in the arms of another man never occurred to Eddie. He never accounted for her even being interested in other men. He always thought she was above physical attraction to men. River was better than that, in his mind. He had seen her shrug off male attention their entire lives. She didn't have time for them. She was too focused, too driven. She wanted to be a healer. She wanted to be an agent of the Lord. She wanted to do the right thing all the time. He saw too often how men would bring women like her down. River had a purpose to serve and she was going to walk in that purpose for the rest of her life, with Eddie by her side—or at least that's how he always imagined it. When his grandfather built their church, he started a legacy for Johnson men. One that his father has honored, and one that he planned to honor as well.

But Edwin wanted to reach more than Freedman, Georgia. He wanted to minister for churches larger than the ones in Savannah and Atlanta. The Reverend, Dr. E.H. Johnson would be a household name someday. He wanted to study medicine with a focus on Negros and be a leader in the church and pillar of the community. Eddie wanted books dedicated to his brilliance. He wanted schools erected in his name. He was going to be the person to put Freedman, Georgia, colored-town, on the map. Every Black man, woman, and child would take a train to Savannah before making that long pilgrimage to the small town of Freedman because that's where he was raised. He could see it, so why couldn't she? Why did she see him as the same, skinny kid who got pushed around defending her? Shouldn't she be thankful for him? Shouldn't she feel attached to him?

He walked up to the church, stopping out front. *Why him? Why Dexter?* That was what he wanted to know the most.

Dexter was big, arrogant, and ignorant to be frank. All the education in the world wouldn't be enough to get rid of Eddie's country, southern drawl, but at least he spoke like he had read a book – Dexter had probably never even seen a real book as far as E.H. could tell. Eddie didn't walk around town in dress suits on Saturdays like Dex, and Eddie certainly didn't entertain loose women. E.H. was respectable. He was everything a woman like Charlotte needed to guide her. So why Dexter and not him?

Pastor Johnson interrupted Edwin's deep thoughts. "What's goin' on in dat brain uh yours, son?"

"Can I be honest with ya, Pa," Eddie asked while looking up at the church.

"I reckon it's better than lettin' it eat chu alive, so out wit' it nie, boy," his father replied.

"I'm in love with Charlette Montgomery."

Pastor Johnson remained quiet. The man's round belly heaved upward as he took a deep breath and let out a sigh. He patted his son on his shoulder and started up the steps to the church.

"That's it, Pa? Just a pat on the shoulder?" Eddie followed his father. They entered the church and walked straight up the pews into Pastor Johnson's office. He went behind his large oak desk and took spectacles from the drawer. "Daddy?"

Pastor Johnson was annoyed and made sure to make a show of his annoyance. "What you want me to say, boy? Dat da sky is blue and Jesus saves souls," he asked with irritation.

Eddie was confused and made sure to make a show of his confusion too. He sat on the arm of the chair in front of the desk and looked at his father. He stared at his father urging him to elaborate. Pastor Johnson continued.

"I knows you love dat girl. I knows she love you too. I

knows dat Jesus died for our sins, and dat God say He'll return Him to the world one day. Hey! I knows I'm yo' pappy, like I knows you my son...I knows dat, E. H. Now tell me what's really goin' on in dat brain of yours." The pastor continued to pull and more things from his desk. He stood up and touched his son's shoulder. The two men walked around the church and prepared for bible study. They dusted hymnals and swept between the pews, all while talking about the scene at the Montgomery home from that morning.

"I feel stupid, Pa. I feel like I should have asked her to marry me before goin' to Atlanta like I wanted. I should have never left her here," Eddie admitted. The tall, round man walked over to his son and sat on the pew in front of him. He grabbed his son's arm and looked at him with reassurance.

"You did the right thing by going to school. You couldn't afford no wife and baby, and you can't afford one now either, but at least you have roots. At least you have a foundation." Pastor Johnson outstretched his arms and looked around the room. "All dis here is yours. Dat church you work wit' on campus is yours. You the catch here. Not dat girl. She got the body of a temptress, but the soul of a saint. Between me and you, son, it don't get no better dan dat. God done created dat girl to please body and soul, so I can understand bein' down behind her. But remember, you are the one who got education. You the one who has the full following of da church and community on yo' side. She just a pretty thang to look at when she walk by. I named you Edwin-Hendricks for a reason. Named for your mother's father who you never got to meet, and myself. What you call da child is what he'll live by. You got the first names of two great men. She got da name of some water. Lift yo' head, son, and either get what you want or get on by." Pastor Johnson spoke candidly with his son.

He intended E.H. to be a man of incredible confidence. His intentions were always to ensure that his son knew that he was a man of great power, who could will anything he wanted because he was born a man and because he had God-given authority. Pastor Johnson was no stranger to the hardships of life, nor was ignorant to the plight of Black men. He knew that they were Blessed to live in their own paradise, to live in Freedman. But he wanted E.H. to be bigger than their safe haven. And to be bigger than Freedman and enter the rest of the world, E.H. needed the audacity of men who didn't have the precursor "Black" in their title. That is the confidence Pastor Johnson meant to instill in his son. That is who he intended Edwin-Hendricks Delroy Johnson to be. Eddie's arrogance and distorted sense of entitlement was just an added benefit. Pastor Johnson was proud of those qualities. He preferred seeing Eddie with those attributes than this pathetic "woe-is-me" attitude he had taken on.

Pastor Johnson exited the pews, starting towards his office. He turned to his son as if he had a final thought but decided to tap the wall and give him a reassuring smile instead. Bible study was a few hours away, and Eddie knew his father needed to prepare. Eddie knew what he needed to do. He knew exactly what needed to be done. His plan started with the local 'good time gal' Shelly Hicks. She was at the general store.

"Hey dere Miss Shelly. How you doin' this fine afternoon?" Eddie asked with a smile.

"Oh, nothing really, just watchin da sto' while Mr. Brooks is gone. Can I help you?" Shelly replied.

Eddie had always thought Shelly was a pretty girl. He remembered her being smart too. When they were kids, she was like everyone's big sister. She was maternal and friendly, bossy as hell too. She was such a good girl. But that's the curse of being a woman, Eddie figured. It's only a matter of time before they're true character surfaced. He knew that women were naturally inclined to bend to the will of men–it takes a woman of discipline and virtue to overcome temptation. That's what Eddie was taught. And on the other side of that, it was a man's nature to push the limits of a woman's virtue–and it takes an equally disciplined man to not abuse that authority.

But despite who she used to be, despite what he used to think of her, he had to use what he knows of her now. She was a whore. She was easy. Easy to talk to, easy to be brazen with, easy to manipulate. All he had to do was pretend to be interested, which wouldn't take much pretending, and she'd probably tell him all about her escapades with Dexter.

"You can help me understand why Brooks has such a pretty thing like ya self workin' in his sto' for one." He grabbed the girl's hand. Shelly blushed, coyly. Eddie walked from one end of the counter to the other. He stepped around the corner and walked towards her. They were standing closely to one another, but not so close that anyone would think anything of it.

"Well, I helps around here every now and then so Brooks can be with his sick wife. My Ma is wo' low, so I knows the burden of tendin' to the ill. Plus, he pays me, and it helps me take care of the house, wit Liza gone to Savannah to sing and all."

Shelly leaned over the counter, leaning towards where Eddie was leaning against the counter. The whole time Shelly spoke, E.H. followed her eyes with his own. She went back and forth between looking in his eyes and at her hand. He only heard every other thing she said, but he wanted Shelly to think that he was hung on every word she spoke. Shelly blushed again seeing how attentive he was. "What you need, Edwin-Hen. You ain't come in here to be sweet on me."

"Why ain't I?" he asked.

"Cause I'm me," she replied. They chuckled and stepped closer to each other.

"I'll be honest, I came in here lookin' for you, but not to bump gums about the sto' or Brooks' sick wife, God bless her soul." He stared down his nose at her with a suggestive grin. "I just wanna ask you somethin'."

"Sure." Shelly looked at him with wanting eyes.

"You ain't sweet on that Dexter Alexander, are you? 'fore I go and start somethin' I'm not 'posed to." Shelly sighed and stood up. She walked to the other end of the counter and greeted the people who walked in. She looked over her shoulder at Eddie and shook her head. It felt strange. He could tell she had something to say, but she seemed afraid, or maybe ashamed, to say it. He didn't know if he should be concerned for her or not, but he was excited to know that there was a story there —a story he could tell River and the rest of Freedman.

"He ain't do you nothin' did he," Eddie asked. He inched closer to Shelly.

"Naw..." she replied. She made her way around the counter and started to do little work around the store to avoid the conversation, but E.H. was right on her tail. He started smoothing and folding fabric, pretending to help. Pretending like he cared.

"C'mon now, Shelly, tell me what's got ya goat, girl? I won't say nothin' I just want to make sure I ain't startin' no trouble with a new friend is all."

She took a deep sigh and turned on her heel. She grabbed Eddie's shoulder and pulled him into a corner. She stood on her tip toes and looked over him to make sure no one in the store was in earshot of their conversation. Then, she began her story.

"Look, I don't likes talkin' 'bout it because I still don't understand it myself." Eddie's brows furrowed, and his posture relaxed. He looked over his shoulder and stepped closer to the girl.

"What happened with y'all that you can't make out or understand it," he asked her, confused. Shelly shook her head and rolled her eyes. Her body was as stiff as a board. Eddie started to hug her, but he didn't want to comfort her too much. He wanted her to feel safe enough to share, but not so safe that she didn't still feel pressured to say what it is she was keeping secret.

"Well, I was comin' in here to help Mr. Brooks out, when Dexter came in. He said he needed some work and had been doing little odd jobs around town, but he needed to make real money. I didn't want ol' Brooks to give away my job, so I interrupted him. I came from behind him and put my hand on his shoulder hopin' to get his mind in other places. 'Dat's my job.' I say wit' a smile. 'I helps round here when Brooks is off to tend to his wife, and I don't need no help or distraction while I work.' Dexter gave me dat pretty smile and tipped his cap to me. He say 'I'on mean to put da lady of of job, but I could fix somethin' up if need be.' Brooks takes 'em round back and made a list of all the things that need tendin' to round this old ass sto'. So, Brooks leaves and it's just me and Dexter."

Taking a deep breath, Shelly looked down in shame. She held her breath for just a moment, giving herself the chance to draw the strength to continue her story and delve into the dark corner of her memory. She looked back up at Eddie, his eyes glowing with anticipation. He stared at her intensely and waited for her to finish. Shelly touched her lip, searching for comfort in the familiarity of her own skin. She closed her eyes once more and drew in more air. When she opened her eyes again, they were distant, focusing on a moment far beyond the present.

"Well, 'specially now that summer's approachin', I figured I'd take a moment outback to feel fresh air on my skin. So, I went to the back porch and started to undress a bit. I pulls my skirt up to give my legs some air, and Dexter come out behind me. I saw him seein' me, and he saw me see him. Then he came over and asked if I wanted a cold drank from the icebox in Brooks' office. I don't normally tarry round Brooks' office, but Dexter just got day smile. He just smiled dat pretty smile at me and he just so kind, so I went in dere wit' 'em. When he got me alone in da office, he–"

Shelly interrupted her own story by blowing out sharply. She tried to breathe but the pain of her memory blocked any semblance of relief she may have been able to give herself. Eddie walked up to her and wrapped his arms around her neck. She held his waist tightly and sobbed. Eddie figured it was from shame. He knew that he had her right where he wanted her. He rubbed her back and patted her hair while imagining what she and Dexter could have been doing in the back office.

E.H. imagined Dexter undressing Shelly, his fingers deftly sliding the fabric from her shoulders, revealing her smooth, coffee-colored skin. He envisioned her face contorting in a mix of pain and pleasure, eyes fluttering shut as waves of ecstasy coursed through her. He pictured how breathtakingly beautiful she must have been pent beneath Dexter. Her hair cascading around her face like a curly vail, framing her delicate features and accentuating the softness of her dimples.

It didn't take long for Eddie to envision himself being the one enjoying Shelly, only she was atop of him; her movements fluid and graceful, every curve of her body illuminated by a soft, glowing light. He could almost hear the breathy whisper of his name on her lips, the sound was a tantalizing caress in the quietness of the empty store office. He felt the phantom touch of her hands against his chest, the playful push and pull, her voice a mix of laughter and protest as she told him to stop.

The fantasy unfolded with such vivid clarity that he became lost in the depth of his longing, the vivid imagery blurring the lines between reality and desire. It wasn't until he felt the stillness beneath his hands that he was jolted back to the present, realizing with a start that Shelly was no longer crying, and his grip had become suffocatingly tight around her.

He released her from his grips and turned around to see if anyone had noticed the commotion. The couple who had come in earlier had left the store and some coins on the counter.

"Sorry there, Shelly, I just slipped away thinkin' on what

he could have done to such a petite woman like yourself," Eddie admitted. Gasping for air, Shelly's eyes went from Eddie's face to his pants, then back up at him.

"What da hell is wrong wit you," she asked before stomping away. Eddie turned beet red and rolled his eyes as he adjusted himself.

"Now, Shelly—"

"Get outta here! Get outta here before I go in the office and get Mr. Brooks' double barrel," she shouted.

Eddie lifted his hands and stepped back. "You wouldn't know how to shoot it if ya got it," he said as he walked backward out of the store. He had heard enough and what he didn't hear, his imagination filled in the rest. He felt the tightness in his groin and huffed in annoyance. He thought again about how pretty Shelly was. Her bright, brown eyes. Her pouty mouth, the perfect roundness of her nose.

He realized that he had never seen her hair free before. It was always pinned up into tight curls, or she'd have it in pigtails when they were younger. It occurred to him that he didn't really know what her natural hair looked like–but one thing he *did* know about Shelly, or her hair rather, was that it never had any silver streaks in it like it did today. He saw her and Dexter coming from behind the store together just two days ago, and her hair had no grays in it then. *What happened between then and now?* Eddie wondered.

Silver hair aside, he learned everything he needed from Shelly. He was ready to talk to River and confront Dexter. He was going to the river to find him and Charlette and make Dexter tell him everything Shelly didn't. He wanted him to say how he fucked an unwed, impure, full-figured and experienced woman like Shelly Hicks. He wanted him to admit that all he wanted was to do the same to River. He wanted vindication.

CHAPTER 7

E.H. walked through town in a rush. He saw Henry Stitts and asked if he had seen River or Dexter.

"Seen 'em goin to dat river bout half an hour ago," Henry said.

E. H. made his way through the field and started to approach the trees when he heard rustling coming from the foliage. He didn't know if it was a raccoon or a wild dog, but it could have been River and Dexter, so he followed the sound. He pushed through the brush of shrubs and hanging leaves, and walked up on a small rabbit. When he realized that it was just a little bunny making the noise, he turned to walk away. As he took a step to head in the next direction, he realized that the rabbit was sitting on its hindlegs.

"Was that rabbit staring at me," he asked himself. E.H. turned around slowly, just to see if the rabbit was still sitting there. He found the creature stuck in the same position. It wasn't looking in his direction or staying still to avoid confrontation. The rabbit was staring at Edwin directly in his eyes.

E.H. took a step back, and the rabbit hopped forward. E.H. took two steps back, and the rabbit mirrored his movement, closing the gap with an eerie precision. Eddie jumped and fell backward, his heart pounding in his chest. The rabbit, its eyes gleaming with a sinister light, hopped closer until it stood directly in front of him. Eddie lay on his back, supporting himself with his elbows, his breath coming in ragged gasps. He looked at the rabbit through the space between his knees, its gaze unnervingly fixed on his.

Neither moved. The stillness stretched into an agonizing eternity, each second dripping with a palpable dread. When E.H. finally tried to stand, he found his body unresponsive. He pressed his funny-bone against the ground, attempting to push himself up, but he didn't budge. He planted his hands for support, but his fists remained clenched, as if frozen by some unseen force. The rabbit, a dark harbinger, had hopped even closer.

Being the son of a pastor, E.H's first instinct was to pray. He wanted to bind the rabbit and send whatever malevolent spell he was under back to the sender tenfold, but his lips were sealed shut. He tried to plead the Blood of Jesus over his mind, to ask God to shield him from this tangible evil, but his mouth wouldn't move. The rabbit crept closer, its presence heavy with an unnatural weight, until it was sitting on Eddie's navel. E.H. half-expected the demon animal to speak or reveal some grotesque, human-like expression, but it remained unnervingly silent, its nose twitching sporadically.

A cold, paralyzing fear enveloped E.H., his body trembling as he closed his eyes and started to cry. The sound of a low, guttural moan echoed around him, a disembodied lament that sent shivers down his spine. He opened his eyes and found himself on the floor of Mr. Brooks' office, disoriented and confused. Shelly was atop him, her weight pressing down, her movements feverish and frantic. His body felt febrile, his skin slick with sweat, his breath coming in shallow, panicked bursts. His hands gripped her waist, the sensation foreign and terrifying.

E.H's senses were overwhelmed, his mind a whirl of horror and disorientation. His toes curled, his knees bent, and his lower body tensed uncontrollably. His eyes were squeezed shut so tightly that tears streamed down his face, mingling with the sweat and fear that consumed him. The boundary between nightmare and fantasy blurred, leaving him trapped in a horror he couldn't escape.

"Look at me," a seductive feminine voice commanded. *"Look at me, Eddie."* He knew that voice and it wasn't Shelly's. Out of horror and curiosity, Eddie opened his eyes. Much to his surprise, and to a great pleasure that instantly started to move within him, E.H. found River looking down at him. He was mesmerized. Whether it was by how *fucking* beautiful she looked on top of him, or by the rhythm with which she grinded against him, he couldn't tell, but he was hypnotized.

He couldn't help himself; he wanted to feel her, every inch of her. *Matthew 26:41,* he thought. *The Spirit is willing, but the flesh is weak.* He took one hand and grazed it up her torso, taking time to feel the smoothness of her wet skin. She grabbed his wrist and placed his index finger in her mouth. E.H. threw his head back in pleasure, curling his toes so tightly that he thought they'd lock. Her mouth was soft, wet, and warm. It was hot, unbearably hot. His finger was burning.

With a gasp, he snatched his hand away and opened his eyes. He was back in the woods, but a suffocating darkness had fallen over the trees like a navy-blue cloak. River was still there, but she wasn't herself. Her hair was as thin as it was long, now gray and straight. Her body had become frail, her eyes were dark voids that seemed to swallow all light.

E.H.'s heart pounded in his chest as he tried to push her off, but she — this old, frail, hollow-eyed woman — pushed down harder, her movements frantic and unrelenting. His body began to betray him, responding against his will. *"Eddie,"* the woman rasped, in a voice that was decaying and brittle. He pushed harder, but his arms were weak, as if the strength had been siphoned from them.

"Eddie," she cried again, her voice a grotesque parody of the woman he loved, moaning his name in a nightmarish fit of pleasure. The woman grew skinnier, her wrinkles deepening, her appearance more corpse-like with every second. Her skin felt paper-thin, tearing at his touch, her hair falling out in

clumps around him. *"Eddieeeeee,"* she groaned, her voice a muted eruption of unholy satisfaction.

Tears streamed down his face as his body convulsed in an unwilling release. With a final, satisfied huff, the decrepit shell of a woman collapsed onto his chest. He opened his eyes to find himself staring into the skeletal remains of the woman he wanted to profess his love to, her empty eye sockets boring into him.

With a scream, he jumped up, his heart pounding in terror. He was back in the woods, facing the rabbit again, the nightmarish vision seemingly a cruel trick of his mind. He turned frantically to look around, the oppressive darkness pressing in from all sides, but nothing seemed out of the ordinary.

He took a step away, his breath rugged and uneven, but a morbid curiosity made him glance back. Slowly, he turned his head over his shoulder, dreading what he might see. The rabbit was gone, leaving behind an eerie silence that seeped into his bones. The terror of the encounter lingered, a chilling reminder that he was not alone in the pursuit of River's affection.

THE NEXT DAY

Charlette woke up feeling refreshed and full of life. Between the moment she drifted to sleep and the time she woke up, she was washed of her shame. Her creator was a God of grace. She was reminded that, despite her newfound abilities, she was human and humans are curious. She was assured that she was still a girl on the heels of becoming a woman. It was only natural of her to be swept into temptation, but like the good and faithful servant she was, she did not yield to the desire of her flesh. She did not waver from the commitment she made to herself and to God.

So, River dressed, braided her hair, and sat under the window above her bed. The wind caressed her face as it entered her room. The smell of honeysuckle filled the air. *Today is going to be a good day,* she proclaimed to herself. Her mother had already left for work, and her father was still asleep. River wanted to take advantage of not having to speak to anyone. She reveled in the freedom of not having to smile, or laugh, or sing, or pray for anyone. She enjoyed this rare moment of solitude so much that she skipped going to the New George River that morning, and decided to enjoy her peace at home.

She sat on the porch of her home and thought about how she had spent the last nineteen years. Her mind allowed itself to reflect on years of unquestioned obedience, to her family, to God, to the community. She thought of all the people she had prayed for, all the jars of Blessed oil she made, all the manifestations she had scripted in her prayer journal. After a few minutes of allowing her mind to shift from blissful reminiscing to focused remembrance, she realized that very little of her spiritual gifts were used to grow herself at all.

She couldn't remember ever asking for anything other than strengthening her discernment or empowering the spirit that lived within her. Never once had she asked God for an A on a quiz, or for a financial Blessing for her home. She wondered, had she never asked for these things because faith always blocked her worries or because she knew the Jehovah Jireh had always proven himself to be a provider. Or was it because she never prioritized her own life, her own desires.

River sat and watched the road as she thought. Her mind was lost in itself until she remembered that her birthday was the next day.

When Eddie's mother was alive, she'd make a cake for River and Eddie. She would always wait until dinner before taking it to the Montgomery home with Eddie. It was River's favorite birthday tradition before Mitsy passed. Charlette stood up and dusted her white linen dress before strutting towards the church. She gathered herself and held her head high. She was happy to be nineteen tomorrow, and she was excited to celebrate it with Eddie.

Last year, he was in Savannah the whole summer preparing to go to school. He stayed with his mother's sister and worked with her downtown in a diner that had an all-colored staff. He spoke to the few Black professionals to pick their brains. He was gifted a copy of *The Souls of Black Folk* by a man who owned and sold property all around Georgia. He let River read it when he came home in July before going to Atlanta in August. Charlette was excited to see what Dexter would do for her birthday since this was the first one they would spend together, but she really wanted to spend the day with Eddie. If nothing else, then to catch up with him. She hadn't realized how long it had been since they had seen each other, but she knew where she could find him.

The church doors swung open and presented River standing in the center of the door frame with a ray of light shining on her like the angel Pastor Johnson thought her to be. He smiled.

"God told me he would bring a blessing today, River Montgomery. But it ain't never crossed my mind that it would be with your beautiful presence." He embraced her with a hug. He lingered and rocked her from left to right, just once before letting her go. "My God, today. What a lovely gal you is."

"I didn't want much Pastor." Charlette said as she sat on the back pew. "I came looking for Eddie, but I realize now that my birthday falls on a Sunday. You think it's too late to ask for a song to sing?"

The pastor grabbed her hand and sat next to the young woman. "As long as I'm Pastor, you ain't never gon' need permission to praise the Lord in this house. I ain't da kind to keep folk from dey callin' and sanging is surely yours, Miss River."

Charlette blushed as she pulled on the tail of her braid. She didn't know why, but she was nervous. Something about the whole interaction felt awkward. She didn't like being around

Pastor Johnson alone anymore. Not since what he said in Brooks' store. "Eddie not 'round here, I reckon?" she asked.

Pastor Johnson shook his head. "Naw, he ain't neither. Done forgot 'bout my own boy, I did. Come to thank 'bout it, River, I ain't seen him all mornin'. I reckon you don't know where he been?"

River shook her head. They looked at one another waiting for the other to provide more information, but neither of them had a clue where he could be. Pastor Johnson had fallen asleep early that night, but when he woke up that day, he just assumed his son was in his room asleep. Did E.H. ever come home, he thought to himself. And if he hadn't come home, it was strange that he hadn't seen Charlette either. After a moment of uninterrupted silence, River stood up and began to say her goodbyes.

"Nie, wait on right dere, a minute River, I wants to talk to you." Pastor Johnson announced. River sat back down. She knew he was going to take this opportunity to make an appeal on Eddie's behalf. She could already hear him saying not to think much of his absence and to give him grace because he was a young man who needed time to expel his earthly desires before settling down and answering his calling. River was already annoyed, but it wouldn't be a visit with Pastor Johnson without him trying to hook the two of them up, somehow.

"I hear you goin' round town fancyin' that Alexander boy that blew in here. Dey say he walk you to and from dat New George every day, and when y'all ain't dere, you's followin' behind him like a lost puppy."

River shifted her weight in the seat and patted her lap before looking the Pastor in his eyes. She was praying that he didn't sense her aggravation. He straightened his posture and lifted his chin acknowledging her indignation.

"River, I met the man, and I got to say, he pretty charmin'. But he ain't da man for da likes of you. You just mo' beautiful den any colored woman in Georgia, and you smart as a whip, stubborn as a mule at times, and you got da voice of an angel, gal. I understand, he tall and easy on da eyes, but he just a simple man with a dream. If you wanted to be a preacher's wife, you could just marry my Edwin-Hendricks."

River knew he meant no harm, but she truly was uninterested in what he had to say. She had known Eddie her whole life and never saw him the way Pastor Johnson wanted her to. He and her mother had been trying for years to get them together, and it hadn't worked. Only recently had River begun to realize that it may never work. She's a young woman now, ready to enter the world on her own. She didn't need anyone to tell her what to do or who to love. God brought Dexter to Freedman for a reason, and Charlette was beginning to think it was to get her out of there.

"Pastor, I love you and respect you, but this here is my life. Now if it's okay with you, I'm gonna go on to the New George and practice for tomorrow," she replied as gently as her voice would allow. They stood up and Pastor Johnson let out a discouraged sigh. She reached out for a hug, but the round man clapped his arms in front of him and shook his head. Charlette took a step back and placed her hands on his hip.

"Now I know you ain't just decline a hug, Pastor Johnson," she questioned. He opened his arms and River stepped in for a hug before bidding the man adieu.

She still wasn't ready to go to the water, so she set out to find Eddie instead. She walked towards the town square and prepared herself for the people she would see. As she made it into eye shot, Hop Wilson jumped down from the porch.

"Hot damn! Dere she is! Dere she is!" he said, announcing her presence. He smiled like a proud father as River walked over to him and the few men that were with him. He put his hands around her shoulder and faced her towards the crowd of people loitering in front the stores.

"Nineteen years ago tomorra, dis here angel was given to Cleo and Cecilia Montgomery. Being her daddy's best friend and all, I was da first one to know of her arrival."

Cleo Montgomery hated Hop Wilson, but Hop continued with his tall tale.

"Da doctor pulled her from 'tween Cee Cee's pretty brown legs and handed her to me. 'Mighty fine baby you got dere,' Dr. Bailey say. I say, 'She ain't none of mine. Cleo big ugly ass be dis baby Pappy, but thank you jus' the same." Everyone around laughed and clapped as Charlette blushed and pulled on her hair. They all wished her a happy early birthday and asked if she'd go with them to Hop's brother's juke joint later that night.

"My Ma would knock me into next week if I went to a juke joint with y'all," she replied. Truth be told, River never wanted to drink or go to parties or hang around with people outside of being cordial. She never wanted to do anything but sing, read, and pray. River didn't think much about what her life would look like as an adult. She liked being told what to do. It gave her the opportunity to follow instructions and follow them correctly. She honestly enjoyed doing *right*. It drove her. It grounded her. There was a security in being obedient. Most people view submission as a forfeiture of control, but she thought of it as the opposite. She saw submission as shifting fault on to someone else.

"Aw girl, you'll be a full growed woman tomorra. Don't be so focused on where you go in death that you miss happiness in life," Mr. Jenkins advised from the porch. She blushed and instructed herself to take that advice.

"My Ma would say that she liked to enjoy flowers while she can smell 'em. Say dey ain't no use to her dead." Hop added. River understood what they were saying and was thankful to have people who cared about her happiness, but she heard too many stories about whores and simple men. She wasn't looking for comfort in the bottom of a bottle or love between the sheets of strangers. She wasn't looking for anything other than what she had.

"Thank y'all for the offer, but I just came 'round her looking for Eddie-Hen. His daddy say he been gone all morning. I ain't even see him yesterday, when I think about it."

"I seen him follow behind you and Dex yesterday when y'all was going to da New George. Y'all ain't see em?" Mr. Jenkins added.

"Naw. He ain't followed none of us down there. We woulda seen him," River replied.

"Well, he crossed that field and walked through dem trees. What he did after dat, I can't say, but I knows dese ol' eyes seen him walk dat way," Mr. Jenkins told her. River remembered going to the water and talking to Dexter for hours before actually making him leave so she could pray. Eddie never once joined them. He didn't even show up peeking behind trees.

"That's mighty strange because we never saw him," she responded to her old friend.

"I'm sho he somewhere lookin' fo' you too, River. Gon' on and find him. We'll be here tomorra wit' gifs," Mr. Jenkins announced.

River smiled and waved to everyone as she walked off. Still not ready to go to the river, she ran back to Hop Wilson. "Dex still at your house?"

"Now wait jus' a damn minute, gal," Hop said as he crossed his arms across his chest. "You ain't finna be wit' dat man alone in my house. Not so yo' daddy big, black ass can come clean my clock after Dexter get you in a bad way."

River's color flushed. "I—I didn't mean, I—I wasn't suggestin…" River stammered and struggled to grab the tail of her braid as she spoke. Hop and everyone else fell into a loud, rhythmic laughter at River's expense. She was so embarrassed. Her hands were shaking as she tried to soothe herself by stoking her hair. "Daggone Hop," she thought to herself, unable to curse even if no one would hear it.

"Aw, I'm jus jokin', gal. I knows you'd sic da holy ghost on em 'fo you let 'em lay you down before marriage. Stay pure, baby girl. He's a good man. He'll wait. He might still be dere, dat's where I left em this morn' and I ain't seen 'em since." Hop gave River a wink and reassuring smile.

After the red in her cheeks mellowed to an even brown, Hop told her again that he meant no harm and apologized for embarrassing her. She knew he was just joking but the embarrassment was there for a reason. He was right, she *would have* had a fit if Dex or any other man tried–really tried– to pressure her into something she wasn't ready for, but that's what she *would have* done. *Now*, with *him*, she wasn't so sure that her flesh wasn't weak.

River enjoyed her walk to Hop's house, each step light and buoyant. The air felt cooler than usual, and the grass seemed to shimmer in a brighter shade of green. The closer she got to Dexter, the happier she felt. Anticipation and excitement danced in her stomach like blue and purple butterflies. Her abdominal muscles tightened and flexed the nearer she drew to the shack. She realized just how much she wanted to see Dexter, her body physically aching for his presence. She stopped in front of the one-room shack, trying to calm the fluttering in her belly. *"Is this how girls feel when they like a boy? Is this what happens when you're falling in love?"* she wondered.

River's thoughts raced as she tried to steady herself before knocking on the door. Inside, Dexter watched her through the window, grinning and silently laughing. He felt the same way—excited, giddy, like a little boy again. Whenever they were near each other, euphoria was inevitable. In each other's eyes, they saw their future: a life filled with their heart's desires. She was gifted and beautiful, loyal and faithful, more powerful than she realized. To him, she was perfect, exactly who he needed.

River let out a sigh and walked toward the door. Just as she lifted her fist to knock, the thin wooden door flew open. Dexter stood there, his eyes sparkling with the same excitement and longing that filled her own heart. Their smiles mirrored each other's, a silent testament to the connection that pulled them together, stronger than any force they had ever known.

"You done thinkin' and talkin' to ya self," Dex asked with a teasing smile. He leaned in the door frame with his right elbow supporting him and his hand holding his tilted head. Charlette looked from his smile to his coffee-colored arms to his broad, bare chest. She blushed, her heart fluttering.

Dexter stepped aside, inviting her in. "Just need to throw a shirt on and some shoes. I'll be ready in two shakes."

River sat on the cot in the corner as Dexter buttoned his shirt. She shifted her sight from one small object to another, distracting herself as Dex dressed. She let her eyes wander around the small space that was Hop Wilson's house. It looked like an old slave's quarter with everything all in one room. Her gaze flitted from the cold kettle on the stove to the spoons and knives dangling from hooks on the wall. She looked from there to the rickety table and the old wooden chairs. She started at the floorboards and all the dust that covered them, which led her to Dexter's feet. Her eyes traced up his legs, taking in his high-quality slacks, then moved to his neatly buttoned shirt, and finally to his thick, strong neck.

Before she realized it, she was staring into his eyes. *Had he been walking toward her the entire time she was looking at him,* she wondered. He was closer now, standing right in front of her. His long arm reached out, his hand gently cradling the back of her head. She stared up at him, losing herself in his gaze. Lost in the burning of his eyes, she saw everything he was thinking because she was thinking it too.

The air between them crackled with unspoken desire. Without a word, Dexter pushed her back onto the cot. He began unbuttoning his shirt as River fumbled with his belt. There was no hesitation, no second-guessing. Deep down, they both had wanted this moment to happen.

Their movements were frantic, filled with an urgency that neither of them could deny. As his shirt fell open and her hands roamed his body, they surrendered to the intense, magnetic pull between them. It was a moment of pure, unfiltered passion, leaving no room for thoughts, only the undeniable connection they shared, only their instincts.

"You–you hear dat?" River asked Dexter. Dexter didn't hear a thing. His eyes were focused on her full, brown lips. For all he knew she could be hearing the sounds of Gabriel's horn, signaling the rapture, and even then, he wasn't going to let that ruin this moment between the two of them.

"Hear what?" he responded. The door opened and Eddie walked through. The three of them frozen in time, suspended from nature, stared at one another. River's eyes started to water from shame. She was caught. Eddie could see her. He could see all the sin that she had been lusting for since the day she met Dexter Alexander, and she could not deny it ever again because she was caught. Because Eddie had caught her. All for his viewing pleasure, Eddie could see her hands on Dexter's waistband and her legs wrapped around his. *Matthew 26:41,* she thought. Only she, and she assumed Eddie did too, knew that her flesh was more than weak, but also willing.

After a few seconds Dexter started to stand up just as Eddie charged him.

"EDDIE!" River shouted. She got off of the cot before it collapsed under the enormous weight of the two heavy men. Eddie was choking Dexter and Dexter was hitting Eddie anywhere his fists would land. The tears whipped back to

River's ears as she dashed to get between them. Her heart was beating so quickly she thought she would fall out and die right there. Eddie released Dexter's neck and punched him in his left eye.

"EDWIN!" River cried. Dex kneed Eddie between his legs and grabbed his collar before he could fall back in pain. He pushed down on Eddie's shoulders and used him to stand up. Dexter landed two punches to Eddie's right eye before dropping him to the ground.

"DEXTER!" River yelled.

Eddie laid on the ground in pain watching as River dashed around the shack looking for something to patch Dexter up with. He was hurting but not so much that he couldn't move. He rolled over on his back and turned his head to see Dexter looking at him from a chair in the kitchen. They locked eyes and stared at one another. River took a damp towel and pressed it against Dexter's left eye. Eddie could feel tears forming in the wells of his eyes. Just as he started to close his eyelids, he saw Dexter grin.

He's done it. Eddie thought. *Dexter Alexander, that stranger who strolled into town only a month ago had done the thing every young man, elder, and child wanted to do for years: He got Charlette Montgomery.*

River never made it to the New George that day. After the whole scene at Hop Wilson's house, she went back home. She patched Dexter up before walking Eddie home and going back to her own house. Eddie tried to apologize, but that turned into the two of them arguing and her crying. She spent the whole day replaying that one part of her day. She sat, legs crossed, in the center of her bed thinking about how she had almost given her body to Dexter. She laid with her head over the edge of the bed thinking about Eddie punching Dexter so hard she thought she could feel it. She turned towards the wall and thought about Dexter striking Eddie twice in the same eye, leaving a gash on her best friend's handsome face. And she laid flat on her stomach and sobbed as Eddie's words rang in her mind: "You don't love me no mo' because he's turning you into a common whore!"

She saw the rage and pain in his eyes as he yelled it. Pastor Johnson walked up as he said it too. River felt gutted. She couldn't move after he had said it. All sound was muted, and her ears started to ring. *Whore.* Pastor Johnson tried to speak to her, but she couldn't hear him. She could barely see him through the tears that welled in her eyes.

She felt lower than the dirt at the bottom of their shoes. Seeing her best friend so angry, so hurt, and all because she had fallen for another man. All because he had seen her *with* a man. She never thought Eddie could make her feel so bad.

Whore.

It echoed in her mind as she watched Pastor Johnson pull Eddie away. The rage in Eddie's eyes scorched her soul as he scowled at her when he walked away. She wanted to go to the water and pray. She wanted to lay in the water and be cleansed of her sin. She wanted to go there and stand in front of God and ask him why she was suffering and why she was wavering. She wanted to know what purpose all this turmoil served. She wanted to know why she was being tempted. She wanted answers.

The next morning, Cecilia entered Charlette's room with a cup of coffee, a bowl of grits, two small hoe cakes, and ears ready to listen. She heard River crying the day before but knew not to bother her. She figured she was feeling a deep sense of anguish. For her daughter to cry in bed all day rather than at the river praying for clarity and peace, it must have been a faith-breaking pain that she was suffering through, and Cecilia knew through lived experience that nothing a person says to you sticks until you're close to being on the other end of healing.

"Wake up, pretty girl. Time to thank God for a full nineteen years of favor, grace, and a joyous life." River rolled over and faced the wall. She completed her nineteenth year of life. She wanted to celebrate, but she was still hurting.

"I know you're singin' in church today, so I want you to be up there full and focused. I got you a proper breakfast right here." Cecilia never knew River to not jump up at the mention of singing in church, so her daughter ignoring her only confirmed that she was beyond reach, but still she felt a glint of annoyance in herself that would not go away with parental understanding. Cecilia sat the tray of food on the edge of the bed and placed her hand on her daughter's head. "You don't feel warm, Charlette, so I need you to get ya narrow behind up and get ready for church. Can you get up for that reason, at least?"

River rolled over and laid on her back before covering her face. Cecilia threw her hands over her daughters as River started to cry. Cee Cee pulled her child's petite hands down slowly and looked at her tears. She kissed River's face before asking what happened.

"They got into a fight, Mama, and it's all my fault!" The words fell out of her and released a heavy wail behind them. Her chest heaved up and down as groans and cries left her mouth.

Cleo shot into the room and nearly sat on the tray at the foot of the bed. "Baby, what's the matter? What happened?!" he roared with deep concern. He tried to gentle his heavy voice, but his fear and anger could not be hidden.

"Sound like Dexter and E.H. got into it," Cecila explained.

"Oh hell," Cleo said with a shrug as rolled his eyes.

"Nah, they got *into* it. They had a fight."

"Aw… hell." Cleo sat back down.

River shot up and wrapped herself around her mother. Cecilia held her close and rocked her. Cleo grabbed her foot and held it, thumbing over the veins under her cinnamon skin.

"We got to get ready, Letty. We got to go to church." Cecilia reminded River.

River stood front and center of the church desolate and sullen. The choir sat behind her. She opened her mouth to sing, but no words came out. She shook her head as one tear fell.

"Dats alright" A woman cried from the crowd.

"Let 'em work" Pastor Johnson followed.

River sighed and tried again. *Oh no...* she thought. The world around her faded. She was transcending. She was losing consciousness. She was about to give way to a spell of divination. Her body felt weightless, and her eyes rolled backward. She started praying. Her eyes were closed, but she felt them fly from left to right rapidly under her eyelids. The pounding of her heart sounded like a horse galloping unrestricted and free. Her body stiffened, and her throat opened. She tried to listen to what she and the congregation was saying, but she only heard her heart.

"Oh God...Please Father...God of mercy I call to you!" she shouted. A loud, long "YES!" rang from the crowd. She heard people clapping and crying, but she still didn't see anyone. "Use me, God..." She heard herself say and repeat. She came back into her body. She fell to her knees and tears burned her hot face. "Father God, I thank You!" She shouted. She could see and feel again, but she was not in control of the words she was saying. People all over the congregation were shouting. She saw her mother with arms lifted and shouting praises to God. Miss Tolbert was bent over touching breast to knees with one arm outstretched behind her as she yelled "Thank Ya! Thank Ya!" repeatedly. River stood up still giving God praise and made eye contact with Eddie. His right eye was swollen shut, but his left eye was perfectly fine. He saw the fear in River's eyes and stepped towards her.

"Father, You come in and use this place... Be seen here Holy Ghost...We yield to Your will, O God! We submit to Your mercy, O God! Let Your presence take hold of everybody in this place, O God, and let it be known that Jesus! Lives! Here!" Pastor Johnson shouted.

The second Eddie wrapped his arms around River, she collapsed. The church fell silent in confusion.

CHAPTER 8

After church, Pastor Johnson stopped River and Cecilia to invite them to his house. He wanted to thank River for such a beautiful, spiritual moment in church and the rest of the congregation wanted to wish her a happy birthday. River felt weak and confused, but her mother insisted that they at least show their face at the Johnson's house since it was a gathering in her honor. They went home before going to the Johnson's. Cecilia grabbed the pie she baked the night before while River washed her face.

"Ma, I really don't think I can do this. I feel sick," River explained.

"Just the spirit movin' in you." Cecilia replied. She wrapped her thin arm around her daughter's shoulder and squeezed her tightly. She wasn't listening to River. She wasn't paying attention. Even if she actually wanted to go to the Johnson household, she couldn't. Her body was still recovering from the spectacle in church.

River shook her head. "Nah, Mama. It feels like something took over me and hasn't given a part of me back yet. I don't think the spirit does that to you," River said. She tried to put it plainly so that her mother understood how afraid she was. River had been trying to figure out if her ability to float and be absent of her body was connected to her gift of discernment or her ability to will things into existence by nothing but faith alone, but the weakness she was feeling in the moment was almost a confirmation for River that what she was feeling, was from a spirit that did not have *Holy* proceeding its name.

Cecilia realized River was more than nervous or

embarrassed by her episode in the church. She saw that her daughter was shaken and scared. For a second, Cecilia was scared of whatever made River afraid too. Charlette was never afraid of anything. If her daughter was shaken by something, then Cecilia should be terrified. But the moment was fleeting. Her empathy was temporary.

She didn't feel concerned for River or her well-being. She was annoyed with nineteen years of pampering and coddling her daughter. She was tired of being overruled by her husband. Cecilia's fear was replaced by anger, rage even. She had felt something within her that she had been trying to extinguish for years, but the flames of irrational indignation consumed her.

She used to love people's admiration and awe of Charlette. She loved people stopping them and saying how blessed River was and how lucky she and Cleo were. She loved their jealousy. But now, seeing River's fragility and weakness, that admiration turned to resentment. Cecilia's view of her daughter started to shift around the time River turned fifteen or sixteen. She loved her daughter and supported her through everything, but she was sick of coddling her. She was tired of River always needing shielding, protection, and comforting. Everyone thought she was so strong and her faith so big, but they knew nothing of her fragility.

River acted like every little thing was a damn sin. Before Charlette could speak, Cleo could drink any man under the table, but after a while, all he heard was a little girl in the back of his mind reminding him, "Don't forget that drunkards will never inherit the Kingdom of God, Daddy. First Corinthians chapter 6, verses 9 through 10."

Cecilia didn't know who to blame more, herself or her husband. She wanted to instill faith in River so she could use it as a source of strength when the world got hard. That's how she survived the worst years of her life, so she wanted to pass that down to her daughter. But Cecilia knew plenty of people who could have fun and let loose and still remain obedient to

God's word. Why was Charlette so uptight and holier-than-thou? Cleo did that to her. Always telling her that she was better than something, that she was made for a bigger purpose, always shielding her eyes when strangers kissed or covering her ears when old men cussed. Yeah, he ruined her. He spoiled her and made her an unlikable, insufferable, self-righteous little brat, and Cecilia was sick of her daughter's sanctimoniousness.

There were times when young boys or old men would come around, and Cecilia wanted to yell, "Take her ass 'round back and learn her somethin'!" She hated herself for feeling that way when she did, but she wanted something to pull River's head out of heaven and bring her down here into the real world. She wanted her to be hurt, to feel disgusted, to feel sorry and sad and broken. She told herself that she felt that way because she wanted River to be ready for the world, but in truth, she was jealous of River too. Just like the people whose envy Cecilia used to find pride in, she too was envious of the ever-so-perfect Charlette Montgomery.

Cecilia grabbed River's chin forcefully before landing a burning slap across the girl's smooth, red skin. She stared at River with disgust. Her daughter looked up at her with tears in her eyes. The corner of her mouth turned, and her nostrils flared. Cecilia didn't even care if her daughter saw her contempt. The more hurt River became, the more disgusted Cecilia felt.

"It's the least you can do for Pastor Johnson after getting his boy beat up because you decided to be fast in the ass for some new man," Cecilia spat, giving River one last look of pure disdain. Then she stormed out of the house, slamming the door behind her. River stood leaning over the sink, listening to the fading echoes of the thump the door made against its frame. She shook her head, stood up, and followed her mother out the door.

Before knocking, Cecilia turned. She grabbed her

daughter's hand and squeezed it. "I'm sorry, Ladybug."

"It's okay," River replied. There was so much unsaid, so many feelings left unspoken. River yearned to understand what had just happened–what had been happening. She wanted to beg her mother to tell her what went wrong and why (and when) she started to hate her. But she knew that her mother's apology meant that it was over, and the slap, her mother's repulsion, River's fear, would never be acknowledged from that point on.

It's okay. The words came out of her mouth in defeat. She wanted to suck them back into her throat and have the burn in her stomach acid, erasing them from ever being spoken. She needed help, she needed guidance, she needed her mother. But this was over. This was done.

The gathering at Pastor Johnson's house was much more fun than River anticipated. The whole town was there. Cecilia, Miss Tolbert, Mrs. Gray and a few other women started to cook after they realized more people than just the church members were arriving. Hop made his way to Mitsy's old piano and started to play every hymn and spiritual he knew. Mr. Jenkins sat out back and lied to anyone who listened. River sat back and watched it all. Her strength was renewed, and her heart was full. She was grateful to have a community of people who truly cared for her and who she cared for in return. She noticed Eddie standing by the back door eavesdropping on Mr. Jenkins and decided to walk over.

"Whatchu doin back here, Edwin-Hendricks?" she asked with her head bowed.

He looked over his shoulder at her then back to the men. "Listenin' to Jenkins 'nem tell old stories and lie." He drank the hooch that he doctored to smell and taste like a tart lemonade then stepped outside.

River followed him. He wasn't getting out of this conversation so easily. They needed to talk about what had happened. They needed to clear the air between the two of them, otherwise they'd never be able to look one another in the eye again. And that's what River wanted. That's what she desired most from Eddie, for him to be her best friend again. Her life felt like it was starting to spiral out of control and all she wanted right now was normalcy, and who better to give her that than the person who she knew best in the world? He could walk away from her all he wanted, but Charlette was going to stay hot on his trail.

"We ain't talked about yesterday, Eddie." He looked over his shoulder again and ignored her. He sat on the bottom step, passed everyone else, and left River to the trap of old men that she was stuck in.

"Dere she go! Dere she go!" Mr. Jenkins shouted. All the old men wished her a happy birthday and gave her hugs. "How proud yo' Ma and Pa must be. Nineteen years lived with no babies, finished school, still sang like a angel. My God today! You got some lucky parents," he said, singing her praises. River blushed and pulled on her hair.

"I heard you sang yo' self happy up in dat church dere. Say you was sangin' den shoutin' speakin' in tongues, all da stuff."

"Speakin' in tongues?" River asked.

"Yeah, say you spoke in a way not even the elders heard. Say you called Jehovah befo' you and got to shoutin'," Mr. Jenkins informed her. River didn't remember speaking in tongues, she didn't hear herself saying anything that she couldn't understand. And Mrs. Tolbert was always able to understand what people were saying when they spoke in tongues. She was something of a translator in that regard. Why couldn't she make out whatever it was River was saying. Was she really speaking in tongues?

River pondered over the information Mr. Jenkins shared with her, when suddenly Eddie threw his empty cup and walked off towards the chicken coop.

"Dey also say yo' Dexter Alexander beat him pretty bad yesterday," Mr. Jenkins explained as he watched the boy walk away. River dropped her head.

"Don't be shamed, baby girl. Dat ain't none of yo' fault. Men got to be men sometimes. Sometimes we just wanna know who dick bigger at da end of da day. Ol' Dex showed 'em dat. Now he takin' it out on you," Mr. Jenkins shared. River stood again pondering over his insights. Mr. Jenkins was wise beyond what most people understood or realized. What they heard as an old man rambling, River appreciated as wisdom.

"You love 'em?" Mr. Jenkins asked.

"Who?" River replied.

"You tell me." Mr. Jenkins responded.

River didn't understand that time, but she didn't want to ask him to explain himself. A clock is right twice a day, so the word around town about Mr. Jenkins rambling was true a lot of the time. River figured this was one of those moments.

"When I ask if you love 'em, who you think of dat made ya heart drop?" Mr. Jenkins asked.

River dropped her head and smiled. The clock had gone from noon to midnight, and she understood what he was asking before. She leaned down and kissed the side of the old man's forehead before stepping off the big wrap-around porch, following Eddie into the chicken coop. Eddie was standing behind the hen house kicking rocks and cursing.

"In all my years, Ion think I ever heard you cuss befo'," River said.

Eddie threw his hands up in frustration and faced the young woman. "What I gotta do to get rid of you, huh? It obviously ain't makin' an ass outta myself trying to protect your honor!"

River sensed that he wanted her to be afraid or ashamed,

but she was neither. She reached out to him just to see if he'd pull away. When he didn't, she hugged him. Warmly. Tightly. She pressed her cheek between his chest and squeezed his body fiercely. Eddie didn't want to hug her back, but he couldn't help it. He wrapped his arms around her and reciprocated the loving embrace.

He melted in her arms. He let out a sigh and felt himself loosen. He shut his eyes tight to fight back tears, but they flowed from him like a stream. They let go of one another and stared. River looked him in his one good eye, and he peered into her with it. Without thinking or hesitation, he planted a kiss on her lips. She tried to pull away, but his mouth followed hers every time she moved her face.

"Eddie Stop! Get Off—" she struggled to speak between his wet pecks. "Eddie please!"

When he finally released her, the palm of his right hand smacked her face. She fell to the ground and stayed there with her face hidden from his anger. "The fuck is wrong with you! WHAT. THE FUCK. IS WRONG. WITH YOU, Charlette?! I'm tryin'! I'm fuckin' tryin' and nothin's workin', and I feel like givin' up. I oughta let you ruin yo'self and your reputation. Like I oughta let him get between ya legs den run around telling everybody what it smell like!" Eddie screamed at her, his voice cracking under the weight of his frustration.

He felt broken, shattered by her rejection. In his mind, he was giving her a chance to make it right, to mend the rift between them, and yet she was declining his offer to kiss and make up. He couldn't understand it. He had always believed he deserved her– her forgiveness, her affection, her submission. His sense of entitlement blinded him to her pain, to her perspective. Instead of seeing River's attempt at mending what little semblance of friendship they had left, he saw only defiance, and it fueled his anger even more. He felt like he was losing control, grasping at the remnants of his pride, unable to accept that she had the power to say no.

River wanted to cry but she couldn't. Her heart wanted to pour out in front of him, but stun had set in her bones. She felt it so deeply that it ached and pained her teeth. She was paralyzed by shock. All she could do was sit in the dirt, holding her stinging face, staring at him.

"Look, Letty, I'm sorry," Eddie pleaded. He walked over to her to help her off the ground, but River scooted backwards. "Stop playin' now, girl. Let me help you." River moved back farther. Every time he took a step she went back farther. "Fine!" he yelled.

By then the group of old men and a few other people had gathered around. Eddie pushed past them and went inside. Everyone just looked at her. They mumbled, shook their heads, but didn't try to help her. For the second time in her life, Charlette felt shame. She didn't know why this time, but she felt it wash over her in waves. As bad as she wanted to look away, her eyes went from one person to the next, taking in their pity. She wanted to curse them. She wanted to say something that would make them all drop dead in front of her. And she probably could too. She probably could have hit them with a King David level curse, something pulled directly from *Psalms 109*.

She could feel her heartbeat in her throat and fire behind her eyes. Her shame had turned to white-hot rage. How dare they see a girl in need, a girl who had helped them and prayed for them, saved them and their souls, with such little compassion. How dare they. She felt the injustice of their indifference burning inside her, fueling an inferno of anger she could barely contain. Even with all the fury she felt, she could not move and was unable to speak. All she could do was lay there, welted and heartbroken under their hurtful gaze.

Finally, Hop Wilson walked up and told everyone to move around. As the crowd stared back towards the house, Mr. Jenkins reached to her for help off the ground. She couldn't thank either of them because she was worried her words would spew out of her like venom. She couldn't find her mother and ask to leave; she couldn't say goodbye to Pastor Johnson and express gratitude for his hospitality. She couldn't do anything but get the hell away from that house before she asked God to open up the earth and swallow it whole, with everyone there still in it.

River ran home to find her father and Dexter Alexander on the porch talking. They both stood up and stepped towards her as she ran up. Cleo stretched his arms out to hold her, but she flew past him and landed in Dexter's arms. Cleo sat down and nodded to the man, understanding and accepting the new role he played in his daughter's life. But all River could think about was the searing rage that still burned inside her, a fire that would not be quenched until she found a way to reclaim her dignity and her power.

"Charlie, what happened? What's the matter?" Dexter asked.

"It's Eddie!" she sobbed, tears scorching her face.

"What about 'em?" Dex asked.

"He—he—" She stuttered.

"What the hell he do, Charlette?" Cleo demanded.

"He say Dexter is out to make me a common whore, and he said I never loved him," River said, not really lying, but omitting parts of the story. She knew not to tell her father that E.H. had hit her. She knew that her words carried power but so did her father's rage. She had strength to keep from hurling curses at undeserving strangers, but her father had very little restraint. Cleo stood up again as he saw Cee Cee and Pastor Johnson walked towards the house. He soared off the steps and stood toe to toe to the tall, round Pastor.

"What's this 'bout your boy callin' River a hoe!"

"Hoe?" Cee Cee echoed.

"Now wait just a minute, Cleo. I ain't here 'bout no name callin'. I came because E.H. said she fell pretty hard behind da coop today." Pastor Johnson threw his hands up and took two steps back as he spoke to Cleo. River glanced over her shoulders at the three adults, relishing in the safety of Dexter's embrace.

"Look, Cleo, I don't know da full story but some old men and Mr. Jenkins say Eddie hit Charlette. And I'm here to say that we know he'd never do dat."

They all stared at one another. Cleo rubbed his chin and slowly turned to his copper-toned daughter. Since she was a little girl, even if she just bumped into a table, River's red skin would welt and bruise easily. She turned her cheek deeper into Dexter's body. She squeezed him tightly around his waist, trying to hide the evidence of Eddie's offense.

"Letta go, Dex," Cleo started. River tightened her grip around Dexter's waist. "Pusha off ya if you got to, Dexter, but let her go." Dexter gently tried to push River off of him, but she held on to him tighter.

Cleo marched towards the house and up the steps and spun River around. Sure enough, the lower half of her cheek had a glowing, raised handprint debossed into her skin. Cecilia stepped in front of her husband only to be pushed to the ground. Pastor Johnson started after him and tried to ask him to not move with anger but instead to seek God's advice. Cleo ignored him and started to run to keep himself from ripping the Pastor's esophagus from his throat. After sprinting all the way to the Johnson home, Cleo ran into the house where a small group of women were still gathered cleaning and a few men who were too lazy to leave were at the table talking. Hop Wilson stood in front of Cleo and asked him to calm down.

"You seen my baby get hit by that pansy ass boy and didn't do shit about it, Hop?" Cleo said quietly, furiously. Hop stepped aside and nodded towards the backdoor. Eddie heard

Cleo yelling at people to move from the inside, and tried to calmly rush away before Cleo could catch him.

Just as Cleo made it to the last step, Pastor Johnson stood in front of him with the barrels of a shotgun pointing at his head. "You git from 'round my house befo' yo wife and daughter have to plan a closed casket funeral," the Clergyman said.

The two men stared one another down. Cleo saw in Pastor Johnson's eyes that same thing Pastor Johnson saw in his. It would take God himself to stop either one of them from protecting their children. Both men respected one another too much to let this go further than it had, but they both knew—silently agreed that even—that if things went any further, they both were willing to kill if necessary.

Cleo spat on the ground near Pastor Johnson's foot. He pushed the gun from in front of his face and walked home. Cee Cee tried to console her husband, but he put his hand up telling her he was in no mood to talk. Back at the house Dexter was pacing in the kitchen cussing and planning what he'd do to E.H. if Cleo didn't kill him. River leaned on the sink with a damp towel on her face, praying. She asked God to bring peace to their small town and into every room of her household. She asked that He gave Dexter and her father peace and asked that Eddie found a place in his heart to forgive her. Dexter turned and saw her mouth moving and walked over, putting his forehead to hers.

"Let me pray with you," he suggested. They grabbed hands, closed their eyes and prayed. Shortly after, the Montgomery's walked through the kitchen door. Cleo blew past the young couple and went to his room. He slammed the door so hard the whole house shook.

"Ma, tell me he ain't kill him," River asked, running to her mother.

"Nah, but Hendricks Johnson nearly blew his head off," Cee

Cee explained.

"What?!"

"Brought out his double barrel and pointed at your daddy's head," she looked from River to Dexter. "I think you best be gettin' home, Mr. Alexander. You causin' too much strife 'round her." Cecilia didn't have an issue with Dexter, she actually liked him–*a lot*– but Charlette had been different since he came to town. Staying out until after dark, ditching her best friend, not going to the river. Something about Dexter made Charlette different, and Cecilia wanted him away from her home.

"Now Mama, Dexter ain't tell Eddie to choke him at Hop Wilson's house and he sho ain't tell him to hit me." River watched her mother roll her eyes and walk away.

"Don't matter no mo'. I talked to Eddie and he say he saw you up under'im. 'Sides I been knowin' dat boy his whole life. I don't feel right with the man who blacked his eye sittin' in my house. Gon' nie, Dexter, git." Cee Cee walked to her room and shut the door behind her.

The next morning Dexter was standing outside of Charlette's window holding a bouquet of flowers. "I walked up to Savannah at the crack of dawn to get these for ya. Got you some chocolates and a toy too." River grabbed the teddy bear, the flowers, and the chocolate all in one swoop. Then, she leaned out the window to kiss him. They smiled at each other.

River stared at the toy with a weak smile. She looked at its soft, kind brown face, its round, shiny black eyes. *What should I do,* she thought to the bear, as if he'd hear her and reply. *What should I say to him?*

She knew it would probably be best to send him away, reminding him that her mother banished him from their home yesterday, but she wanted to climb out of her bedroom window and run away to the woods with him. She looked up from the teddy bear, finally, and made eye contact with Dexter.

He was so *handsome*. He was so charming. She smiled a little more sincerely, then let out a sigh.

Something about Dexter made her feel at peace. It was what she liked most about him. But she was weary of it too because in moments like this when she knows exactly what the right thing to do is, his smile tells her to do something different. To make matters worse, she always wanted to do the wrong thing with him.

Dexter's smile always warmed her heart and his voice always eased her mind. His skin was rich and familiar and his body was basically a symbol of protection. Surely following her heart wasn't wrong, River thought. Dexter's influence of her following her instinct was no cause for concern, she assured herself. Plus, the inner voice of the righteous was actually the voice of God, she affirmed to herself. If leaving the house with Dexter is what she felt like doing, then it was God telling her to do it. Yes, that's what was happening. She was listening to the voice of God; the Holy Spirit was guiding her. No harm was being done. She closed her eyes and thanked God, feeling the weight of her decision lighten–though there was a part of her that knew that all she had done was rationalize her own decision.

"Thank God indeed," Dexter said as he leaned in for another kiss. He stretched out his hand, encouraging her to climb through the window and run away into the woods with him, just as she had been thinking about doing.

Without thinking, River grabbed his hand and started to climb out the window. Dexter's face lit up like the sun at high noon. She smiled back at him for just a second, then realized that she was still in her nightgown. "Don't worry 'bout yo clothes, Charlie. Just come with me," Dexter said eagerly.

"Let me meet you 'round front. I won't take long getting ready," River said to Dexter. He freed her hand from his and stepped back as River closed the window. She had just closed the curtains when it finally dawned on her that she hardly said a word just then, but Dexter responded to every thought she had. A chill ran down her spine as she took a step back and stared at the thin curtains in front of her. Though she couldn't see Dexter, she knew that she was looking directly at him, and that he was staring directly at her. An unnatural force seemed to compel River to walk back to her window. Her feet moved to their own accord, drawing her nearer to an unseen source.

As if possessed, her hands reached for the curtain and slowly started to draw it back. Time seemed to crawl, the seconds stretching as the curtain moved inch by agonizing inch. Her heart pounded fiercely as the glimpse of a satin-blend shirt came into view. She fixated on the shirt, dread pooling in her stomach, as her hand continued its slow-motion task.

Her eyes, almost against her will, began to travel upwards. She imagined a face she had never seen–a face unsettlingly similar to the man she was falling in love with. In her peripheral vision, a dark silhouette materialized in the corner of her room. A wide, lopsided smile formed in the shadows, sinister and menacing. Panic surged through her as her eyes darted between the figure outside her window and the apparition inside her room.

Her heart pounded violently, each beat echoing like a drum in the eerie silence. She could feel the malevolent presence growing stronger, the air thick with its heavy energy. Her breath hitched as she realized she was not alone; someone, or something, had invaded her sanctuary.

Just as she let go of the curtain, ready to confront the shadow in the corner, her bedroom door swung open. River jumped.

"You goin to see dat man, ain't you?" Cecilia questioned.

"Yes ma'am," River replied. She didn't feel the need to lie. She didn't care if it made her mother angry because her mother didn't care about hurting her. Besides, she had bigger things to worry about, like who or what was just standing in the corner of her bedroom. River was more worried about whether or not she was losing her mind.

"Be back befo' sunset," her mother replied. "I decided you not grown just yet, so I want you in the house befo' da sun goes down."

A slow smile crept across River's face. Her mother was being kind again, she was back to being herself. The two women were hugging and laughing before Cecilia could even get her sentence out. River kissed her mother's cheek before closing the door to dress, and her mother gave her backside a swat as she scurried out of the door

Maybe this was going to be a good day. Maybe her imagination was just getting the best of her.

River and Dexter walked into the square and had breakfast in the diner. Dexter worked overtime to put a smile on River's face, but her spirits were low. The eerie silhouette from that morning lingered in her mind, casting a dark shadow over her thoughts. She wanted to shake herself free from the unsettling memory, but something about the shadowy figure felt both familiar and deeply wrong, a chilling echo that distracted her from Dexter's charm.

She picked at the food Dexter had ordered for her, her appetite lost in the turmoil of her thoughts. Each bite tasted like ash, her mind replaying the morning's events in a relentless loop. The presence had felt so real, so menacing, its familiarity gnawing at her. Why did it remind her of Dexter? The question gnawed at her, adding to her unease.

After pushing her plate away, River decided she needed to go to the river. She craved solitude, a space to reflect and confront the force that had invaded her room. She wanted to cast it down and send it to hell, to seek protection and lay her worries at the altar. She longed to put her mind at ease, to reclaim her peace.

"Hey, I think it's bout time I head to the New George," she said, her voice tinged with a desperation she couldn't quite hide. "I think I need some time alone."

Dexter's face fell, but he nodded, sensing her unease. "Alright, Charlie. If that's what you want, we can head that way."

"Dex, I think I want to go alone." River spoke with her head down, staring at her hands in her lap. She couldn't bring herself to look Dexter into his eyes, not after what had happened that morning, not after telling him she wanted to be alone.

They walked outside and were greeted by Hop Wilson and a few other men who didn't have jobs. That end of the square was older than the rest. The windows had a thick permanent film on them, a mixture of age and dust that could not be wiped away. The wood and bricks of the buildings were old and brittle. Something about the setting matched the crowd. Well-intentioned and comforting on the inside, but the exterior was hard and dingy.

"You sure I can't come witcha," Dexter asked River just as they made their way outside. All eyes were fixed in the young couple. The pressure of everyone staring at them nearly made River break out in a sweat. She smiled at Dexter who had been giving her the warmest, pleading, desparate eyes.

"I don't see why not," River replied unconvincingly. To the crowd of on lookers it seemed like they couple had been flirting coyly. In reality, Dexter was taking the opportunity to use River's need to save face against her, and River's reluctant agreeing was her falling dead in his carefully laid trap.

"Dat's a good man you got dere, River. And an even finer woman you got in her, Dexter." Hop announced. They both smiled.

"You ain't got to tell me Hop," Dexter replied with a glowing smile. "Dey say good women have the sweetest secrets, and trust, I intend to uncover ever one of them."

CHAPTER 9

The walk to the New George River was normal, until Shelly Hicks came running from the trees, onto the dirt path leading back to the field that separates the woods from their small town.

She was barefoot and afraid. She looked like she could have been walking around outside for days. But Freedman was a small town, not big enough to miss anyone. River didn't understand how anyone would let Shelly wander around in the woods for days, especially when the thin stretch of trees fenced in their town wasn't thick with enough foliage to even be considered "the woods."

"Shelly, you alright," River asked. She ran over to Shelly to help her get her footing. Shelly pulled away and stumbled. Dexter approached the two women slowly, Shelly inched farther and farther from River as the distance between them grew shorter.

"Yeah, River just come with me please," she begged. She had such a firm grip on River's wrist, River thought she may leave a bruise. Her eyes went from her wrist to Shelly's face. Shelly was hyper focused on Dexter. Her sight on him never broke, not until River stepped between them.

"Hey, Shelly, are you okay? How long you been out here?" River asked her question while guiding Shelly past Dexter, always standing between the two of them. She didn't know what Dexter may have done to Shelly to make her so afraid of him, but she could all but smell the fear radiating off Shelly's skin. Suspicion clawed at River's insides. She grabbed Shelly's face, her voice trembling, "Look at me, Shell. You okay?"

Shelly's eyes darted, wild and unfocused, unable to settle on River's gaze. Her breathing was rapid, her eyes painted with terror. Shelly couldn't focus on a central point in River's gaze because she was too worried about what Dexter was doing. She grabbed both of River's elbows and closed her eyes. She was praying. River, overcome with a rising tide of dread, closed her eyes and did the same. As their foreheads touched and their hearts opened to Christ, River began to hear a familiar voice echoing in her mind.

"Lord, please let this girl listen to me. I don't have time to explain this shit to her like she a child. God let her listen to me. I can't save me, her, and Mama if she don't listen. I can't save none of us if she don't listen." River could hear Shelly's prayer. "If it come down to it Lord, and please forgive me, I will kill Charlette Montgomery if I have to."

River jolted back, her heart pounding in her chest. She had just heard Shelly profess to God, God almighty, the creator of all things, their very maker, that she would kill her if necessary. Shelly locked eyes with River, silently pleading, her eyes filled with a desperate intensity.

"C'mon, baby, I'll explain it all on the walk home, just come to the house with me real quick. You can, uh, you can come pray for Ma for me, just come to the house with me please," Shelly begged, her voice breaking into sobs.

River felt her anger surge. Was Shelly really trying to guilt her into a trap, River thought. Was she trying to get her alone so she could hurt her? River's posture straightened, her face tightening with suspicion. Shelly reached for her arms to pull her closer, but River jerked her hand back.

Dex smirked proudly in pure satisfaction, watching the scene unfold. River didn't trust Shelly; she was unmoved by her tears, unconcerned with her fear.

Dexter swaggered over to River, standing behind her with his head held high and his shoulders straight. Now smiling, he looked down at Shelly who was trying her best to ignore him. "Think it might be best you get from 'round her, Miss Shelly," Dexter said, his voice dripping with menace. If looks could kill, the one Shelly gave Dexter would have taken every ounce of life out of him right then and there. She looked back at River, who was staring at her with disgust.

Shelly closed her eyes, took a step back, and looked at River one last time. "Be careful," she said ominously, her voice filled with a mix of warning and resignation, freeing River from her disillusioned cloud of judgment. She watched Shelly walk away hurriedly, looking over her shoulder every once in a while. Had River misunderstood her prayer, she asked herself. What did Shelly mean she couldn't save them?

River took a step, nearly calling out to Shelly, but she was too far gone. *When did Shelly grow gray hairs*, she wondered, remembering the haunted look on Shelly's face when she came through the trees. Dexter placed a hand on her shoulder.

"Come with me Charlie, I want to show you somethin'," he said, his voice a chilling blend of seductive authority and disheartening deceit.

Dexter had led River down to the South side of the riverbank. River was familiar with this part of the water, but not nearly as much as she was with the Northern end. It was an unfamiliar familiar for her. A place she only visited in memories but almost never in person. Dexter offered to carry her on his back so she could cross the water without having to take off her boots.

"People don't really go over there. The old folks said it wasn't no good across the water," River warned in an attempt to discourage him from exploring the other side of the water.

"Aw, Charlie, it's the same land separated by a stream that ain't more than 12-feet wide. Going 'cross that water won't hurt you," he said.

River looked at Dexter searching for right or wrong in his face. He was right. It wasn't like it was on the other side of an ocean; it was just a river. People crossed the river at the North end all the time. What was different about crossing there than crossing where they were?

"Okay, but let's pray about it first. I heard bad things 'bout that side of the land," she said to Dexter. Too many weird things had already happened today. The shadow in her room, Shelly Hicks on the path. River didn't want to leave anything to chance. She wanted to let it all be determined by God. As she outstretched her hand to encourage Dexter to grab hers for prayer, she couldn't help but think about how she almost told him to walk away from her window this morning, and how different the day would have been had she done that.

With every head bowed and every eye closed, River lead the two of them in prayer. She asked God for protection and direction. She asked Him for guidance. She asked Him silently to bless her as she trekked through forbidden land. She squeezed Dexter's hand as she asked God to order his steps trusting that this prayer would be a guiding light for their well-being. She pulled him closer to her and asked that Dexter would be wise in the decisions he made and discerned the voices he heard. She was just about to ask God to cast down that evil being from her room that she still felt lingering, when Dexter hurriedly dropped her hands saying, "In the name of Christ our savior, Amen."

River was stunned. She was cautious too, but she figured he was just impatient from excitement. Projecting her own feelings onto Dexter, she thought that maybe Dexter wanted to get her alone on the other side of the New George and away from Freedman so they could finish what they had started in Hop's house.

She imagined how pained he must have been to caress her, to smell her. She envisioned him stroking her hair and holding her face. She just knew that he wanted her as badly as she wanted him. She could almost feel his breath against her neck and her body under his. The thoughts of their unfinished business made it hard for River to focus on Dexter who had put a sizable distance between the two of them.

She watched Dexter with a mix of desire and caution. As he guided her through the dense woods, her mind teetered between vivid daydreams of their future together and an insistent voice urging her to retreat to the safety of her mother and father. She navigated thick tree roots and felt vines whip against her calves. River stopped to rub her ankle to soothe the sting of fresh sap on her skin. Standing there, nursing her ankle, River's thoughts drifted to how exhilarating it would feel to finally have Dexter inside of her. She paused, startled by the intensity of her own longing. River was sheltered, but she wasn't ignorant about sex. However, it was something she had never thought about. In all her years, she had never imagined its pleasures until Dexter Alexander came into her life. She glanced up, realizing he was nearly out of sight.

Determined, she sprinted to catch up to him. As she struggled to close the distance between them, the sound of her own labored breathing made her heart race, not just from the exertion but from the intense thoughts of Dexter teaching her things she would never learn in Sunday school. The juxtaposition of church and carnal desire made her think of Eddie. She couldn't help but chuckle. The idea of Eddie as her lover was amusing. It was comical. Eddie was just Eddie. But Dexter was a man. And though she wasn't well-versed in the art of intercourse, she knew instinctively that kind of intimacy was something she only wanted to share with someone who embodied masculinity, and for her, Dexter was the epitome of that ideal *man*.

Finally catching up to Dexter, River asked how much longer they would be walking. They had been maneuvering through the woods for just over five minutes, and River was bored. Dexter hadn't once pulled her against a tree to kiss her or stopped her where she stood to hold her in his arms. She was disappointed. Before they were separated, all Dexter had been talking about was the odd jobs he had worked around town and how angry he was with Eddie. River didn't want to hear about any of that, she wanted to feel him, to touch him. She needed Dexter to distract her, to give her conscious rest so that she didn't have to think about how excruciatingly loud it was telling her to avoid Dexter and go home.

"You been runnin'" Dexter asked, completely unaware that he had left her behind. River rolled her eyes as he continued to speak, but beneath her irritation, a storm of unease brewed. She took a deep breath in and let out a sigh when, without warning, a snake dropped right in front of her. She gasped loudly, jolting backward as it slithered away. Her eyes tracked its movements as it vanished beside a tree and disappeared into a hole beneath the trunk. The sight of the snake rattled her deeply. It wasn't just the creature itself—it felt like an ominous warning.

Her heart pounded as dread seeped into her bones, affirming every anxious thought she had been trying to silence. Every fiber of her being screamed at her to run, to break free from the woods, from the presence of this man who was ultimately a stranger, and seek refuge in the safety of her home. The urge to flee and pray for protection consumed her, every instinct clamoring for her to escape. Yet, despite the overwhelming fear, there was a persistent whisper within her, telling that she had all the protection she needed in Dexter. This conflicting inner voice left her torn between her escalating suspicion and a fragile trust in the man leading her deeper into the woods.

"Charlie, you good back dere," Dexter asked. He had been watching her watch the snake. He was growing impatient by the second. He was on a mission. This thing that he wanted to show her was more than something he thought she'd like to see, it was the very thing that would seal his fate, bringing the both of them closer to their dreams. He didn't see it the first time he visited the other side of the river, but when he found it, he knew it was exactly the thing he needed to win River over. Dexter figured he could earn River's affection based on the strength of his charisma and appeal alone, but the day he stumbled upon this treasure, he knew that he wouldn't have to fight so hard for her love. Though he wasn't threatened by E. H., he couldn't ignore the tenderness River felt for him. E. H. was no competition for Dexter, but if he were, Dexter knew he had nothing to worry about because he was the one who had a gift and a calling. He had a goal, and River was exactly the person to help him achieve it.

As annoyance surged through him, the voice who had been silent for a while spoke again. *"Befo' you do dis, you might want to consider something else,"* the inner voice warned. Dexter shook his head and walked over to the girl.

"Nah, this is exactly how I wanna do it," he replied internally.

"It's yo funeral. Just don't be mad when the last words you hear is me saying' 'I told you so,'" the voice said before leaving Dexter to his own thoughts. Charlette had made her way to him. He smiled at her, taking in how truly beautiful she was. Her perfect brown skin, her warm, almond shaped eyes. She was the perfect blend of sultry and sweet, exactly the way her power balanced her obedience. His smile stretched across his face in genuine adoration for the woman standing before him. She blushed.

"Come wit' me now, Charlie. It's just on the other side of these trees."

CHAPTER 10

They stopped abruptly. River, still focusing on her steps and not the man in front of her, ran into him. She felt like the wind had been knocked out of her when she hit his back. She fell backward and landed square on her tail. She brushed dirt and moss off her hands and looked up to find Dexter's body being framed by a tall, dingy, vine covered church house.

"My God," she quietly expressed. Dexter was standing in front of the door looking up in awe.

"Dissit, Charlie! Dis is exactly what God was leadin' me to when I walked into Freedman. What he was leadin' us to." Dexter spoke to River with genuine passion and jubilance in his voice, his excitement palpable. River, however, felt a stark contrast to his enthusiasm as she grasped his hand and gazed up at the imposing building before them. The church's wood looked sturdy and strong, but its age was evident. The white paint was chipping in some places and completely missing in others, giving it a worn, neglected appearance. Vines wrapped around it like the earth was trying to reclaim it, and thick bushes and overgrown grass surrounded the building, forming a green moat that seemed more like a barrier than protection.

The doorway was wide and intimidating, composed of two heavy wooden halves forming a pointed arch. Huge, round, wrought iron handles, nearly the size of River's face, added to its foreboding presence. The steeple loomed above them, like a daunting tower that seemed to pierce the sky. The windows, though intact, were so thick with dust that seeing inside was nearly impossible.

River glanced at Dexter, who was beaming with excitement.

She forced a smile, trying to mirror his joy but feeling a gnawing sense of unease. The building was undoubtedly beautiful, with an air of grandeur and history, but something about it felt off. It didn't feel like a church—at least, not like her church. The sense of sanctuary she associated with her place of worship was absent, replaced by an unsettling feeling that she couldn't shake.

"Remember when I said I always wanted to be a reverend of some kind? Ya know a preacher or Deacon or something?" Dexter asked. River shook her head. "Dis is it. Dis is our church. Dis is our future. The Lord didn't want me to get close to Eddie and Pastor Johnson because he wanted me to lead my own ministry, and, Charlette, this is the church I'ma do it in, wit you by my side."

River was frightened and excited all at once. Seeing him being absolutely elated made her soul shine. She smiled so big her cheeks hurt. Hearing the joy in his voice made her inspired. She wanted to support him. She wanted to be exactly who he was imagining her to be. She thought back to the dream she had the night Dexter came to Freedman. She saw the two versions of herself again and imagined both husbands. Which one was Dexter? She could see him being both; the man who had honor and respect from the community, the man who made her a mother and situated her as a pillar of the community, but she could also see him being the one who built her up to be this powerfully confident version of herself. On the other side of that, she couldn't imagine him being the man who neglected her, nor could she imagine him ever leaving.

Dexter brought both of her hands to his mouth. He planted the softest, most gentle kiss on her delicate knuckles. He looked into her eyes. She gazed back into his trying to read them the way she had been able to read people's eyes her whole life, but her sight was blocked. Her foresight was being impaired by something in Dexter that she could not identify.

"Baby girl, I'm gonna clean this church up, make it new,

and I'm gonna bring my word to Freedman. River—Girl—GOD!" He shouted so loudly that the trees trembled and the leaves danced.

River jumped when he shouted, startled by the dominance of his voice. She laughed at herself for being so jumpy, so wary of him. All day she had been battling between not trusting Dexter and wanting him to take her right where she stood, when all she needed to do was relax and let God be in control. Look at him, as giddy as a child because he found an old church building that he could minister in. River thought to herself, *what evil presence would be so bold to perverse the word of the Lord in a church?* Dexter began to laugh with her. The two of them shared a moment of laughter together, neither one knowing what amused the other. River was at peace, her heart was calm. She laughed and laughed, then stopped to smile at Dexter who had ended his laughter just before her. She grinned at him and he smiled back, locking his joy filled eyes with hers. Their gazes met only for a second because just as River's eyes met his, Dexter became fixated on something just behind River.

"What you lookin' at," she said in a chuckle. Dexter didn't respond but broke his smile into a quiet laugh, as if he had seen something behind her that reignited his fit of laughter.

"What is it," River asked, as she turned her head slowly, her voice still shaking with laughter. Her gaze shifted from Dex to whatever could be behind her. Standing so close that she nearly fell, River spun around to face the decaying corpse of Annie Jones. Her heart pounded in her chest, and her breath caught in her throat. The sight was grotesque. Miss Annie's jaw hung unhinged from the rest of her skull, her mouth eerily agape, and her eyes were wide open, clouded and lifeless.

River was literally petrified, paralyzed by terror. Her body fell motionless to the ground beneath her, her legs unable to support her. The world fell silent. She could not move. Her eyes glanced past Annie's swollen purple feet, their ghastly appearance contrasting starkly with the lush green of the forest floor. Desperately, she tried to focus on something in the distance, hoping to escape this nightmare, even if only in her mind.

From the corner of her eye, she saw a snake, black as night, slithering into view. It approached with a slow, deliberate grace, its tongue flicking out as if tasting the air. River didn't feel danger; instead, she felt a bizarre sense of hope, as if the snake might save her.

The snake seemed to beckon her, its presence both sinister and oddly comforting. She strained to hear something, anything, a whisper of telepathic communication, but the silence around her was deafening, a void that swallowed all sound. She closed her eyes, trying to center herself, to pray, but her thoughts were fragmented, scattering like leaves in a storm.

A sharp hiss cut through the silence. River's eyes snapped open to see the snake coiling itself around Miss Annie's left foot. The serpent's movements were hypnotic, its scales glinting in the dim light as it tightened its grip around the rotting limb. The snake's black eyes blinked slowly, fixing its gaze on River.

"What are you trying to say?" she thought desperately. River strained her eyes, trying to find some message in the snake's gaze, her ears aching for a direction in the thickness of the heavy silence. But there was nothing.

Then, as if the world collapsed in on itself, River was enveloped in total blackness. Her senses were obliterated; she felt nothing, heard nothing, saw nothing. She was in total blackness. The void consumed her, in its utter nothingness. No sounds. No thoughts. No God.

CHAPTER 11

"Charlette?" Dexter cried out.

River opened her eyes and saw nothing but nature in front of her. Tall grass and a tall, old tree. She could hear locust in the distance, the wind rustling the leaves, and the sound of Dexter's heavy feet running towards her grew louder as he came closer.

He scooped her up from the ground. "You scared me, girl. One minute you was here laughing at nothin', da next minute you was on the ground passed out. You okay?" he asked with concern in his voice.

River dropped her head. She didn't know what was wrong with her and she was starting to realize that she shouldn't trust Dexter. Since he had come into her life, she had been fainting, having dizzy spells, and feeling weaker everyday. All her life she was grateful for her connection to God. She always had the ability to feel Him, to hear Him, but this floating thing was beginning to feel more and more like a curse. It took a toll on her physically, and she didn't know why. Could Dexter be doing something to her, she thought. He did come to town the same day she began to levitate.

"I haven't been feeling well lately, Dex. I think something's wrong with me," River said weakly. She tried to walk away but stumbled after a few steps. Dexter ran to her side and offered her support. As he held her, he squeezed River tightly. A surge of comfort shot through her bones, warm and inviting. River couldn't make sense of her feelings. Too much bad happened since this morning for her to ignore the signs, but her body had never felt so safe in another person's arms.

Dexter raised her to her feet guiding her back to the church. River shook her head and turned away.

"I need to go home, Dex. You stay here at the church," she said sheepishly. Her body was weak, her voice was feeble. Dexter reached out for her, but dropped his hand at the sight of her fragile nature. The thought of her falling for a man who meant no good hurt River. She had been so focused, so cautious, only to end up with a man who had an air depravity about him. Surely, he was unaware of this evil that surrounded him, and perhaps it was her assignment to pull him out of it, but right now she needed to recharge. Today had drained her and she needed rest.

"Nah, Charlie, you good. Just sit out here a bit, then we can head inside," Dexter said as he moved her to sit on the steps of the church.

"I just feel exhausted, and confused. I like you Dex, a lot, but maybe Mama was right, maybe we need some time apart," River expressed. Tears started pour from her eyes. Her throat was burning, and her ears were hot. It felt like someone had tied a fiery rope around her neck and started to slowly pull her throat closed. "I— I—I don't know, it feels like maybe God doesn't hear me no more. Like I'm out here fightin' demons on my own." She could hardly speak the words. From the tension between her and Eddie, and the sudden bouts of disdain from her mother, River had been feeling terrible. Her life was completely different now than it was just a month ago. And now she's seeing dark visions any time she's around the one person who offers her any kind of solace and consolation.

Dexter wrapped his arms around her and rested his cheek on her head. He began to rock her lovingly. He really did care for Charlette. He knew the day he saw her alone at the river that he wanted to get to know her in a special way. His intentions at first were not as innocent as they seemed, but by this point, he truly intended in making an honest woman out of River and laying a foundation for himself, and the family he'd raise with River someday, in Freedman. Everything just needed to go according to plan. Everything just needed to stay its course.

"Listen to me, Charlie. I know I'm addin' to your pain too. I know I done came in and ruined what you had wit' yo' best friend. Done fought him, pissed ya mama off. Charlie, I'm sorry," he said apologetically. He kissed the top of her head, stealing a sniff of her hair. He held her tighter. "Please, Charlie, let me make it up to you."

River knew he was being sincere, but she didn't feel like he had heard her. She didn't think he really understood the gravity of what she was saying. She didn't feel a connection to God anymore. She felt like he had left her to figure out how to navigate all her problems on her own. That was no small thing. How was she to address falling in love with a wolf disguised in lamb's skin alone? How was she supposed to handle her best friend abandoning her and their friendship because she wasn't attracted to him? And Shelly's losing her mind, Fred Jones is telling people Miss Annie has lost her mind, and somehow it all comes back to Dexter–who she really was starting to love. Surely, he misunderstood how severe her situation was.

"I know you said you wanna go home, but what about going to the river, River? You don't feel like prayin'?" Dexter asked

"No, I don't actually. Ain't no need," she replied dry.

River walked away, leaving Dexter standing alone in front of the decaying church. He followed after her, determined to keep her in the forest, fixed on having her inside the building that held their future.

"Don't go talkin' like dat. Don't let go of ya faith. Ain't no sense on turning your back to God," he said, watching her walk away. River's body stiffened; her temperature rose. *"Don't turn your back on God."* She hadn't, not once had her faith faltered, not once did doubt creep into her heart. It was just then in her time of need that *she* felt abandoned, not that she had abandoned Him.

River rolled her eyes in an attempt to calm the fire he had ignited within her. The audacity of him, the boldness with which he said it. His ignorance fanned a flame that she had been struggling to contain. With a self-soothing sigh, River squared her shoulder, releasing the tension that coiled within them. She let out another reassuring breath and started to walk away again.

"Charlie!" His voice sliced through the air, pausing her escape. "What?" she shot back, irritation and frustration mixing in her tone, scorching her throat as she spoke.

"You sure you'on wanna stay here a while? Let's step inside to pray. Or we can just go inside to sit and talk for a while," Dexter said, his voice tinged with a hint of desperation. He peered into River's eyes. Rage and confusion met his gaze, swirling inside of River in a fury that could not be tamed by his lopsided smile or silky charm.

"Told you dat girl was bad" the voice inside said to him. *"She hotter than a two-dolla pistole right nie."*

Dexter gritted his teeth in frustration, letting out an annoyed sigh. He reached out towards River but she stepped away, walking back towards the New George.

"I don't wanna do nothin' anymore, nothin' at all. I want to go home, crawl into my bed, and let this day go," River's words trembled out as tears began to form in her eyes, the rage and confusion dying down into fear and frustration.

"I just blacked out, Dex, and you want to look around in some old church house, just sit around bumpin' gums, planning the future. I want to go home!" With each word she stomped her heels into the ground, her frustration growing. The force, the authority and command in her voice coming to a shock even to herself. She felt something surge within her, something powerful, something bigger than her; something telling her that enough was enough to stand up to Dexter then or always fall victim to his charm.

"Charlette, what happened back dere?" Dexter's voice carried concern as he spoke. He outstretched his arm again, offering comfort to her. but in a stubborn silence, she walked away, her gaze focused ahead. She could hear the distant rush of the New George, a beckoning call pulling her towards home, encouraging her to not relent in her efforts to escape this conversation and Dexter's undeniable pull.

"What happened?" Dexter said, his patience worn thin. He grabbed her arm in an attempt to snatch her in but caused River to stumble backward into a thicket of blackberry bushes instead. Struggling to free herself from the prickly embrace, River rejected Dexter's offered hand. After a few seconds of watching her struggle, Dexter told her to stop acting like an old mule and let him help her. Instead of accepting the offer, River grabbed a handful of berries and ground them into his trousers with fierce determination.

Kicking and thrashing, she fought against the bush, her cries of frustration pouring out, echoing through the forest. With each attempt to free herself, River's angry grew until it erupted into shouts accompanied by tears and screams. She lashed out blindly, hurling leaves and berries into the void, her limbs flailing in a desperate release.

Dexter knelt beside her silently in support, giving her the space she needed to unleash all that she had bottled up. With each kick or quiet sob, he remained steadfast by her side, offering the solace she needed. And when her cries eventually subsided into exhausted huffs, he tenderly rubbed her ankle, his thumb tracing soothing circles as they lingered in a shared moment of vulnerability.

As time stretched on, for what felt like forever, they remained locked in their embrace. In reality only minutes had passed, and River's fury had cooled. Finally, with a defeated sigh, River extended her hand in a silent plea for assistance. "Can I have some help please?" she said with her head lowered, defeat in her voice. Without hesitation, Dexter jumped up, gently tugging her free from the entangling bush. As she stumbled into his arms, he pressed a tender kiss to her forehead, entrapping her in a comforting embrace.

"Think I oughta be headin' home," River said.

Dexter, carefully not to show his annoyance, managed to summon a reassuring smile. With deliberate tenderness, he pulled her closer, squeezed her tighter before reluctantly releasing her.

"Dex, I'on mean no harm, but could I have a few days to myself? I–I got a lot on my mind," she said, gently pulling away. Her voice was nervous but sure. She needed time alone.

"Sho thang, Charlie. Anything you need," he replied, indignation in his voice. They shared a sweet peck on the lips, bidding one another goodbye.

As she walked away, the weight of the day's encounters pressed heavily on her shoulders. She couldn't shake the feeling that something dark was watching her, waiting.

CHAPTER 12

She had been trying to hold herself together since Eddie and Dexter fought in Hop Wilson's house, but at that point, after a day like yesterday she had to let it out. Unconcerned with the rest of the world, River let out a deep, guttural wail. She screamed into her pillow, she punched her thighs, she bit down into her blanket and released everything that had been pent up inside of her. Her throat burned from being worn and raw. With each scream, each punch, she felt the weight of abandonment crushing her soul, leaving her hollow and alone. Soon there were no more tears left to cry, no remnants of a voice left to yell with.

She had laid it all out in her bedroom. She had nothing left to place on the altar before God. Her head pounding from the time she spent crying, River forced herself to her feet. She opened the door of her room and found that she was home alone. Barefoot, she drug herself into the bathroom. She stared at herself in the mirror. She looked the same, but so different. Her skin was smooth, soft, supple, but her smile lines had turn downward from all the time she had spent crying. She turned her cheek to see if the precious brown freckle that adorned her face singularly was still there.

She touched it, admired it, and reminded herself who she was. The urge to pray filled her heart, but her mind told her it would be a waste. If God were still with her, he wouldn't be putting her through so much turmoil. If he still had plans to prosper her, he wouldn't lead her down a path that required her to fall in love with a man trapped under the enemy's spell.

Just as she had begun to silence the voices in her head that were both trying to reassure her of God's unconditional love and convince her that she had been doomed to a life that required sight over faith, she caught a glimpse of the back of her hair as she began to braid it. A thin strip of hair, just behind her ear, had turned a dark shade of gray, marking the decay she was starting to feel inside, deepening her sense of desolation.

In the silence of her empty home, River looked back at her reflection, and whispered what she accepted as a bitter truth: "you're alone in this world, Charlette Marie. And don't you ever forget it."

After her long hair had been plaited into two thick, poorly done braids, Charlette decided she needed time alone. She walked out of her house, up the newly paved road, and deeper into the stretch of old homes that led opposite of the direction of town. She found herself in a familiar grove where the memories of her first kiss with Dexter lingered in the air like false hope and unspoken promise.

She grabbed her right arm in her left and hand and watched her feet kick dirt. She didn't want to think about Dexter, she didn't want to think about Eddie either. She only wanted to be alone with the earth. She needed a minute to just be, to just take in all of creation and calm her nerves.

Caressed by the Spring's breeze, Charlette allowed herself to be embraced by the comfort of the warm winds. She wanted to feel free again, to feel safe again. Standing there, alone in a field of trees, under the rustle of the leaves and the dance of the Sun, Charlette allowed her spirit to be liberated from the prison of doubt and fear that she had placed herself in. Any intrusive thoughts about Eddie calling her a whore, or Shelly's ominous behavior, or the vision of the snake around Miss Annie's leg, were cast down and ignored.

The only way she would get better was if she allowed herself to be better, and in order to do that, she needed to spend time figuring out who she was. She didn't want to be River: the girl who had supernatural abilities and a Christ-like spirit. She didn't want to be Letty: the supportive, maternal, emotionally strong best friend. She didn't want to be Charlie either: the love stricken, virgin whose infatuation blinded her view of reality. She wanted to be Charlette, but she didn't know who she was, she hadn't figured her out just yet.

The effects of the week weren't something she could shake in a day; she was going to have to sit with her feelings to understand them. She was going to have to draw inward and explore herself. Charlette laid out in the grass; her face turned to the sky. She replayed every conversation, every interaction. She was searching for a catalyst, a cause for all this strife she was feeling. She had been relating everything to Dexter's arrival, completely disregarding the fact that Eddie had showed up in Freedman the same day.

Could all her issues really boil down to one of two men entering her life and causing strife, she wondered? Was the answer as simple as God abandoning her?

After laying in the grass thinking about the last three days, something inside her told her she'd get more answers in town. Charlette had gone against her inner voice too many times to not listen to it when it spoke to her. She got up from laying on the ground and made her way to the square.

She had walked past the small neighborhood of houses that lined the newly paved road, and was just about halfway up the dirt trail to town. The church was behind her now, and she was starting to approach the small farm land where the older, bigger houses of Freedman stood.

Fred and Annie Jones' house was coming into view as she approached their 2-acres of land. As she moved past their garden, walking near their backyard, she couldn't fight the feeling of eyes being on her. She turned her head in the direction of their home and thought she may have seen someone moving around the back of their house, but as she got closer, there was no signs of any life in their backyard. She had made it past the garden and wild mules that lived in the edge of the yard and the backyard was now clearly in her view. She tried to look ahead, uneased by the possibility of another shadowy figure invading her peripheral view, but against her will, she noticed a figure by the backdoor again.

Charlette stopped. She had a decision to make. She could either walk up to the door and find out who was back there, or she could continue to live her life afraid of things that moved in the corner.

"Miss Annie," she called out. "Is that you over there?" No one replied. She approached the yard and looked around but she didn't see anyone there. "Miss Annie," she shouted, leaning over the gate. The back door was shut, the wired gate was locked. Charlette should have been able to find comfort in knowing those things so she could sum everything up to her imagination, but her sixth sense told her otherwise.

Charlette went to the front door and knocked, but no one answered. She knocked again and waited a little longer, giving whoever may be home time to get to her. After a few seconds, Charlette felt annoyed and banged on the door just once, before it swung open from the force of her fist.

Just like in the woods before, her senses tingled with an urge to turn and run away, but she had to know for sure that there was nothing to be worried about inside her neighbors' home.

"Miss Annie," she called. "Fred?" No one replied. The house was neat but dusty. Like it had been cleaned just before being abandoned. She walked past the living room and went into the kitchen. "She probably up in Savannah with that designer lady," she thought to herself. Charlette slowly ran her index finger across a side table and rubbed the thick layer of dust between her pointer and her thumb. "But where is Fred at though," she questioned.

She walked back to the vestibule and scanned the dimly lit

living room one last time. Taking a cautious step, she peered into the kitchen, looking for anything that may be out of place. Though nothing raised concern, Charlette couldn't shake the creeping sense of unease that she felt. Just as she turned to leave through the front door, a flicker of movement caught her eye, and her heart sank. There, by the back door, stood a figure, lurking in the shadows like the specter from her bedroom.

Unsure if she should leave without acknowledging the figure or if she should confirm that it was just a disoriented Annie Jones, Charlette stood frozen with uncertainty.

Her mind raced with questions, doubts clawing at her sanity. Had they been there all along, watching her every move, she thought. Did they see her cautious exploration of the house? Her nerves were on edge as she grappled with the decision of whether to confront the shadowy being or slip away unnoticed.

As she considered her next move, a shiver ran down her spine at the sight of the figure's eerie grin, an unnerving silhouette of gray light against the dark figure. Their features obscured, she could only discern a chilling glint in their eyes, presenting as a silent threat lurking in the shadows. With a trembling hand pressed against her pounding chest, she whispered a desperate prayer for protection. "God drench me in the blood of Jesus and shield me from evilness," she chanted quietly as she mentally planned her escape, the words tumbling from her lips like a lifeline in the darkness. As "Amen," quietly pierced the choking silence, Charlette snapped her eyes opened and ran for the front door.

But before she could reach the threshold, the figure lunged forward with supernatural speed, knocking her to the ground in a violent blur of motion. Panic surged through her veins as she grappled with her unseen attacker, the air thick with the presence of fear and determination. In the midst of the struggle, she could hear the guttural snarl of her attacker, a primal sound that chilled her to the core.

As she fought for her life, blocking blows and throwing punches anywhere they'd land, Charlette envisioned the ghostly creature hurling towards her. She remembered seeing a dress sailing behind it as it came towards her. She pictured its ghastly grin and dark eyes.

"Miss Annie?" she questioned. Though she was unable to see the face of the assailant, she was sure it was Annie Jones. "Annie, Miss Annie, Miss Annie! Let me go, Annie Jean, turn me loose," she cried out frantically. In a desperate bid for escape, she kicked the woman off of her with the strength she could muster, her every instinct screaming for survival. Just then Fred Jones kicked the back door open. "Get outta here, River" he shouted. He ran over to Miss Annie and held her down. "River, get out," he demanded loudly.

With a final burst of adrenaline, she scrambled to her feet and bolted out of their front door. But even as she fled into the safety of the daylight, the memory of that haunting encounter lingered like a shadow.

She ran past the houses, up the hill, and through the middle of town. She wanted to be near people, she wanted to be in the safety of a crowd. Charlette ran until she reached Mr. Brooks' store. When she entered, she doubled over and grabbed her knees. She was out of breath, but she was safe. She came there to speak to someone, anyone. She knew that Fred Jones had been going around saying Dexter possessed Miss Annie, and after her vision in the woods, and what just happened at the Jones' home, she believed his story was more than an old drunk's rambling.

"What da hell wrong wit you?" Mr. Brooks asked as Charlette caught her breath. "I'm sorry Mr. Brooks, I was just attacked by Annie Jones."

Mr. Brooks and everyone else in the store stopped what they were doing and gathered around Charlette. She had scratches on her arms and rips in her clothes. Her face was dirty from dust and sweaty. Hop Wilson, Mr. Jenkins and the rest of the old men all came into the store to see what was causing such a commotion.

"You get in a fight wit a bobcat girl? Da hell done happened to you," Hop asked as he pushed past nosey bystanders. Charlette told everyone what happened, and they all listened. "Y'all know dat Fred Jones stopped going to work. Say he workin on a plan to kill dat Alexander boy." Charlette couldn't tell which old man said it but she looked at Hop Wilson for an explanation.

"Look, River, it ain't nothin to worry 'bout. Fred Jones say your man's da devil and his wife done been possessed." He placed a hand on her shoulder.

"Hop, that don't make me feel no better," she said. "From what I saw that lady very well may be possessed and honestly, Dexter might have something to do with it."

Hop pulled her aside and asked her had Dexter ever given her a reason to think he was Satan in human form. Charlette wanted to say something but a hitch caught in her throat and no words came out of her mouth. Hop planted his hands on her shoulder and advised her to go home and get some rest, maybe drink some whisky if she needed. "The Joneses done both lost they minds, baby. If Annie attacked you, and it looks like she did, it's just because she ain't da same woman no mo'" Hop said to her, gentleness and sincere disappointment in his tone.

Everyone in the store told her not to worry about Dexter and to stay away from the Jones house. They all tried to comfort her, but Charlette couldn't shake that something was wrong. That's when she noticed Shelly Hicks.

Shelly had been listening the whole time. She stood in the back shaking her head, listened as Charlette recounted her story. Charlette saw in Shelly's eyes that she had something to say. After that scene on the road and the way they left things, she knew Shelly had something to add to the story.

Deep down, Charlette knew Dexter wasn't the devil and she didn't care how crazy everyone thought Fred Jones and Miss Annie were, but she saw what she saw--in Dexter and in the Joneses–and she had a feeling that Shelly might have seen it too.

Shelly walked out the back of the store and stood on the porch. Everyone stood around Charlette asking questions and examining her injuries. She rushed them off as fast as she could so that she could speak to her old friend. She wanted to know what Shelly knew about the Joneses, and most importantly what she knew about Dexter.

"Hey Shelly," Charlette said noticing how thin Shelly had gotten over the last two weeks. River thought she must have been incredibly distracted when she saw Shelly on the dirt road yesterday afternoon because not only did she miss Shelly's new size, she also missed how much longer, brittle, and gray Shelly's hair had gotten. "Hey, River, I was just 'bout to leave," Shelly said as she stood up and stepped off the porch. Charlette followed.

"River, I don't like talkin' much these days, what is it dat you need," Shelly said as she spun around annoyed.

"We need to talk about yesterday. What you know about Dexter and the Jones that I don't know?" River asked Shelly. She drew in a breath and focused her eyes in the center for Shelly's eyes. She was doing to her what she had done to people her entire life, she was reading her for answers she knew Shelly's mouth did not want to give.

Shelly jerked back. She shook her head and turned to walk away. Charlette called after her, but Shelly kept walking away. Shelly threw up one finger and shook it. Charlette yelled her name and demanded that she spoke to her, that she opened up and let her help. The authority in Charlette's voice shocked even her. Shelly continued to ignore Charlette until finally Charlette said: "enough." Shelly stopped in her tracks. Her body turned slowly towards Charlette. If it weren't for the sheer rage and annoyance she felt, Shelly would have been afraid, but being moved by a power unknown to her didn't surprise her these days.

Once fully facing Charlette, Shelly marched up to her and spoke candidly. "Dat Dexter of yours ain't no saint. Somethin wrong wit em, River girl." Her eyes were pointed and red from anger. She held a finger to Charlette's nose and spoke with disdain and contempt.

"I ain't sayin he da devil, but I am sayin dat after what he done to me in Brooks' office, dere ain't no God in em! Look, I tried to tell you yesterday but you decided that you wanted to put on big girl panties and go cake in the wood's wit 'em," Shelly began.

"I ain't trying to start no mess or ruin what y'all got going on, but he's no good, River. Dat's da truth. I haven't been the same since the one encounter I had with Dexter Alexander. I ain't been right, and it's because of him."

Charlette nodded towards a tree and both of their feet moved in unison towards it. They stood under its shade and spoke beneath its limbs as if its leaves protected them from anyone interrupting their conversation.

"What did he do? How have you changed?" Charlette asked, encouraging Shelly to speak further. Shelly didn't want to speak to Charlette because when she tried to tell her yesterday, she was too holy, too smitten to hear what she had to say. As far as Shelly was concerned, Charlette decided on that dirt road yesterday that she was going to be on Dexter's side no matter what anyone had to say.

"Speak," Charlette commanded, and Shelly spoke.

"He took me in da office and did somethin to my mind." Shelley said. "I felt trapped, stuck in my own body. I couldn't move, I couldn't scream. I was stuck, just standin' there frozen.

I couldn't see anything around me but him, 'cept he wasn't his self. He was taller, skinnier, and he was so ugly lookin." She placed her hand on her heart to soothe herself as she thought about what she saw. Her face furrowed and frowned, but she kept speaking. "He looked so scary, so, so scary. Like he was dead. His skin was kinda gray but kinda green. It was saggy and his eyes was sunk in. He still smiled and it still curved to the left." The hairs on Charlette's body stood as she saw goosebumps form on Shelly's arms. "He just smiled but I could hear him speak to me. I could hear him trying to get farther into my mind, like he wanted to be in my body."

She sucked air in through her nose and tried to shake herself free of that feeling, her anger calmed by fear. She turned towards Charlette and looked at her, pleadingly. Her eyes were dark, with rings around them that were so red, they were nearly purple. The dark halos under each of Shelly's eyes told Charlette that she hadn't been sleeping. Her collar bones were prominent and protruding. Her hair was lazily tied behind her with fly-aways going in every direction. Charlette saw how frightened Shelly was and started to feel scared herself.

"What was he sayin," Charlette whispered. "I don't know," Shelly replied. "I don't know if I don't remember or if I couldn't understand him, but I know he was saying something and I was scared." Shelly leaned on the tree and threw her head back. She shut her eyes and opened her mouth to say more, but all she could do was cry. Charlette walked over and embraced her in a hug. She didn't speak. She couldn't speak. Shelly shook her head in disappointment and continued.

"I tried to scream, I tried to run, but I couldn't move. Then he started coming toward me, he started getting closer. I thought I was gon' die, River, I didn't know what to do. I kept trying to swing my arms to hit him, but he kept getting closer, and closer. My heart was beating so fast I just knew it was gon' burst. I felt like stone. Like only my eyes and heart worked. I could feel myself trying to scream, my lungs was bout ready to give out from all the yellin' I was trying to do. Then he was right up on me, I mean square in my face. All I could do was cry. I closed my eyes but I could feel his breath." Shelly started to shake as she spoke. Her whole body vibrated. River reached out to comfort her but Shelly's body vibrated with such intensity that it startled Charlette, causing her to jerk her hand back. "I could feel his hot breath, I could feel his long, thin finger graze my face."

River's stomach turned over as she imagined, cold, dead skin brushing her cheek. She turned green and leaned on Shelly for support. "I pissed myself, River." Shelly looked over at her from the corner of her eye. "Huh," Charlette asked. "I was so scared I pissed down my leg. I couldn't do nothin else. Then as suddenly as it had all started, it ended." River was confused.

"What do you mean," she asked.

"Das it. I was stuck there, frozen and pissy, then out of nowhere we were back in Brooks' office, staring at his ice box. He asked me if I was okay, and I said I wasn't thirsty no mo' and ran out of the office. I didn't even want to go back to the sto' the next day for work and I didn't. But I gotta take care of my Ma and I need the money, but River, I'm so afraid of him. I'm afraid of everything. And these dreams I been having. I don't think we safe here, River, not while he's here."

Charlette just stared at her. Shelly wiped her tears, but Charlette just stared at her. She didn't understand what Shelly had just told her and she was trying to make sense of it all, but it didn't seem like there was any sense to be made in her story.

"Shelly, are you eatin'? You done lost half a person, Shelly, I wanna know if you eatin'. If you takin' care of your self, if you sleepin' because you sound crazy. Plus, you was runnin' around in the woods, barefoot. Shelly, are you okay?" Charlette herself didn't understand what Shelly's diet, or lack thereof, had to do with anything she just learned from her. She just wanted to stop thinking about everything Shelly had just said. She wanted to change the topic and question Shelly, maybe even make Shelly question herself. She just didn't want to think about Dexter being a willing participant to all the chaos that had been unfolding around her.

"I just told you dat I had a dream or vision or some weird shit about your weird fuckin man being dead, trying to get in my mind or my damn drawls, and you askin' if I done ate?!" Both of the young women's chests were heaving up and down as they stared into one another's eyes.

"Maybe I was wrong, maybe you and Fred Jones and Miss Annie really have lost your minds. That sounds crazy, Shelly. He was dead in front of you?" Charlette was shocked by herself, she was disappointed. Shelly and Fred Jones were convinced that Dexter was involved in something sinister, and Charlette had been brushing off their concerns, despite her own suspicions. But she was afraid to confront him, afraid of what she might uncover.

"Nah I ain't ate! I ain't ate, I ain't slept, I barely even want to bathe after what he done to me. What has he done to me, River?! What did he do? Help me!" She was screaming, just on the verge of tears as she shouted. Charlette didn't know what to do, she didn't know what to say. She put her arms around Shelly's frail frame, and slid down the tree with her.

"River, I just don't know what to do anymore," Shelly's voice cracked as tears streamed down her cheeks. "None of y'all care! You don't care. Hop think I'm losin' my mind, think I'm making everything up. And Brooks don't even notice how much I been strugglin'. None of y'all care about me!" Shelly fell to her knees, sobbing forcefully.

She paused, taking a shaky breath before continuing. "And then there's E.H.," she said defeatedly. "When I tried to tell him 'bout what happened, he didn't comfort me. He tried to have his way wit me," Shelly choked on her words, on the memory of she and Eddie that day in the General Store.

"What did Eddie do?" Charlette asked with genuine

concern. She didn't want to burden Shelly with reliving the moment, but she wanted to know what she meant by Eddie trying to have his way with her.

"He was turned on by it, River. I told him how me and Dex was alone in Brooks office, and before I could tell him more, he was standin' there harder than week old bread. Imagining Dexter being filthy wit me, I guess, I don't know but it was disgusting, River! I feel like I'm drowning. Like Dexter is going to kill me and you too, but no one cares." Shelly buried her face in her hands, shoulders trembling with the weight of her pain.

Charlette stared at her. She was stunned by the distress in Shelly's nature and the disgust she felt from hearing her story. Kneeling there with her hand on Shelly's shoulder, Charlette wanted to know what the hell was happening with the men in her life.

CHAPTER 13

Charlette walked Shelly home. Neither of them saying a word to the other, both burning to say more. When they made it to the house, Shelly told Charlette that she was thinking about moving to Savannah with her sister Eliza and that she could come with her if she wanted. Charlette considered it for a second, but remembered that Freedman was her home. Her mother and father lived there, her church was there, her future was there too. She couldn't let Dexter or Eddie intimidate her or keep her from her calling. Her purpose was to be there for that community, and though she felt like Jesus had taken a break from interceding, Charlette had no problem filling in. She couldn't go to Savannah with Shelly because she still had work to do in Freedman.

Shelly understood and asked her to come in and pray for her mother. She asked that she'd pray that Mrs. Hicks would survive the trip and that Shelly would be able to earn enough money to get them out of town by the end of the month.

Charlette did as she was asked, despite her belief that God no longer concerned himself with the issues she presented him with because deep down, she knew he'd never forsake his children – she still believed that even if she could not get him to work for her good, they were still close enough for him to do a favor for a friend.

So, she prayed with confidence and conviction. It felt as if God himself had come down and prayed with them. The holy spirit entered the Hicks' home and took hold of them all. By the time Charlette had finished praying for her, Mrs. Hicks was sitting upright and crying. Her arms were lifted and all she could do was cry "Hallelujah" and "Thank you, God." She tried to pay Charlette for the prayer, but River said that the Lord's grace is free to all who believed.

Mrs. Hicks and Shelly both hugged her before she left, and Shelly held on extra tight. "Please be careful with him, River," Shelly said as they embraced. "I know by the way we didn't speak about Dex on the way home that you think you still love him, but a wise woman once told me to stop hurtin' myself behind men. I think you'd benefit from hearin' dat yo self right now." Charlette smiled and thanked her old friend, but she had no plans of steering clear of Dexter. She needed to speak to him and find out why there were at least two people in Freedman who were saying his name in such close proximity to the Devil's.

Charlette could not stop thinking about what Shelly had to say. She couldn't stop thinking about Miss Annie attacking her. Her mind was moving a mile a minute, and nothing she could do would make her focus on one thought at a time. Everything was floating around and running into each other in a thick haze that was fogging her mind. Normally, she would have visited the New George to clear her mind and leave her worries at the altar, but she was so consumed with all that had taken place, that the thought never crossed her mind.

She was in such a daze that she was completely unaware of where her feet were taking her. She walked past the old, grand homes, onto the new concrete pavement, and right to her front doorstep. Charlette wasn't even ready to go home, but her body, devoid of its own mind, had taken her there.

When she walked through the side door, into the kitchen, her mother was home just about to start cooking. "I seen Dex walk by earlier, but I ain't see you wit him. Where you been?" Cecilia asked.

Charlette shrugged her shoulders and flopped into a chair at the table. She folded her arms and planted her face into her elbows. "Mama, I been to hell and back."

Cecilia walked over and rubbed her daughter's back. "Eddie came lookin for you," she said in her daughter's ear. "I told him it's probably best he don't come 'round here for a while."

Charlette's head shot up. Her eyes followed her mother across the kitchen before rolling in frustration. She closed her eyes and threw her loose curls over the back of the chair. Why was Eddie looking for her now, she wondered. The last time they saw one another was nearly a week ago, and he had just struck her across the face.

Cecilia walked over and planted a kiss on her daughter's forehead, a kind hearted attempt to quell the storm brewing in her daughter's mind. "Sun still up, least for another hour. You ought to go see him. Talk to him and have him walk you home in the sun set," her words a gentle push towards reconciliation. But Charlette's thoughts were elsewhere, weighed down by a burden too heavy to lift. Guilt had begun to creep in. A shadow cast over her as she thought about her recent prayers for Mrs. Hicks. Although she prayed with fervor, she couldn't deny the lingering tension that existed between her current self and the devout woman she once was just a month ago. The tension wasn't between herself and her past, but with her faith—there was a struggle for control that started to unravel her spirituality.

Despite whatever hold the spirit had over her recently, Charlette could admit that she loved God. She loved the relationship she had with Him, the Son, and the Holy Spirit. She felt something that transcended even the highest honor for God giving her the gifts she had even before her most recent abilities. But the weight of her secrets—the ability to levitate, the haunting dreams and visions—pressed down on her, suffocating her sense of self.

She felt trapped between her desire to embrace her

spirituality and the fear of losing herself to it. She let in a

sulky breath and mulled over her conflicting emotions and the turmoil she was finding herself succumbing to. Then, in that moment, Charlette realized she wasn't trapped at all. She was stuck. Just like Shelly said, *"stuck."*

"Ma, what do you do when you don't know what to do," Charlette asked.

"You pray," Cecilia answered.

Charlette was on a mission. She walked out the door, up the road, and towards the Johnson home. She wasn't sure what exactly she expected Eddie to shed light on, but he had been trying to tell her about Dexter and Shelly, and now, hearing Shelly's version of the story, she wanted to hear Eddie's.

What on earth could he have seen or heard that made him believe that Shelly and Dexter had been together, she asked herself. What about his version of the story could have turned him on? Her feet hit the ground harder as she turned off the main road, onto the dirt path leading to the stretch of houses and farms behind the square. Determination had set into her bones. Eddie knew something about Dexter that she didn't, and Charlette was going to find out what it was.

As she began to approach the first house on the country road, Charlette heard whistling just beyond a small patch of trees. She recognized the whistling to be Dexter. She inhaled sharply and stepped a little harder, moving faster. She had no time to speak to him, to let him distract her with his dazzling smile and suffocating charm. She didn't know if she could trust him yet, she needed to speak to Eddie.

As the sun dipped below the horizon, casting a warm glow over the small town, Dexter leaned casually against a worn wooden fence that bordered the large houses' land. His smile was like a flickering flame, drawing her closer despite the warning she felt under her skin.

"I've heard whispers in the wind, darling," he murmured, his voice smooth as silk. "But rumors are just that whispers. Let me show you the truth."

Charlette hesitated, torn between the undeniable pull of his presence and the cautionary tales that swirled around him like a dark cloud. Yet, she found herself inching closer, drawn by the promise of something forbidden.

With a flourish, Dexter produced a small bunch of hydrangeas from behind him. Their velvety white petals a stark contrast against the backdrop of uncertainty. "For you," he declared, his eyes alight with an intensity that sent shivers down her spine.

But as she reached out to accept the offering, her fingers hesitated, hovering just inches away. "Your words are pretty Dexter, so are these," she whispered, her voice barely audible above the gentle rustle of the evening breeze. "But as pretty as all this is, I still need time to make sense of all this ugly."

For a moment, his mask slipped, revealing a flicker of frustration in his steely gaze. But just as quickly, it was replaced by that charming, left-leaning smile. He took her hand in his, pressing a gentle kiss to her fingertips.

"I'll leave you alone," he breathed, his voice a seductive promise hanging in the air like a lingering scent. "But let me show you something first." And in that moment, she knew she was lost, caught in the web of his charm, even as doubt gnawed at the edges of her heart. Charlette's feet were carried away on a wind of desire.

CHAPTER 14

Charlette never made it to Eddie's house. She and Dexter walked to Hop's house instead. His old shack was the first house off the main road, you had to pass it to get to the Montgomery home. They sat on his small wooden porch all night.

Dexter knew how to make her smile, make her laugh. He was the word comfort personified. She loved being near him, she loved being around him. And the command he had over people made her heart swell.

He had every man and woman that was sitting in Hop's bare yard dying with laughter. Everybody who was there that night left with a story about how funny that damn Dexter Alexander was. Hop told Dexter that he was alright with him, that nothing anybody had to say about him mattered because he knew what kind of man Dex was for himself.

"Man listen, and listen good too, y'all. I've been living in Freedman since I was a six-year-old orphan. Henry Stitts' mama Mary Bell, God rest her soul, brought me here from Atlanta when she was a young woman. Pregnant with no husband either. She was leaving there to come here after her low-down uncle knocked her up," he paused his story to apologize to Henry for sharing the shame of his conception.

"She used to work with my Ma befo' my Ma got sick. Ma Bell knew dat my Pa had run off and left me after Ma died. So, she came and got me from my shack, which wasn't as fancy as the one I live in now, and packed me up in her buggy and we rode for four days until we got to Freedman."

"I'm tellin y'all this because there wasn't a single man in this town that was kind to her back then. The women were good – helped her find work, set her up in that old house over yonder, fed me and Hen Dog here – but those men were low down. I'd curse they named if I wasn't just like 'em. Now, the niggas my age, we all are good, we all were raised by some good, prayin' women, so it might be a shock to hear about the bastards befo' us. But there was one man, one good man that loved Mary Bell despite her having two sons. Our Pa, God rest his soul, Cato Samuels."

"He married Ma Bell, bought her dat house Hen Dog is in now, set my Mama up so that she neva had to work a day in her life. His being here made them ol sorry niggas like Jenkins get up and find some act right. Dexter, you got the same stuff Cato Samuels had. I believe you would kill or be killed for' dat woman, for any of us."

"And if someone got something to say bout you, den to hell wit 'em," Hop shouted. He ended his drunken monologue by telling Charlette to never let anyone in their business. That in order for a couple to survive the times they had to keep their relationship tight. Don't even let her mother and father set asunder what God brought together.

"Those whom God hath put together, let no man set asunder." Matthew 19:6.

The words rang in Charlette's head.

"Come wit me," she heard Dexter say. Only, it couldn't have been Dexter, she thought, because he was standing next to Hop who had taken him under the tree to speak to him privately. Dexter looked over his shoulder at her, nodding his head towards the road. Without thinking Charlette stood up. She walked to Dexter, standing behind him waiting for his conversation to end.

"Remember what I said, nie, girl," Hop said to Charlette with a wink. She smiled back at him, his words echoing throughout her mind. *Those whom God hath put together.* Did God want them together, she asked herself. She never imagined loving someone would be this hard. Though it wasn't an immediate concern of hers, Charlette always knew she'd be a wife and mother someday. She always knew there would come a point where her mother and father would sit her down and tell her to find someone to marry, but she never imagined it would be this hard.

She never considered the fact that God would put someone in front of her, with all the opportunity, all the freedom to fall forcefully, passionately, quickly in love with him, only for Him to turn around and put doubt in her heart about that very man. She always believed everything in her life was either appointed or approved by God, so why would He have her fall in love with someone she should not be with, she questioned.

Those whom God hath put together, let no man set asunder. That was God's word through his Son, Jesus Christ. She did not search for Dexter, he was placed in front of her. She was not looking for love, but love found her. God had put them together, and the rumors of bored townsfolk, even the suspicion in her own mind, would not set them asunder.

"Hey, Hop, I 'preciate what you said back dere, man, but if it's all the same to you, I'd like to take Miss Charlie here back to her Ma 'fore they think I'm trying to get her in a bad way," Dexter said to his friend. Charlette looked up at him with a smile. He glanced at her with a smirk.

The couple said their goodbyes to the people still settled in Hop's dry, sparse yard. As the evening's shadows lengthen and the sun inched lower, the couple made their way to the Montgomery home. The air was heavy with unspoken tension, a silence so thick that it was almost tangible, hung between the two of them. As the sun made its final descent beyond the horizon, they approached the family's porch, lingering just outside the door, the sound of locust providing a backdrop to their conversation.

"I had a good time over at Hop's house with you, Dex," River said through a faint smile, lowering her gaze from his warm brown eyes to the dirt that had been blown on the porch. "I always enjoy time with you, you know that, but...I still need space. I need to not be doing this," she said, her words coming out more as a murmur.

Dexter's smile fell, disappointment crossing his features just before he gained his composure. "I understand, Charlie," He replied, his voice thick with longing and persistence. "But I did want to steal you away to the church 'for it got any later. I thought you might like to see the inside, get a feel of what it's like to be in dere."

River's brows furrowed in confusion. "It's too late now, Dex. And it's too dark to be tryin' to cross the river and walk through the woods."

Dexter outstretched his hand, offering to take hers in. It hovered there between the two of them, River staring at it hesitantly. "I'd never let no harm come to you, baby girl. Swear 'for God," he said earnestly. But River shook her head. "I said no, Dexter," she said firmly, her resolve unwavering.

Dexter, undeterred, pressed on. He bore into her eyes, attempting to sway her decision. Unseen to anyone but River, he took the opportunity to delve into her mind, to influence her thoughts, bend her will. But as he probed deeper he found something that made him recoil, startled by the power that existed within her. He didn't see it, but it was a force within her that was formidable.

With a sudden shift in demeanor, Dexter smiled, adopting his usual charm. He threw his hands up in a sign of renounce. "Can't argue wit a no, now can I?" he said playfully, as he walked backward off the porch.

"You know where to find me when you ready to start lookin' for me," he said as he left.

River watched him as he left, her heart heavy with uncertainty. The whole exchange felt off. She could never make out Dexter's true intentions, yet she remained hopeful. Was this suspicion her instinct making her aware of caution, or were they a product of being so new to the affection of a man.

Charlette wasted no time going to the river the next morning. She didn't speak to her mother, she didn't drink coffee, she dressed and headed for the river. She woke up early, just as the sun was rising, still sitting on the horizon. The grass was wet with dew, the air hovered in a visible fog above the ground. The banks of the New George were the same, but felt unfamiliar.

Charlette sat on the muddy earth in a pair of old jeans that she hadn't worn in years. She left home in a rush, having no time to braid her hair. The thick curls danced freely in the wind, untamed by the confines of careful styling.

She closed her eyes, taking in the crisp morning air and embracing the peace that hung over the world at this hour. The world was peaceful at this hour. Listening to the chirp of the birds and the croak of the frogs, she took a moment to appreciate the bluish-yellow atmosphere that surrounded her. The warmth of the still rising sun began to thaw her cold skin as rays of light shone through the trees. She was hearing God. She was feeling him near her again.

Her heart felt whole, her Spirit was refreshed. It was as if order had been restored again. Before she knew it, she was crying. She was on her feet with her hands outstretched, her body shaking with joy. "God, I thank you," she cried. "O, Lord, I thank you. I Bless your Holy name." She was inconsolable. As her thankful tears transformed into a wrenching sob, Charlette felt like a stranger in her own body. While she was grateful to feel God's love, and to be in His presence again, this reaction felt like a lot.

She began to jump, clap, shout out in exalting the name of Jesus. She was overcome with emotions – gratitude and thanksgiving – but these feelings were not her own. Before she knew it she was floating, hovering above ground against her own volition.

She figured that she had to be at least five feet above the ground, stomping, walking, jumping on the atmosphere beneath her. Her body was not her own. It felt as if she were watching herself from the outside, sitting on the river banks, marveling at the sight of herself. This sensation was eerily similar to what Shelly had described, but this time, her body was actually moving. It was her mind that felt fastened, unable to break free from the grip of something unseen.

Unable to move a muscle, Charlette seized the opportunity to retreat inward. Though her body was frozen, her mind remained alert. So, she delved deeper into herself, clinging to the memory of her surroundings with each determined breath. Painting a vivid picture in her mind, she saw the thick fog, the blue-yellow hues of the twilight sky, the murky earth, and the telltale grass stains from sitting in grass on her old jeans. And in an instant, she was there, transported by her consciousness to the very scene that took place before her - watching her body, devoid of its mind, floating so still above the water that it almost looked lifeless.

Scanning the riverbanks, peering behind trees, Charlette searched desperately for any sign of him. It couldn't have been a coincidence that she and Shelly both felt the same sensation of being cemented after encounters with him; Dexter had to be nearby, but despite her attempt to find him in the shadows, he was nowhere near. Could she have been wrong about him? Was Shelly, she thought to herself.

Immediately following the thought, she felt a violent, rushing sensation that launched her back into her body, washing over her like the crash of a sudden wave. Still floating, she continued the conversation with her thoughts. Maybe she had fainted from the heat and dreamed it all. Maybe Shelly was confused from the stress of her mother's illness. Maybe that's what happened: Shelly was stressed, just like Charlette. The thoughts came to her in a welcoming affirmation. They were stressed and Dexter was not evil. That explained it all.

After a while she was back in control of her body. Hovering over the water, with her eyes half shut, she wondered if she could move herself while in the air, the same way she does when it's something – or someone else – doing it.

She decided to use the same technique that drew her mind inward, pushing her consciousness outward, to try to move. She thought about how she was going to move. With a few deep breaths she withdrew from the moment, focusing on the distance between the air beneath her and the water.

Her eyes were still closed, Charlette imagined herself gliding above the water. She pictured her legs being crossed, her hair floating in the wind, and the feel of the wind whipping around her smiling face. She saw her soaring northwards up the New George, stealing kisses from the flickering sun as it touched her skin. She saw herself reaching down, dangling her index finger in the water, slicing through its surface, nearly wincing at how cool it was this early in the morning. She smiled as the scene played out in her mind.

Opening her eyes, Charlette found herself on the brink of being face-to-face with a water moccasin, its sleek, black body, dangling from a quickly approaching tree branch. With quick reflexes, she veered to the right, narrowly missing the curious encounter, just avoiding the slithering creature's grasp. She glanced back, watching the creature grow smaller as the distance between them grew, and wondered — could that have been the same snake she'd seen before?

Shaking off the brief moment of unease, Charlette whipped her head forward and smiled in amazement at the earth shifting beneath her, seemingly moving towards her. She was moving

— flying even. Well, not exactly flying, she thought, but certainly hovering, floating on some force that chose to remain hidden from her.

Charlette threw her head back in a sudden burst of laughter, the thin rays of leaf-shaped sunlight shone on her face. In that moment, surrounded by the whimsy of nature, she felt an overwhelming sense of peace settle over her like a warm embrace.

"Charlie," something cried out softly, abruptly ending her moment of solace. She opened her eyes and looked to the left of her, but nothing was there. *"Charlie,"* she heard it say again. She didn't know what to make of the voice because it spoke in a soft whisper, like they were speaking directly into her ear, but she could sense that the thing calling out was in the distance, just on the other side of the water. *"River, river!"* She stopped.

CHAPTER 15

In one spot over the water, Charlette sat in the air, looking into the woods to the left of her. She stared. In her search to find who or whatever had been calling her, she strained to see anything beyond the sea of green that enveloped her. Though there was nothing there to see, she could feel its presence. It was undeniable. Leaning forward, she attempted to pierce through the dense foliage for whatever was just beyond her field of vision, but the thick canopy of trees remained a barrier that obscured whatever was in the forest.

Still, Charlette persisted, her determination driving her to the brink of exhaustion as she strained her eyes more and more for something beyond the shadows. The world around her seemed to blur, to spin, almost as if the world was tilting–it sent her into a dizzying, whirlwind sensation. Charlette leaned forward, stubborn and determined, searching for the thing that had called her. She leaned forward, her body contorting until it seemed like she was about to fall into the water. The world had shifted her view until the sky and earth seemed to swap places in a whirl of disorientation.

Then she realized the rustle of the wind dancing through the trees had silenced, that the foliage in front of her was uncomfortably still. Looking down into the water, Charlette found herself confronted by the sight of her own reflection. Beads of sweat glistening above her brow, her chest rising and falling with each labored breath. She leaned closer, her reflection mirroring her with unsettling precision. "Charlie!" the voice boomed in the distance, the sound bounded off the tree, shaking the earth itself. Startled, Charlette's reflection looked up, peering into the distance, then looked back at her.

Charlette flinched, falling into the water below her. The water at this end was deeper, coming nearly to her neck. She bobbed in and out of the water fighting nothing but her mind. She spun and turned, trying to see if anyone else was in there with her. Finally, she waded through the water and made it to land. She came out on the left side, the other side. *"Charlie...."*

After walking aimlessly for what felt like an hour, the land started to look familiar. She was trying to walk south towards Freedman, so that she could cross at the shallow, narrower part of the water. But somewhere along the bank of the river, she found herself moving further and further into the woods, beckoning her closer to somewhere she had been before.

The tall, decaying church loomed in front of her, grand and daunting. *"This is what was calling me,"* she thought. *"This is where that voice came from."*

Charlette walked up the concrete steps and reached for the doorknob. She paused. *"River, this place isn't like any other church in Georgia,"* she heard in her ear. She stretched her hand out again, pausing before touching the door. She closed her eyes and turned away. "That was God," she said silently as she descended the stairs. Just as her foot touched the hard earth below the step, Dex appeared from behind a tree.

A chill went down Charlette's spin as she saw him swagger towards her. "Was he the one calling me," she asked herself. "He is the only one who calls me Charlie. But that voice was soft, feminine; it couldn't have been him."

"I sho' been missing you Miss Charlette Montgomery," he said with a smile. He walked right up to her and lingered closely, before walking towards the church. River's blood ran cold, but her skin was hot. "You comin'," he asked over his shoulder as he pushed the heavy doors open.

The way River saw it, she had two options: listen to her instinct telling her that God was telling her to leave that church where it stood, or listen to her heart and believe that God brought Dexter to her for a reason, and even more so, that he's calling them to lead a congregation.

"Charlie," Dex called. She spun on her heels and ran up the steps.

The inside of the church was dark. Very little light broke through the dingy windows, the room stunk with the smell of wet wood. River felt a presence there. It was like a familiar sense of uneasiness. She stayed close to herself; she stayed close to Dexter.

As Dexter stepped into the hallowed sanctuary, he found himself struck with a sense of awe. Everything his eyes touched showed him the promise of the church's glorious potential. The cobwebs that clung to weathered pews looked like silken cascades of smokey, silver satin, draped there for some grand ceremonial occasion. His gaze drifted to the choir stand, its once majestic velvet now decorated with mold and decay. Yet, in Dexter's eyes, he envisioned Charlette standing at its center, her beauty radiant, her voice ringing with angelic purity. He could almost feel the wash over the assembled congregation, their hearts moved to tears by her voice.

And then there was the pulpit, a towering monolith of wood and stone that commanded the attention of all who beheld it. Its imposing presence spoke to him, telling him of trials endured by faith, a symbol of hope and redemption--a testament to the enduring power of faith that sustained Dexter.

Charlette followed Dexter as he inspected the old, empty building. He was glowing, beaming with pride and excitement. There was a heat radiating from his body that comforted Charlette but scared her too. She tried to silence the voice telling her that this was strange, but she could not shake it. This was strange. Something had called her out of the water, to the church, and directly in Dexter's path.

It all felt off. It felt too much like a plan and less like a coincidence. God spoke to her often, that was a known fact, but it was very rare that her Spirit was this loud about something. Her hands were shaking, her body was tight. Any time she was even just three feet away from Dexter, she felt a lifeless chill that seemed to steal the warmth from her skin. This was all too much for Charlette. She turned to Dexter with the intention of telling her that she needed to leave.

But as she spun around, he was standing directly behind her, so close their bodies nearly touched. Her heart sank to her feet. She started to walk backward, attempting to put distance between them. "What's the matter," he asked as he mirrored her every step with uncomfortable precision. Charlette tried to speak but words fell out of her mouth in a disoriented stammer. "You alright, dere, Charlie," he asked. Charlette choked on every word she tried to speak. Finally, she stumbled on a dirty pew. She almost fell, but Dexter grabbed her. "You scared or some," he asked with a furrowed brow.

"Dexter, I'm leaving," Charlette said, her voice betraying the facade of confidence she was adopting. She tried to move towards the door, but he grabbed her. "Charlie, what's goin on," he asked as he pressed her arms against her body firmly. She wiggled, shifting her weight to free herself, but nothing worked. "Dexter let me go," she said firmly.

He released her in a huff before taking a step back. They stared at one another. His eyes traced the outline of her body and glowed red with desire. River took a step back. He stayed where he was but his gaze never left her. Suddenly, River felt all the warmth in her body. Her skin felt hot, her breath was short. She took another step back. Dexter slowly moved towards her.

This time she was the one who didn't move. Her short breaths grew shorter. Her body grew hotter. She felt sweat beading around the edges of her head, as her eyes followed Dexter as he circled around her.

"Charlie, why would you be scared right now," he asked. "It's just me."

"I'm not," she lied.

"Ain't no need for lies and fallacies, baby girl. You know I can read you," arrogance drenched his voice.

River felt butterflies again. He smiled at her as he walked between the pews.

She felt the same sense of nerves and excitement she would feel when she saw him in the morning, back when they first met. The feeling didn't manifest in her stomach though, but she could feel it everywhere else—in her fingertips as she imagined how they'd feel on his wet skin, on her neck as she pictured him breathing down it, and most alarmingly, she felt it somewhere between her thighs, dripping with anticipation.

"Dex," River said softly, her voice catching in her throat as she caught sight of him seated near the entrance of the church, a soft sigh escaping her lips. Her heart fluttered seeing his figure bathed in the soft light of what little sun broke through the dingy windows. It was then that she noticed that his shirt was only buttoned halfway up, a subtle invitation that flush of heat in her cheeks.

"Com'ere" he said, chuckling softly, his smile tilting to the left in a way that never failed to stir something within her. A flicker of apprehension lingered in her chest. She did not move. "Come. Here," he demanded, his voice low and enticing. Charlette hesitated, but her right foot copied the action of her left foot, pulling her closer to Dexter, unable to resist his magnetism. Something unsettled her in a way that she didn't quite understand—it wasn't fear but something bigger, something irresistible.

She didn't want to be near him, not when she knew the walls she had carefully built around her purity were in danger of crumbling before her. In that moment, her flesh had finally weakened and her fall from grace was upon her.

She walked in front of him, standing there with a mix of reluctancy and anticipation. He placed his hands on her waist. "Why you so wet, gal," he asked with a grin. "Huh," River asked. "Your clothes. I been meaning to ask you why ya clothes was wet, but this place gets me so," he paused. "Excited," he groaned as he shifted his weight downward while thrusting his hip upward. "I fell in the river," she whispered, her voice dripping with hesitant desire.

He grabbed her, pulling her between his legs. "You wearin pants," he asked, unbuttoning them. "Yeah, I—" River couldn't finish the sentence, distracted by feel of his mouth pressed against her stomach. She rolled her eyes to close them. *"Lord, I'm tryin'"* she thought. *"Please, don't make this hard on me."*

He pulled her into his lap and put his finger under her chin. He kissed her, she reluctantly kissed him back. She turned her body towards his, placing her hand behind his neck. He placed one hand in the center of her back and rested the other on her thigh. He stopped kissing her to look her in the eyes. River saw an appetite in him, a craving for something only she could give him. It burned inside him like a fire. Golden, rageful flames that cried to her desperately. Her brows furrowed, the corners of her mouth turned downward, forming a longing frown–a silent signal that her body had held out for as long as possible and had started to anticipate the desperate, vigorous, satisfying sensations that were waiting for her on the other end of this interaction. If they could have swallowed each other whole in that moment, they would have.

That isn't to say that one didn't try their hardest to consume the other, but such pleasures are not entirely possible. Their mouths interlocked, their tongues shyly, sneakily grazed each other's. Charlette felt heat beneath her skin, the passions of desire igniting her every sense, so much so that she thought that the wet shirt on her back had started to produce steam. She pushed off of Dexter, frantically unbuttoning her shirt. Her fingers struggled to connect with the buttons as her hands shook from the excitement of it all. Dexter calmly, but urgently, grabbed the bottom of her shirt before yanking it over her head. He placed his hand on her stomach, slowly inching lower and lower until the tips of his fingers hovered just below her waist.

She grabbed his wrist. He kissed her cheek, a gesture of comfort that both eased her mind, and to distract her from the fact that his hand had slid behind the band of her unfastened jeans. He slowly inched lower and lower until something inside River awakened. She had never even touched where his fingers had settled. She jumped. He paused. They looked at each other, frozen in the moment. His eyes that were just glowing red eyes were brown again. They were pleading, inviting, telling her that she was safe in his arms. His eyes were telling her to relax, to trust him, so she did. His middle finger followed his ring finger, as they continued their expedition. They traveled inside her, moving carefully, diligently, as if her body were hiding pure gold.

She bit her lip to hush the exhale that still escaped her shakily. With the hand that was supporting her, Dexter leaned her back softly. She rested in his arms, her mouth slightly agape, her body waiting. He pressed further and the breath Charlette had been holding on to suddenly disappeared. She didn't breathe out, nor did she breathe in—the breath was just gone. He pushed harder, shifting the acid that had rested in her stomach. River's cheeks were hot, her ears were stinging, her body quivered as he moved, then...

"What," she questioned worriedly, not sure what to make of her sudden descent. Dexter kissed her neck, "let it happen," he whispered. The room grew darker, her vision started to blur. "Look at me," Dexter said to her. Charlette's frightened eyes met his, blinking rapidly.

"Dex," she cried.

"Look at me," he repeated.

"I'm trying to but I can't see. My–my sight. Its–" she couldn't focus on her words. Charlette was too focused on being present in the moment.

"Yeah, dere you go. Dere you go, Charlie, just like that," he said, his voice rough but soothing. Charlette didn't know what he was talking about, what he was praising her for doing. Her consciousness was disconnected from her body, trapped behind the barriers of her mind.

"I got you, baby, just keep looking at me," he said.

Charlette decided not to speak, or even think. She wanted to be silent, she wanted to listen. All the color flushed from her body as she heard herself moaning. She tried to set herself free, to regain control. *"Dexter,"* she screamed inwardly. *"Stop,"* she shouted to no one.

She kept fighting, but nothing happened. She had fully retreated into herself. It was the first time she had ever been intimate with a man and she wasn't even there to experience it. Charlette withdrew. She gave up.

"Charlie," She heard Dexter say to her. "Charlie," he called again. Charlette could tell that the voice wasn't really Dexter, or at least not the one talking her body through an experience she wasn't having.

"Charlette," she heard him say. She tried to bring her consciousness forward, but she had gone so far within herself, she couldn't determine a way out. "Follow my voice," he called to her. "We're almost at the end."

River's mind followed the echoes of the Dexter that existed in the physical world telling her to be louder. She trailed the sound of herself crying out in pleasure, panting, begging, reaching. She envisioned herself walking towards a light. Reality started to become tangible, she was almost there. "You sound so good, baby. You're so close. Keep coming, Charlie, you're almost there,"

She got closer, so close to being back in her body she could reach for it. Then she stopped, halted in her tracks by a sensation in her body so powerful that even she could feel from the recesses of her mind. Her breathing labored, her heart raced. Without any further thought or effort, Charlette found herself back in her own body, overcome by the surge of senses that beckoned an imminent eruption. She tried to brace herself for what was coming, but nothing could have prepared her for the explosion that reverberated through every fiber of her being, electrifying her with its raw, unbridled intensity.

Dexter kissed her sweaty forehead, "you looked so pretty just now, Charlie." She looked into his eyes to see if he would say something. She wanted to know if he remembered or even realized that he went inside her mind, that his deep dive into her subconscious was the only reason she's present in the moment.

His eyes were doty, beaming with pride and satisfaction. She didn't see anything but him. He started to blush, that's when she realized that either he had no clue what happened to her, or he was a really good actor.

She grabbed her damp shirt from the dirty floor and pulled it back on. She hopped out of his lap, buttoning up her pants quickly. Before he could stop her, Charlette flew out of the door and ran away from the church.

"Wait," he cried out. "Stop," he shouted. River turned around and slapped him.

"I don't know what your plans are or who you think I am, but that was not me," she said with a firm finger pointed directly in his face.

"That was not me. I am not some common whore who spreads her legs for a debonair stranger with a pretty smile!"

She pushed him with all her strength, just for him to barely move his shoulder to the right. He reached out to her, but she slapped him again.

"Okay, now Charlie—" she slapped him again. "Charlette, don't hit me no—" she struck him again. "Dammit, River, if you—" she reached out to hit him again, but this time he grabbed her wrist. She tried to hit him with her other hand, but he dodged the blow before grabbing that hand too.

He spun her around and wrapped her in his arms. He held her as she tried to free herself from his grasp. Dexter couldn't help but laugh at her. She was small and petite. He was tall and very strong. She tired herself out soon, letting out a defeated huff as Dexter rested his chin on her shoulder. "You done," he asked her.

She stomped off in frustration, but only made it about five paces away before Dexter said "Hey, Charlie."

When she turned around, ready to strike, she saw him down on one knee with a ring in his hand.

"Will you marry me?"

CHAPTER 16

THREE WEEKS LATER

Eddie woke up that morning with a terrible headache. He had gotten drunk the night before in the next county over. It was a miracle that he even made it back home to Freedman.

"Gon' and get up, boy," Pastor Johnson said from the doorframe. "Clean ya self up and start lookin' fo a place to stay." Eddie rolled over, looking at his father out of his still heavy, very tired eyes. "I can't let you ruin yo self in my house. I can't watch you die," his father said as he turned to walk away.

Edwin-Hendricks Delroy Johnson, the great "future leader and colored scholar," had become Freedman's prodigal son. Potential wasted. He had all but become a drunk since River's birthday. He had been sneaking in and out of brothels, and he hadn't been to church once since that Sunday. Not for bible study, not for choir practice, not for any reason at all.

"Daddy, what the hell you talkin' bout," he mumbled as he attempted to roll back over. His father snatched the quilt from E.H.'s body, pulling him off the bed with it.

"Don't speak to me like dat boy," his father said with a glare. "Boy, if yo mother was here she'd skin yo narrow hind." The two men stood toe to toe and faced off. Eddie's jaw clenched, tightening in eager anticipation to fight. Pastor Johnson lifted his own chin and clenched his fists, also willing to tussle with his son.

E.H. shook his head before grabbing the pile of dirty clothes that had been gathering in the corner. "I don't have to listen to this shit," he said. He bumped into his father's shoulder as he exited the room. Feeling no need to explain himself or elaborate beyond the one sentence, E.H. walked downstairs and out the door.

He walked around aimlessly, going nowhere, anywhere, just not back to Freedman. He felt nothing as he passed the church his father and grandfather ministered in. There was no nostalgia when he passed the school house where his love for education was founded, no sense of loss when he passed the cluster of buildings that made up their town square. All Edwin-Hendricks Johnson felt was a longing to leave for Atlanta as quickly as he could.

But in addition to the fact that he knew his father wouldn't give him the train fare, school didn't start for another 6 weeks. So, he walked, aimlessly, heading nowhere, heading anywhere away from Freedman.

As far as E.H. was concerned, Freedman was a shit-show now. There was nothing keeping him there. His mother had been dead for years, his father had begun to hate him, and River was engaged to show-boaty, siddity-ass, tacky-ass Dexter Alexander. There was nothing for him in Freedman but rage. Everywhere he went, he found anger.

E.H didn't know what he was going to do for the rest of the summer, maybe walk up to Savannah, stay with his aunt, work with her in the diner, he thought. Hell, he might even find a woman out there to take back to Atlanta and make his wife. That'll show River, he thought. That'll show all of them.

He walked in the heat of the unrelenting Georgia sun, mulling over the last three weeks. Each memory fanned the flames of his desire to leave his hometown-from the fight with Dexter, to the scene in the backyard with River, and most searing of all, the day he stumbled upon her and Dexter by the lake.

There they were laying shamelessly in each other's arms.

Their disregard for his feelings or how it would look to anyone else cut Eddie deeper than any blade could have. Should he have minded his business, E.H. thought, and in hindsight, he probably should have, but in the moment his desire to separate them was stronger than any other feelings he may have had.

"Might fine day, it'nit," he asked bitterly, looming over them, his shadow cast intentionally over their affectionate embrace. The couple stared up at him, both smiling when they saw him.

"Hot, but pretty," Dexter said, pulling Charlette closer to him. "Not as pretty as my baby thought." Dexter's casual reply and unthreatened gaze only added insult to injury. And Charlette's shy smile and bashfulness was like twisting the knife deeper into his wound.

Despite having been emotionally stabbed to death, E.H. used the gall that had always sustained him to sit next to River, ignoring the bruise that had started to form on his already pained ego.

"No braid today? Seem pretty hot to be having all that thick pretty hair hanging down ya back like dat," he asked Charlette cooly. She sat up from the ground wearing a smile that melted his heart. Eddie tried to maintain composure, but her radiant smile pulled at his heart strings.

"I haven't been feelin' like doin' my hair. 'Specially not with all that we have goin' on right now," she said proudly, making no effort to hide her excitement. Eddie took her outstretched hand in his own. His gaze shifted from the modest ring on her finger to Dexter. Still lounging in the grass, still not threatened by Eddie's presence, Dexter smiled at E.H., taunting him. As if his pride hadn't taken enough, Dexter made sure to send Eddie a wink that ignited an all-consuming fire ablaze within the young scholar.

E.H. felt sick, betrayed even. He had loved this woman every day of his life and she threw it all away for a man she hardly knew, for a man who added nothing to her life. It was hard for Eddie not to suffocate on the fury that grew inside him.

"I wanted to say something when he asked last week, Eddie, but my daddy said not to ever go round your house again," Charlette said, her words sliced through the air like a whisper of remorse. She wanted to bridge the gap between them but she knew this only pushed them further apart. She tried to grab his hand but the shock of the sudden touch and the genuine disdain he felt in the moment made Eddie recoil from her touch with disgust.

Turning away from Charlette, he spat in the opposite direction, an honest attempt to rid himself of the bitterness and resentment within him.

"I ain't mad," he lied. "Ain't mad at all." His words fell out with a chill of spite. In the depths of his soul, he was wounded. The scars of her betrayal were deep. He had heard enough. He stood up and tried to walk off before he unleashed his all-consuming emotions on the two of them, but Dexter called out to him. "Hey, Johnson, wait up."

The two men walked away, leaving River alone at the New George. Her first thought was to follow them, making sure they didn't try to kill one another, but there was something else in her that said that these two grown men needed to have a conversation amongst themselves without the threat of a woman trying to contain them. So, she closed her eyes and tried to pray.

Her words felt hollow, like they were devoid of warmth and sincerity, as if there was no love in them. With a heavy heart, she made an attempt to control her breath, guiding her Spirit back to her, back to alignment with her words, but try as she might, the prayers still felt empty, lost of the passion and devotion that once fueled them.

Turning her view upward to the sky, Charlette stared at the

clouds that drifted lazily above her. Their gentle dance and effortless obedience were a stark contrast to the turmoil within her soul. As she followed the movements of their shifting shapes, her memory drifted back to the day she saw the rabbit and snake at the lake.

She wondered if the poor rabbit had a family, and if that family missed it - who would take care of them now? She thought about how unfair it must be to exist as the snake. People fearing you because of how you were created. Wasn't all of God's creation perfect? Was the snake wrong for having its daily bread? Was the rabbit's sole purpose to someday die and be nourishment for the snake?

Still focused on the whimsical dance of the clouds and the serenity of their powder blue home, she considered her own life. She had spent the last nineteen years in a church and a culture that allowed no space for questions, no room for curiosity. She had been happily, devotedly obeying her family, her elders, and the Word of God. But she always was able to speak to God so freely; she was always able to ask questions, to seek insight, and he always answered. The Holy Spirit had always led her in the right direction.

And now, she's been more confused than ever. Conversations with the Lord usually end up with her blacking out or feelings abandoned. Was her purpose not to be a healer and serve God, but rather be the model of the perfect Christian woman? Was she to expand the Kingdom of Heaven, or was she only created to nourish the ego of a man?

CHAPTER 17

"Look man, I hope it ain't no bad blood between us," Dexter said to E.H. as they started up the long dirt road back to Freedman. "I know we done had our issues, but you and River, y'all care for each other. I'm just tryna see how much you care for her befo dis become a problem." Dexter's last sentence came out firmly, a lot less friendly than anything else had ever said to E.H before. Eddie chuckled before realizing that Dexter had stopped walking and was standing squarely with his chest high and his stance opened. E.H. glanced over his shoulder at Dex stopping only for a second. He kept walking ahead and spoke over his shoulder. "Ain't nobody studydin' River. You want her so bad; you can have her." Finally, he stopped, turning towards Dexter. "Besides, it ain't in my nature to fight for a bitch who sleepin' around with another man."

Eddie started to laugh to himself, pleased with the dig he just took at River, but his joy was short-lived. Before he knew it, Dexter had struck him in his face. He landed a perfect punch, square on Edwin-Hendricks' nose. Eddie fell backwards and groaned in pain. He stood up to swing at Dexter but missed. Dexter swung at Eddie. E.H. ducked and was able to grab Dex by the waist. He tackled him to the ground and began to let all his rage, all his frustration, all of his anger out on Dexter.

Eddie's fists flew one after another into Dex's eye, his nose, his lip, his chin, his cheek. Blood covered the young man's bruised knuckles. He wanted to stop himself, but he couldn't. The fire that burned in him had been released. It had to come out at that moment or it would surely swallow him whole.

E.H.'s fists started to sting from the tension of connecting forcefully with Dexter's skull, but still Eddie could not stop. This man, this stranger, walked into Freedman and stole the girl he loved. He came in, smiled at her, and defeated him in an instance. He'd seen old men offer up acreage, money, livestock, everything but the sun itself just to kiss her on the hand. River never wavered. He himself had been nothing but kind to her; he supported her, protected her, loved her fiercely and she didn't want him. What made Dexter different? Why was he worthy?

Eddie raised both his fists, positioning them high above his head. He lingered there looking at Dex. He saw the swelling of his eyes, the gashes on his cheeks. He saw his bruised skin and exposed flesh. The scene was gruesome, making Eddie pause for a second. He thought: *"You're going to kill him, Hendricks. Is this really necessary?"*

With a rough, fast, preparatory deep breath, Eddie used all the strength in his body to drop both fists into Dexter's ribcage, cracking them instantly. Eddie watched as Dexter coughed up blood. Dex tried to roll over so that he wouldn't choke on the warm, red liquid filling his mouth, but his lung had been punctured by his ribs. E.H. stood over Dexter, watching as life left his body. He stayed to make sure his deed was done. And when Dexter exhaled after struggling to take one final breath, Edwin-Hendricks Delroy Johnson turned away jubilantly.

Suddenly the world grew dark, the clouds were black. The earth was eerily still. Eddie stopped, turning his gaze skyward. He looked from the left to the right of him, but everything seemed to have vanished. The trees were dark gray, some of them had glowing orange centers—they looked as if they had all been burned. The grass was charred and melted. The spot where Dexter's dead body had just been laying was singed.

Eddie's breath shortened; his chest tightened. He heard people talking about Fred Jones saying that Dex was a demon, that he possessed his wife, but he never paid attention to it.

Despite his disliking of the man, Eddie always knew that Dexter was just a man. Then his mind thought back to the day he followed Dexter and Charlette to the river, how he was transported into a nightmare. He thought about how different River was when she was with him. Was Dexter truly a soldier of the enemy? Was he something other than man after all?

"What the hell you done to me, man," Eddie asked. Just then E.H. heard laughter—a deep, robust, spine-chilling laugh that made his blood run cold. He felt hot air hurl towards him with such a force that it almost knocked him down. "What is it you think you know about Dexter Alexander," he heard something say.

The voice spoke directly in his ear, as if lips were pressed firmly against his helix. "What is it you think you know about dat damn Dex," the voice repeated. This time it felt as if the words were being spat out and spilling directly to his ear drum. The voice was piercing but deep. It was strained, yet confident. This voice was otherworldly. It was sinister. It made E.H. terrified and immobile.

Eddie shut his eyes and took a deep breath through his nose. He could feel the hot air getting closer. It felt as if something under his skin was radiating, like a primal instinct had been activated, telling him that danger was near. The beat of his heart quickened. His skin hardened. "Tell me what you know," the voice said, right inside his mind—as if it were his own conscience. "Tell me about Dex."

Here stood the son and grandson of the greatest colored Pastors south of the Mason-Dixon, facing off against evil. Satan was in his mind, speaking to him directly. Did this mean that he was being given the opportunity to prove his faith and belief in God? Or was this a testament of how lowly and ungodly he truly had become. There he stood, terrified and confused, the voice of a demon in his head. What was he to do?

Eddie kept his eyes closed, attempting to redirect his fear, but he knew that he was facing his own demise; he knew that death was pulling his card and he had to fight for his soul. "You know he's a bad man, don't ya," the voice said. "You know he's powerful," it continued. "And you know he's gonna fuck River so good, that it would take God Himself to get her from up under him." Eddie started to cry.

"Cry about it, preacher man. Cry about yo loss, yo hurt, cry about yo failure." The voice started to laugh again as the earth around Eddie started to burn. All the dead grass and scorched trees disintegrated, bursting into flames. Eddie opened his eyes. He saw Dexter in front of him, swollen, decomposed, stinking of death, with merciless flames engulfing him like a throne of chaos.

He felt the fire on his skin, the choke of smoke filling his lungs. He felt the existence of hell in that moment. E.H. dropped to his knees, feeling the dewy earth beneath him. Just as suddenly as the world grew dark, it became lively again. He looked over to where Dexter's body was supposed to be laying bloodied and bruised, but no one was there. "Ed," Dexter called out. To Eddie's utter terror and surprise, Dexter Alexander was standing to the left of him, unscratched, unharmed and full of life.

E.H. collapsed, he fainted just from the sight of the man. Dexter stepped over his body and kneeled down next to him. It was only a matter of seconds before Eddie came to. Looking up at the tall, dark, and handsome man, Edwin-Hendricks truly thought he was going to die. His heart had begun to beat so fast he was sure it would explode from the stress. Dexter outstretched his hand to help him up, but Eddie could not move. Finally, with his lips nearly touching Eddie's ear, Dexter said to him, "call my fiancé a bitch again, and see if I don't send Satan himself to yo front doe."

Every day since, Eddie has avoided Dexter, the church, and River. Now he's walking straight out of Freedman, into the unknown. Leaving behind everything he had ever known, he was stepping away from his destiny. He laughed ironically. He came home at the beginning of the summer full of hope, full of life, ready to make a man of himself–to take hold of his future; now he's a smelly drunk who has to pay women in brothels just to breathe in his direction.

E.H. had made it past the town and was about to walk to the north end of the New George, officially moving in the direction towards Savannah. He stopped there. He recounted the last few days again, reflecting on his life. He thought about his mother and how much she loved him, how much she believed in him. He grew up with both of his parents pouring all of their hopes and dreams into him, but they were so different in their approach. His father was stern, strict, using intimidation to teach all of his lessons—focused on ensuring that his own legacy remained untarnished—but his mother gave him grace, patience and an abundant amount of security.

He even thought about how much his mother loved Charlette Montgomery. He pictured the two of them at the piano singing, or in the church praying. He thought about River holding his mother's hand as she took her last breath because he was too afraid to do it himself.

The thought of his mother on her deathbed, the guilt of not being strong enough to comfort her then, crashed down on him with relentless force. As tears slowly escaped, streaming down his face, Eddie felt overwhelmed by the memories of his mother's final moments. Vividly, he remembered Charlette's tender touch on his mother's frail hand, the sound of her strained singing comforting his mother while piercing his heart, the way she and her mother put on a facade of strength not just for one another, but for him. In her final moments, his mother still put his feelings before her own, while Charlette did the same thing as she watched one of the women who raised her draw in her last breath. He didn't deserve them.

Confronted by the depth of his pain, with a raw honesty

that neither entitlement nor ego could sway, E.H. let out an anguished wail. No amount of liquor, no amount of women, none of his vices could numb the pain that ached within him. He had to confront this head on. He had to admit that he was not a good man, that he was not strong, that all the confidence he wore on his shoulder was a feeble distraction from how insecure and weak he was.

"I'm sorry, Mama," he said as his forceful sobs brought him to his knees. Surrendering to the release of grief that reverberated within him, Eddie let out a primal, guttural scream. The sound was so loud and striking that it sent a flock of birds fleeting from their home. Enough was enough. Weary, yet resolved, E.H. rose to his feet.

Standing there, on the cusp of creating a whole new life, Eddie knew that if he walked away from Freedman, he would walk away from River, disappointing his mother.

He closed his eyes and shed one last tear before looking towards the sky. "Thank you, God," he said to the clouds. "Thank you, mama," he said in his heart. He turned back the other way and walked up the riverbank, southbound toward Freedman and headed home.

CHAPTER 18

THE SAME DAY

River woke up that morning anxious. She made herself a cool bath to relieve the tension she felt in her bones. The chill of the water, coupled with the coldness of the porcelain tub offered little comfort. She drew her knees into her chest and rested her forehead on them.

She and Dexter were announcing their plans to start their own ministry in Freedman. They had been planning and reacting for a while. They were going to set up in front of Mr. Brooks' General Store, dressed in their Sunday's best, and Charlette was going to sing in an effort to draw a crowd. From there, Dexter would start to speak. He'd joke with people, make them laugh, grab their attention with his charisma. Once he had their trust, he'd swoop in like a thief in the night and capture their souls with an electrifying sermon. After that, Dexter figured his preaching would call the people of Freedman to his soapbox every Thursday evening–as to not interfere with Wednesday night service or Sunday morning worship.

Charlette chalked the gnawing she felt inside as nerves, when in actuality she felt guilty. She wanted to speak to Pastor Johnson and Eddie about their plans to start a church in the old building they had found, but Dexter told her not to. In fact, he told her to never speak to either Johnson men again.

That day they saw Eddie at the river three weeks ago, Dexter came back to her angrier than she had ever seen him before. "I don't want you alone wit him or his daddy ever again, Charlie, do you hear me?" His words fell out of his mouth both as a command and a threat. Charlette's breath hitched in her throat. She didn't understand the mixture of fear and excitement that surged through her then.

"Dat man sees you as his own little doll that he don't want no one else playin wit. You's a grown ass woman, Charlie, not some little plaything he can toy wit," Dexter spoke to his bride with a sureness that she couldn't question. He told her that if he or Cleo wasn't around, be cordial with them, but not conversational. He said he was sure that they both had strange perversions about her, that they saw her for her beauty and the status she would give them.

Since her soak proved to be disappointing, Charlette left the bathroom and dressed herself in another nightgown, not yet ready to dress for the day. She planned to wear the same white dress she had on the day her parents and Dexter were introduced to one another. Something simple but symbolic–symbolic of purity, of good intentions, symbolic of wanting to make an impression but doing so modestly.

And since her fiancé liked to see it down, she only pulled half of her hair into a ponytail, letting the rest of her curls cascade down her back. She went into the kitchen silently, starting a pot of fresh brewed coffee, as her man slept on the couch peacefully in the next room.

Charlette's parents invited Dexter to live with them since the two were engaged. Cleo didn't want his future son-in-law living with Hop Wilson, where loose women and liquor frequented the small quarters. And Cecilia thought it gave them the opportunity to keep an eye on Charlette and Dexter until their wedding day.

Not wanting to wake him, Charlette sat delicately on the arm of the couch. She watched Dexter as he slept, her eyes gently grazing his smooth brown skin. She smiled imagining what joy it would be to wake up to such a fine face every day. She giggled softly, looking at his mouth hanging open, drool falling onto the pillow. She stood up before kissing his forehead. He grabbed her wrist and brought it to his wet lips.

He sat up on the couch, pulling her into his lap. They shared a short kiss before Charlette rose up from his lap. Dexter stood when she did, watching her walk away with a quiet whisper of suggestion in each step. Noticing that she left the door ajar, Dexter saw an invitation in her actions, and started down the hallway. He stopped at her door, taking a moment to watch her as she watched him. He shifted his weight, leaning against the doorframe, anticipation and lust hanging in the air between them. She pulled her nightgown over her head, lingering in front of him for one – for Dexter, painfully, excoriating – second. Dexter straightened his posture, flexed his jaw, and took a step forward. But before he was able to cross the threshold, he heard the side door to the kitchen open.

River must have heard it too because she flew across the room to slam the door in Dexter's face. Dex heard Cleo pour a cup of coffee as he scurried into the bathroom as a save. He waited there for a while before opening the door only to be face-to-face with his fiancé's father.

"Morning, Dex," Cleo grumbled lowly before turning into the room to the right of him, shutting the door behind him Dexter let out a relieved sigh.

"How you so bad but scared of dat big ugly negro," the voice said to him. "I ain't scared of nobody," Dexter mumbled as he walked back to his couch. *"Sho seem like you scared of him to me,"* the voice replied. "I ain't scared of nobody. I know I just said dat." The voice said ok and Dexter laid back down, waiting for his bride.

Charlette came out of the room fully dressed and asked if everything was alright. "Bout right as rain," he replied with a smile.

The couple walked into town at around eleven that

morning. Dex carried an old leather bible, Charlette held one too. Dexter climbed the steps of the porch while Charlette stood at the bottom of the steps, greeting everyone who passed by. Dexter was fully dressed in a three-piece suit–beige, with a sage green silk tie. He was beautiful, he was admirable, and Charlette couldn't be prouder to someday be his wife.

"What y'all got goin on," Hop asked with a toothpick hanging from his mouth. "We ain't missed the wedding, have we?" Dexter laughed, leaning in for a brotherly hug. "Naw, man, we just gettin' ready to spread the news, Good News dat is."

"Aww hell, you done ruined the girl ain't cha? River, girl, he done got you in a bad way already?" Hop tried to sound disappointed by the thought, but the smile on his face betrayed him. Charlette blushed beet red, shaking her head no.

"Naw, none of that. We just have something special we want to share with ya, Hop. You and the rest of the folks of Freedman," she shared. Her words were like satin, delicate and smooth. There was a presence of serenity in her voice, softer than ever before. Charlette was different. No longer did she wear neat braids or tamed ponytails; now her hair hung freely, strands of gray woven in like hidden threads of silk.

Dexter beamed with pride at the woman before him. She had no guilt, no anxiety, barely any shame at all. She was different and he liked the woman she had become. Meek, mild-mannered, well behaved.

"Well out wit it nie, y'all got a crowd so get tuh bumpin gums," Hop said, his patience wearing thin.

Dexter pulled at the lapels of his jacket, puffing out his chest.

"Well, y'all can recall me saying that I wanted to be a man of the cloth, right? Sayin' I wanted to preach or be a minister of some sort," Dexter started. "Well, I planned to do dat by gettin' in good wit da Johnsons, but we see how dats turned out, huh?"

People laughed and chatted a bit, but settled quickly and waited for the point of this gathering. "Well, God done showed me another way. I'll be honest, I ain't ordained or nothing special, but I gots a gift. I gots a calling, and it's preaching. And while I can't depend on Pastor Johnson or his boy, Edwin-Hendricks, I can depend on dis here book."

He held up the bible and shook it gently. By that time more people had gathered nearby. Everyone wanted to know what the mysterious, soulfully dressed Dexter Alexander had to say, and what was River's involvement in it all.

"Wit da word of God and his faithful servant, my soon-to-be wife, by my side, I reckon I can lead this here town to salvation, if'n y'all will allow me dat," he continued.

The crowd was silent. People looked at one another, whispers passing silently among them. Not anticipating people's reluctant reactions, Dexter looked down to Charlette for support. She smiled at him, shot him a wink, then turned back to the crowd.

"Okay, okay, I get it. Y'all thinkin' 'I ain't ever seen ol' Dex in church' or 'ain't no preacher I ever heard of drink hooch or chew tobacco, they sho nuff don't cuss like Dex do neither.'" People laughed.

"But hey, listen to dis: I'm a human just like y'all. I'm flawed like every other person on dis earth."

"I'ma do it," Charlette heard Dexter say. She turned to look at him, he was smiling at her.

"Did you just—," she thought.

"I did," he replied. *"I'm gon' give dem a taste of my sermon. I can't lose dey interest."*

Charlette turned around, blinking rapidly, struggling to make make sense of the conversation she and her fiancé just had. Her heart skipped a few beats, nearly rendering her unconscious, but she felt a sudden sense of calm wash over her. She straightened her posture, patted the edges of her head, and smiled at the crowd a few times before looking up and smiling at the crowd.

"You see, I ain't like most church folk y'all know or is used to. I ain't uppity, I ain't siddity, I'm just a poor Black man trying to find his way. All I have in this world is my woman and my faith," Dexter said, descending down the stairs, resting by Charlette's side.

"My faith tells me, specifically in *1 Corinthians 12:12,* that ***'For as the body is one, and hath many members, and all the members of that one body, being many, are one body: so also is Christ.'*** 'Nie, what you tryna say by quotin' dat, Dex,' I'm gettin' to it folks, jus stay wit me," he said through a chuckle.

Dexter took off his suit jacket and handed it to River.

"What I mean by dat is dat tha bible tells us that we, the members of the body, or the parts of the body, I guess you can say, all make up the one and only body of Christ, each part as important as the other." River knew which part of the text Dexter wanted to preach from and she saw him taking notes and speaking to himself about it all week; he gave her the general idea of what he wanted people to take from his sermon, but she had never heard him put it all together. She was intrigued.

"Nie, dem people over at the First Baptist Church of Freedman might say 'Mr. Jenkins, you welcome to come to church anytime you need, but since you don't have a pot tuh piss in or a window to throw it out of, we'd be just fine, if not better without you' or 'Henry Stitts, you's a good man, a good handyman, so if you could come by and patch up tha roof we'd be grateful, but if you never stepped yo drunk ass in the church a day after dat, we'd be just as happy."

The people of the crowd nodded and "hmm'd" in agreement. People were locked in, hanging on his words. Even Hop Wilson was tuned into what he was saying. Dexter tried not to grin too hard. He gathered himself quickly so that he could continue what he had to say.

"I don't get dat. Dat don't make no sense to me. Does the ear say to the eye 'you're not a ear and cannot hear and so I don't need you?' Or does the hand say to the foot, 'you are not dressed in jewels and rings, and so you are not as important as me, so I don't need you?' You see in that passage Paul is saying to the church dat they have been wrong in saying 'dis person is special because she can speak in tongues, or dat man is more important because he has dis spiritual gift; Paul is saying dat just as each part of tha body serves his own purpose, so does each member in the church, which is da body of Christ."

At this point, it was so silent, you could hear a rabbit piss on cotton. Every man and woman in Freedman had been captivated by the words and allure of Dexter Alexander. They were entranced. Dexter knew the Word and knew how to sell it to the people. And at that moment, he was preaching to a congregation.

"'I hear ya Dexter, I hear," he continued. "But what dat got to do wit me and you and Pastor Johnson nem down yonder in dey church?' I'll tell ya just stay with me. You see, when I'm preaching, when the doors of my church have opened, you will be valued for the purpose you serve. I know dat I need you, each and every one of you. I don't go 'round shaming folks. I ain't one of them sometimey, wishy-washy, nice-nasty Christians who claims to love folk from afar. I know that I am just but one member, one part, of the body of Christ and I need every other member of the body of Christ to survive. I know dat the loss of one sense, of one man or woman, could mean the failure, or hurt, maybe a disease in the overall body."

"I may say 'Henry, I know you been low lately. I know your hands have worked hard to serve the people of Freedman and the next three colored counties over. I know it's hard tuh come home to an empty house after Alberta and the baby died, and I know dat leads you to drinkin', but Henry I'm glad dat you here and dat you made it to hear God's Word. Allow me to be a set of feet and let me stand in da gap for ya. Let me pray a blessin' upon you and your mind. Rest a while, Henry, and let me be a set of feet that can support the weight of yo burden. Let me, brother, be a pair of feet dat will help you walk in the light of Jesus Christ. Come into this church and let me be the pair of feet that allows you, the tried-and-true hands that keep Freedman, Georgia from falling apart, rest and relax in the peace of knowing that I NEED YOU!"

People were shouting, clapping, agreeing with the Word they had just received. Folks who River hadn't seen in church since she was a child or ever were saying "hallelujah" and giving praise. Henry Stitts was in tears, leaning on another man, saying "thank you, Dex, thank you."

River felt excitement radiating off the crowd, she felt their exuberance. She looked at Dexter and saw the exhilaration exuding from his body. She saw him beaming with pride. She was in love.

He was a fervent, sprightly speaker. He knew how to capture a crowd and hold their attention. He was captivating. He was fierce. He was powerful. She was enchanted by him, purely, utterly captivated by him. She was trapped and had no desire to be free.

Whatever doubt she had, whatever hesitation she felt about being with Dexter, had all subsided. Her fears were laid to rest. Dexter Alexander was the man who would lead Charlette to her destiny. He was the man God said would make her face her calling. In that moment, she knew that she made the right decision. She knew that she wanted to be Mrs. Dexter Alexander.

CHAPTER 19

Eddie was approaching town when he saw the people gathered outside of the general store. He could tell that he had caught the tail end of whatever was going on, but he wanted to see if he could find out what had just happened. People were walking away, smiling, hugging, and chattering gleefully. He was confused. Not by the congregating or the happiness of the crowd, but by how genuinely happy folks were.

The people of Freedman were nice. They had an amazing sense of community and always practiced good manners with one another, but they weren't necessarily happy. Life around there was slow. People went to work, went home, and went about their business. They made time for small pleasantries like card parties and eating together, but they weren't exactly happy. Who would be when they're poor, Black, and living in the South.

Seeing people's delight, their genuine splendor, on an insignificant Saturday morning was very strange to E.H. He walked up on the crowd and was greeted by everyone he passed. They were all smiling, all teary eyed. Everyone seemed full of hope. "Good morning, E.H.," Hattie Jackson said to him. "It's a beautiful day to be a child of God ain't it?" Eddie gave her a smile and nodded in agreement.

As he approached the crowd, he felt a presence looming in the atmosphere that was heavy and distinct. It stopped him in his tracks. The hairs on his arms raised, heat scorched his neck. He knew that presence. He had felt that energy. He turned to his left and saw her staring at him, smiling at him. He couldn't move.

Standing right behind her, with both hands on her shoulder was her fine, statuesque fiancé staring directly at E.H., donning a haunting smile. Charlette had her husband bend down so that she could whisper in her ear. E.H. turned to walk away. Before he could make it far, Charlette shouted his name, as she jogged over to him.

"Eddie," she called out. "Eddie, wait" she shouted, but he kept moving, dodging behind people in an attempt to get away. "Eddie." The voice cemented him where he stood, the same labored, sinister voice spoke to him, directly in his ear. E.H. turned around and was met with a warm embrace. He was scared to hug her back, but she held him tightly. Charlette's eyes started to water as she clung to him. He eventually scooped her into his arms, shedding a single tear too.

In the middle of the crowd, Charlette and Eddie held one another, crying as if there was no one watching. For a moment they were young again. For just a few seconds they were both fifteen-years-old with no complicated feelings, no unrequited love, just two people who cared deeply for each other. In that moment, in each other's arms, they were pure.

"Eddie, I ain't seen you in 'bout a month of Sundays. Where have you been," Charlette asked. She knew why she hadn't seen him; she knew that she was the one avoiding him. But still, Freedman was small and they hadn't crossed paths even once. She was concerned for him and that was her way of asking if he had been taking care of himself.

"Aww, Letty, I just been," he paused. He looked into her big, doe-like eyes. He didn't know what to say. Should he tell her the truth or should he make up a lie. His eyes started to water so he looked down, kicking dirt. She grabbed his chin, forcing his eyes to meet hers. "What's goin' on, Eddie," she asked.

"Talk to me."

Charlette latched her elbow around his, guiding Eddie

away from the crowd. Out of instinct the two of them walked up the road towards the New George. She didn't think about Dexter or his request for her not to be alone with Eddie. All that was on her mind was that her friend was hurting and that he needed her.

As they walked down their familiar path, Charlette's mind replayed some of her worst memories with Eddie–him slapping her, calling her out of her name, all the moments he had brought her pain. His words echoed in her mind, making the muscles in her stomach tighten. *"Maybe I shouldn't be alone with him,"* she thought. *"Maybe Dexter was right."*

"Letty, I can't be seen with you," he choked out. "I respect you and Dex too much to be around you." Tears started to fall, but he continued to speak. "I ain't the man I once was. I been drinkin' every day. I been goin to parties, juke joints, I even been to brothels, Letty. I just been low."

Charlette brought him in for a hug, her heart wept for him but her mind was cautious. She wanted to be there for him, but she couldn't shake the desire to heed Dex's warning

"My pa kicked me out this morning. I was about to leave town. But then I thought about my Mama. I thought about my Ma, Letty, and I just couldn't do it. I couldn't leave, not like this. This isn't what she would have wanted." Charlette rubbed his back, she tried to offer him as much comfort as she could.

She felt his body shaking, his shoulders jumping. Eddie was more afraid than she had ever seen, almost as hurt as he was when his mother died. "I just don't know what to do. You hurt me bad with this one. I went to that school hoping to make a man out of myself. I been workin' hard so I could be the person you need," he said, his words stinging like venom to her soul. River frowned at him. Through bloodshot eyes and watery vision, he stared back at her.

"What is it that you want me to say," she asked. "You want me to confess to some great sin of not falling in love with the man everybody told me to be with? You want me to say that I am a whore and a heathen who went and turned the great Edwin-Hendricks Johnson into a sorry jiggalo!" River scowled at him. Disgust surged through her violently.

"All summer you been puttin' yo mess on to me. All summer I've been some kind of whore or some kind of tramp. I been everything but a child of God this summer, let you tell it, and you know what Edwin-Hendricks, I'm damn sick of it." Charlette's words punctured the small shreds of pride that E.H. had been clinging to.

The water of the New George surged and clouds began to form over their heads. Charlette's compassion shifted into growing frustration. "I'm sorry, River," Eddie cried out, but she was seething. The air cracked with fury, and the storm clouds swelled, ready to cast down an outpour of relentless rain, contained only by Charlette's love for her friend.

"Aww, Letty, don't tell me he done got to ya," Eddie said defeatedly. The force of the wind forced him to his knees. The tranquility of the New George was no more, it had been replaced by a turbulent manifestation of E.H.'s turmoil, and Charlette's righteous anger.

"Letty, I'm sorry," E.H. shouted through a sob. "Look, I just--I just wanted you to feel as bad as I did. I don't want to carry all this on my own, it can't all be my fault. Somebody else gotta share the blame with me," he confessed. His heart stung as if the tip of a spear was slowly piercing it. The words fell out of his mouth in a pitiful admission.

Unsurprised, but astonishingly hurt, Charlette let out a chuckle. "He's sorry," she said to herself. The distance between her feet and the ground grew. The indignation in her face morphed into a a spine-chilling grin, sending Eddie's stomach to the bottom of his shoe.

"You're sorry?" Her question came out as she rose higher off of the ground, bringing E.H. with her. She laughed as she watched the fear grow within him. "He's sorry. He's sorry, Oh, my goodness gracious, Eddie is sorry," she chanted. "He's a sorry ass excuse of a man who was taught to view women as accessories — toys that he's entitled to. He's a sorry ass, pathetic ass, just pitiful little man who's insecure in the presence of real masculinity and authority. HE'S SORRY," she shouted ferociously, thunder clapping in perfect rhythm with her words. "Because he can't get in my head or weaken my self-worth, he's finally admitting just how sorry he is."

A sickening mixture of powerlessness, desperation, and fear had overcome Eddie. He hung suspended in the air, his heart heavy with worry for his best friend's apparent descent into darkness. Choking back his fear, Eddie gave a final apologetic plea: "Letty, I really am sorry. I just don't want to disappoint my mama. I don't want to disappoint my daddy either or fall short of the expectations everyone has for me." Softened by his words, Charlette felt torn by her desire not to hurt her dear friend and her uncertainty about where she should trust him.

As the two descended towards Earth, the rain fell softer, as the atmosphere grew calmer. Charlette met Eddie on the ground and knelt beside him. Clinging to her for support, Eddie allowed himself a moment of genuine vulnerability. Unsure of what else to do, River began to pray.

Just as suddenly as Charlette's emotions raged and calmed, the water of the New George surged again with fervor. E.H. pushed Charlette to the ground and walked to the edge of the water. He lingered there, still, unmoving, unconcerned by anything happening around him. Charlette jumped up and ran in front of him, her feet planted firmly just beyond the edge of the water. "What are you doing," she said through gritted teeth, trying with all her strength to push her friend back to safety. E.H. wouldn't budge.

"Eddie, get back," she said desperately, feeling the water rise from her ankles to her calves. She looked up, her eyes meeting his, to the sight of blacked-out, hollow holes. Eddie was gone. Shaking her head in denial, Charlette tried to push him to higher ground. The water continued to grow, spilling over to dry land, inching closer and closer to their waists.

E.H. shoved River aside and walked until the water was at his neck. He stood there motionless for a second before turning to the only woman he had ever loved. "Tell my Pa, I'm sorry," he said, a glimpse of the real him peering through. "Eddie, no!" Charlette cried. The water swallowed the young man whole, cleansing him of his shame. River jumped in the water behind him, bobbing up and down and the water grew vengeful. "Eddie," she screamed frantically, flailing around in the water to search for him when in an instant the water cooled.

Charlette wasted no time looking for her friend. She stepped over rocks, ducked below low-hanging branches, and fought with slowly calming water. She fell on her stomach into the murky, rough water, tripping over a thick, heavy log. She turned around to kick it in frustration but had the wind knocked out of her instead.

"No, no, no, no, no, no, no," she repeated, sucking in tears. Laying face down in the water was the body of her very best friend. "Eddie!" she cried out in pain, unable to support herself under the weight of her grief. She pulled her body next to his and laid his back to her chest. "I'm sorry Eddie. I'm so sorry, Eddie. my beautiful, beautiful, beautiful boy, come back to me please," she pleaded with his corpse, gently caressing his face. Though people said that she may have been the second coming, or that the Holy Spirit operated with a little more authority in her than the rest, resurrection was not a power she possessed.

She placed a delicate, loving, kiss on Eddie's forehead. "I can't carry you, but I'll be right back," she said unfocused in his ear. "Stay there, honey. I'll be right back."

Clearing the woods, and walking over the pasture, Charlette saw Dexter walking toward her. "Charlie!" he yelled as he sprinted to his future wife. He grabbed her to support her weight, sensing the weakness in the petite woman. She fell into his arms. "Charlie, you okay?" he asked, but Charlette did not reply. Looking up from his wife, he turned his head in the direction of the dirt road leading into the woods. "Where's Eddie-Hen?"

"He's dead," she replied. "I left him in the New George."

CHAPTER 20

THE SAME DAY

Dexter watched as River guided Eddie away from the crowd, walking towards the river. He kept his composure, maintained a level head, but inside he was furious; not because he didn't trust River or even because of his distrust of Eddie, but because neither of them feared him.

People walked up to Dexter, patted his shoulder, rubbed his head, all singing their praises; but it all fell on deaf ears. All he was concerned by was Charlette and Eddie being alone. Just as Henry Stitts walked up to pull him in for a hug, someone shouted "He's a fraud," from the crowd.

Everyone turned their heads towards the man. "It's a surprise he ain't burst into flames. God oughta strike him right where he standin!" The voice came from a disgruntled Fred Jones. People looked from Fred to Dex, but Dex said nothing. He just stared at Fred.

"Get from round hurr wit all dat, man," Hop said to Fred.

"But I can't," Fred replied. "Not 'til he admits to who he is, to *what* he is." Fred locked eyes with Dexter.

Just like before, the crowd turned to Dexter for an explanation, but he didn't say a word. He stayed silent; he stayed calm. "Speak," Fred shouted at the young, handsome man. "Say sum ghatdammit!" Just then Fred pulled a revolver from his back pocket and shot at Dexter.

Everyone dropped to the ground or got as low as they could. Dexter stood tall and firm. The people of Freedman started to scatter; they all ran away looking for safety, but not Dexter.

"Get 'em, Hop," a woman yelled. Hop Wilson and a few other men tackled Fred Jones, wrestling with him while old Mr. Jenkins reached over everyone to grab the gun. The whole time, Dexter stood and watched, never breaking eye contact with the madman.

Fred Jones didn't put up a fight against the men. He let them hold him down and pull at him. He took the punches, preparing himself for each blow, but he never broke eye contact with Dexter; showing him that he was neither intimidated nor afraid.

"Fuck is yo problem, Red," Hop shouted.

"Bastard killed my wife," Fred replied blankly.

"Man, yo ol' lady ain't dead and dat boy ain't the damn devil," Hop said as he pulled Fred from the ground. "Get yo shit together man, people round her think you done lost yo mind like Annie, Fred. Gon' on home and sleep dis shit off."

Fred turned to Hop. "Can't do that, man," he said. Fered Jones snatched the gun from Mr. Jenkins, turned back to Hop, and socked the butt of the gun into Hop's right eye socket before throwing a punch at Henry Stitts. The group of men all started to fight one another while Dexter calmly watched.

Mr. Jenkins was able to grab the gun again and shot into the air. The men all dropped to the ground, releasing one another. Mr. Jenkins didn't speak to the men; instead, he walked over to Dexter and asked him to say something. "Make some sense of dis, son," he said.

Dexter looked down at the old man not knowing what to say. For all Dexter cared, the situation was handled. Everyone thought Fred and Annie Jones were crazy. What more was there to say? "C'mon nie, Dexter, I'm already halfway tuh death as it is. Get it out," Mr. Jenkins said, urging him to speak.

Dexter took a deep breath before walking over to the men. He tried to walk towards Fred Jones, but Henry blocked him with his arm. Dexter looked at the faces of all the men around him. He saw their confusion, he saw their need for a story, for an explanation, and he saw how willing they were to accept anything he had to say to them.

"Look, I don't know what happened between me and Fred. One day I was a guest in his home and the next day I wasn't. I ain't neva been alone with Miss Annie. I ain't neva touched her, I barely spoke to her outside of just bein' friendly. I ain't got nothin' to say," Dexter said to the group.

Dexter spoke confidently, firmly, with enough emotion for everyone to believe what he was saying. The men of Freedman thought it was all believable. They didn't distrust Dexter. They all liked him. They liked Fred too and they knew him longer, but it was no secret that Miss Annie had lost her mind. Fred was the one who told them. Why would Fred lie about his own wife? Wouldn't your wife goin crazy drive you crazy too?

"Tell 'em tha truth, Dexter. Tell dem dat you had her in tha kitchen floatin'. Tell 'em dat you makes her want to kill people now. Tell 'em dat you tryin to make me lose my mind too," Fred shouted as two men restrained his arms, keeping him from lunging at Dexter.

"I'm afraid I on know what you talkin' bout, Red," Dex answered. He walked close to him and placed a hand on his shoulder. "I ain't talked to you since tha day you kicked me out. How you reckon I'm tryin' to make you go crazy from afar?" he asked Fred through a sly grin.

Fred spat in Dexter's face before headbutting him in the chin. Dexter took a few steps backwards before falling. The men all grabbed Fred, attempting to drag him away.

"Look, look!" Fred shouted. "Look at what he done to me,

really look!"

They let go of Fred and gave him a once over. He was thin and his hair was graying. His eyes were dark, his skin was brittle. It looked as though Fred had lived three lifetimes in just under a month.

"Damn, Red, you okay," Henry asked.

"Nah, I'm not. I ain't okay. I'm far from okay! Every time I close my eyes I see his face, and not dat face either. I see tha real him; the one dats dead, the one dats fallin' apart. I see dat demon every damn night. Can't hardly close my eyes wit out seeing his face." Fred diverted his eyes from Dexter's and looked away in shame.

"I ain't sleepin, I ain't eatin', and my hair turnin white, just like Annie's did. Next thang ya know, I'll be eatin raw rabbits and huntin' for blood too. Dats what dat man did to my wife, dats what he's doin' to me! He's gotta go. We gotta get Dexter outta hurr. He ain't no good." Fred's words caused all of their pulses to quicken with fear and concern.

The implications of someone eating wild animals could not be ignored, and neither could the visible signs of stress in Fred. They all felt like the truth was lingering in the air around them, but none of them wanted to believe that such wickedness lived so close to them. Confusion coupled with fear and disbelief clouded the minds of all the men there, none of them knowing how to proceed. Dexter stood up and dusted himself off. He kept his distance from Fred, but he spoke to him openly.

"Look, Red. Ion know what happened between us for you to be havin' dese dreams and feelin' this strong, but I promise, Fred, I ain't do nothin to you or Miss Annie."

Dexter spoke to Fred with softness in his voice, his words seemed sincere. He kept eye contact and was intentional with not touching or triggering him. Dexter softened himself, showing a display of vulnerability that no one had ever seen from him before. As his eyes met Fred's, tears began to well – a silent moment passed between the two of them. The show of sincerity was so well done that, just for a fleeting second, Fred considered that he had only been dreaming and it was all in his head.

Was he losing his mind? Were his nightmares just that? Did Dexter make Annie go crazy or was it the world who overworked her, who used her kindness as a weakness? Fred couldn't decipher reality from delusion. Everything that had happened since the morning he saw Annie in the kitchen flashed before him. His memories felt different—less threatening. Did he make it all up? What happened?

Through tearful eyes, Fred gazed up at Dexter; his empathetic frown had morphed into a boastful smirk. He saw through Dexter's manipulative game. Despite Dexter's attempt to sow doubt, Fred remained sure, confident in his conviction that he was not crazy. A flame ignited in Fred Jones that consumed him, body and soul. He ripped from the arms of the men who had been holding him and rushed Dexter. He drove his right shoulder into Dexter's body, forcing him to the ground.

Fred started to strangle Dexter with all the power he had within him. Hop and Henry tried to stop him. The other men were pulled from their trance and all moved towards Fred with intentions of getting him off of Dexter, but something about the tears that flew from Fred's hot face, something about the anguished sounds that came from Fred's burning throat, something about the sheer rage that he had began to unleash on Dexter made them hesitant to get involved.

So, they watched. They stood back as Fred choked Dex. They saw him force his thumbs so deep into Dexter's esophagus that he could hardly yell for help. They watched as Dexter kicked and convulsed and threw punches at Fred's head. They had seen their fair shares of fights—they lived in the middle of nowhere in rural Georgia. All there was to do sometimes was drink, cuss, and fight their boredom away, but never had they seen two men fight for their lives like this.

Dexter was down, he was on the bottom and Ol' Fred was giving him the blues. But don't assume that Dexter wasn't making him work for it. If Fred was going to do this now, in front of all these people, the fight had to be fair, so Dexter fought fair. He was younger, faster, and stronger than Fred. Fred couldn't kill him without working for it, so he made him work.

Fred had been focusing on one particular vein in Dexter's neck. He watched the vein and relished in how the blood above where his thumb had been pressing down on it started to pool and swell. He watched it as it twitched, pulsating with desperation. He watched as the vein grew thicker, fuller, until finally it stopped. He noticed then that Dex's hits were softer, his kicks weakened, his body had stiffened. Fred didn't want to stop until he knew Dexter was dead, so he shook Dexter's limp neck, tightening his grip just a bit harder.

Finally, Dexter was motionless. The air was tense, the men were silent. As the saying goes, you could probably hear a mouse piss on cotton at that moment. Fred kept his eyes focused on the vein. He looked at it as it faded. He watched as it disappeared under dark, brown skin. He closed his eyes letting a sigh of relief pass through his full lips. The tears of anger had dried on his face, pulling on the skin around them. Fred brought his hands to his face to wipe the salt away. He laughed to himself, silently, pleasantly. Then he opened his eyes.

No one was there. No one was around him. There was no Dex, there was no Hop, no Henry; even Mr. Jenkins and the rest of the men were all gone. No one was there. The sky above him was dark and the sound of the New George was loud and angry. He stood up, walking towards the water.

Fred walked until he could see a couple of figures. Eddie

was walking towards the water and River was following him.

"Hey," he shouted. "Edwin! Eddie-Hen," he called. "River," he yelled, but neither of them turned around or acknowledged him.

Fred tried to move closer, but it seemed like he could never close the distance between them.

He saw the water level rise, as Eddie jumped in the New George, and he saw River jump in after him. Fred fell to his knees in horror. Two kids who he had practically raised were swept away by a vengeful river. He saw two kids that he loved as if they were his own, die– one of whom had been taken by the place she felt safest.

"Aiight, back to bidness," he heard Dexter say. And just as suddenly as he had been transported from the fight, he was right back in it. Dexter landed a solid knock to Fred's right temple, causing the older man to fall over.

The men who had once been petrified by awe, sprang to him and pulled him away.

"Let's just take 'em home," Henry said. "Let's just get 'em a part."

Henry and Hop both grabbed an arm and lifted Fred away. As the town square shrank in the distance, Fred kept his eyes on one spot. Looking past the town, looking past Dexter, staring at the river.

Fred wasn't crazy. Fred hadn't lost his mind.

CHAPTER 21

Pastor Johnson stood in front of the congregation with his head held high. "I stand before you a sad, sad man," he said to the members of his church. "A lonely man with nothing left in this world but this church and my community." He looked down at his son's stiff, gray body. He shuddered as he turned his head to the left before covering his face.

"Take ya time, baby. We understand," Miss Tolbert said from the third row. Pastor Johnson turned back around, wiping sweat from his forehead, and snot from his lips.

"Y'all have to excuse me today, family, this is rough for me." He cried some more before Deacon Brown came up to give the Pastor a hug. "This was my only child, my baby boy. The only connection I had to my wife, Mitsy, and now he's gone too." The church was silent, except for a few sniffles and groans of understanding.

"I—I don't mean to put you on the spot, but Miss River, if you don't mind would you stand up for me." Charlette was sitting at the back of the church between her mother and father with Dexter standing on the wall behind them. Cecilia grabbed her hand for support. She nodded at her, gesturing to her daughter that she would be okay. Cleo put his arm around his child to help her to her feet.

"You see, church, this young woman right dere," he paused and sucked in his lips to keep from crying. "She's a child of God. She and my son have been thick as thieves since dey was knee high to a grasshopper, and she was tha one who found him that day in tha New George." The pastor paused, sucking in air between his teeth and his lip.

Charlette's face turned beet red and her ears started to burn. She fell weak in the knees, but her father pulled her close to offer support. Two tears fell from her left eye before she lowered her head to cry.

"My son had changed before he died. He had become a new man. And dat new man was no saint. He lashed out at people, he hurt folks that he cared about, and he hurt Miss River real bad." Everyone had turned in their seats to stare at Charlette, who had started to tremble from guilt, regret, and shame.

"She spoke to my son. She prayed for him. She was with him that the day he drowned his self." The pastor dropped his head and cried for a spell. "She begged him to think about his father and his mother. She asked him to think about the life he was giving up on and the legacy we had established for him. She believed him when he said he would come home. She believed him when he said he just needed to be alone for a while." Charlette let out an anguished cry that shattered the somber silence that was beginning to fall over the church. Her father, tenderly cradling her weakened body, encouraged her to "let it all out" as she wailed. Cecilia rose from her seat, wrapping her daughter in a loving embrace, and covering her face from shame.

"River went back to the New George to find E.H. after a while, only to see that Satan had won, and my son had died. She jumped in the water and held him," the Pastor said before walking out of the pulpit. A woman, Charlette didn't know who, let out a mournful sob. It sounded like pain. It was gut-wrenching. It was agonizing. It pissed Charlette off – how could she release such a sound from her body, Charlette thought. She wondered if she really knew Eddie, or if she only knew the parts of him that brought her pleasure.

"That is the woman my son loved. That is the woman, Miss Montgomery, soon to be Mrs. Alexander," he gazed at everyone in the crowded church as he paused. "Despite the hurt and pain my son caused her, she loved him for who he was.

She cried for the man she knew he could be. And church, family, this is what I ask of you today. When life has dealt us bad hands, when all hope seems lost, when da bank won't give you no loan to buy some land, or or or when you apply fo a job downtown, dat you know you oughta get, and dey turn you way because you just a little too Black or or when ya old man up and leave because he don't want to be no daddy or ya ol' lady say she moving to the North because she just can't take being po and Black no mo, I ask you church, to remember that God loves you for who you was before life let you down!"

The congregation was on their feet. People were shouting, but Charlette was weak. Her mother clapped softly as tears streamed from her face, and her father held her close while choking back tears. Charlette turned into her father's arms, holding him tightly. "Can we leave, daddy," she cried softly. "Grab Dex and let's go," he replied through tears.

Back at home, Cecilia began to pack a huge meal for Pastor Johnson. Collard greens, candied yams, mac and cheese, pork chops, black eyed peas with salt jowl, pan fried chicken, leftover ham, and leftover seasoned corn. Cleo said he would walk with her to Pastor Johnson's house to make amends for the last time they spoke to one another.

"We'll be gone for just a second, ya hear," Cecilia said to the young couple. They were sitting on the couch in the living room. River was leaning on Dexter's shoulder still crying from the funeral.

"Yes'm," Dexter replied with a respectful nod. Cecilia went over and kissed her daughter on the forehead before placing a polite kiss on Dexter's cheek.

"I know y'all been through a lot these last few weeks wit all dats goin' on with Edwin and even worse now with his death, but I pray that God can forgive us all in the role we played in him taking his life. And I pray that the both of y'all can get on with your life as a new couple too," she spoke to them firmly but with sincerity.

"I still want this wedding to happen, and I want it to happen in two weeks, hear? Don't let this shake you, Charlette Marie, and Dexter don't you let it get to her. Seek each other right now, look to one another for support, and let God guide y'all through this, understand? Do y'all understand me?"

Cecilia's remarks were met with a yes ma'am from the both of them, and with that she and her husband were out the door. River stood up to put a pot of water on the stove.

"I'm gonna draw a bath and soak for a while, can we please not talk much today," she asked. "I— I just don't have it in me to talk or do anything else today." Dexter walked over to her, wrapping his arms around her waist when he met her. "You got enough strength in ya to pray?" he asked.

Charlette rolled her eyes before pushing his arms off of her. "Bold of you to ask me to pray with you after you done made me lie about what happened to Eddie. You and I both know that one of us killed him." She felt herself getting angry with him and feared that she may begin to float. trembling with fury, she clenched her fists tightly, then let out a steady exhale. She closed her eyes and drew more breath, with more composure she turned up the fire on the stove, hopeful to quell the one that was raging within her.

"Dere it go, dats dat power I warned you about," the voice said to Dexter, but he ignored it and began to interrogate her.

"What you mean one of us killed him? I wasn't dere Charlie, and all dat talk about controlling the water and the weather, girl, dats crazy talk. You were scared, you don't know what happened for real," he said, his words coming out surely, though he was internally concerned that Charlette may have figured him out.

"Look I only lied to everyone about how you found Eddie because if you went around tellin' folks you can fly and control nature, hell, they'd burn you like a witch. You want dat? You want dem thinkin' you some kind of witch?" Dexter followed Charlette as she grabbed the pot from the stove and walked hurriedly towards the bathroom.

"You hear me, gal," he shouted from the mouth of the hall.

"You want them thinkin' you done lost yo black ass mind?" he yelled. River slammed the door of the bathroom before dumping the hot water into the tub. She heard Dexter walking towards the door so she pushed a chair under the knob.

"Aww, you done it now, Charlette. Open this door! I ain't done talkin' to you," he said sharply. He banged on the doot, demanding that she let him in. She ignored him and poured lavender oil and bath soap into the water. "Charlie," he shouted. She kept drawing her bath.

Charlette closed her eyes and imagined what the inside of her mind must look like. She thought of it being a field with cornflowers and azaleas. She pictured herself laying there, free from all that awaited her in reality. With just the thought of tranquility, the darkness behind her eyes transformed into a lush field in the landscape of her subconscious.

For just a second, she was at peace, laying back in the comforting embrace of soft grass and wildflowers. The sun was bright, the air was warm. There was no one or nothing there but her. Taking in the satisfaction of being in her own corner of paradise, Charlette closed her eyes again. She attempted to dig her hands in the dirt around her, but had submerged them in a pool of warm water instead. When Charlette opened her eyes, confusion filled her up as found herself sitting in the middle of the field soaking in her bathtub. BOOM BOOM BOOM. She heard reverberating through the atmosphere.

BOOM BOOM BOOM, she heard. Charlette jumped from the sound of Dexter banging on the bathroom door. "Give it up, Dexter! Your Charlie is gone and she won't be back for a while," she said before submerging herself in the beautifully scented water. "*River*," she heard him say in her mind. "*Open the door so we can talk. I just want to talk.*" She ignored him speaking to her and covered herself in the water. She stayed there for a few seconds and imagined her life was peaceful, calm; she imagined being just as safe and relaxed as the world she created in her mind.

She lifted her head from the water, hopeful that her mind had returned back to its utopia, but try as she might, Charlette found that she was still sitting in the bathroom.

She rested her head on the cold porcelain, deciding whether or not she should pray. She struggled to find the words to tell God how she felt and what she needed. Her thoughts were just a cloud of dark chaos. She stared at the ceiling, waiting for something to happen. She waited for words, or a thought, or an emotion to move her but she was drained, completely drained.

Tears started to fall back to her ears, so she wiped them away and got out of the tub. She peeked around the bathroom door to see where Dexter was before tip-toeing into her room, dripping and naked. To her surprise, he was sitting on the edge of her bed with a towel and his eyes closed.

"You must have a death wish," she said to him as she grabbed the towel. "If my daddy came home right now, he'd run you up a tree, and my Mama would be behind him with a torch." She chuckled before going into her closet to dress.

"We need to talk, Charlie," Dexter said dryly. She sighed deeply but did not respond. "I'm serious, we need to talk about dis instead of tip-toeing around it."

She came around the corner half dressed in underwear and a pair of white slacks. "What is it that we tip-toein' around," she asked.

She pulled a shirt over her head before tucking it in. She stood in front of him with her arms crossed and her eyebrow raised. Dexter grabbed her by the arm and guided her out of the room "let's find somewhere to talk."

They walked out to the front porch. Dex sat on the top step, looking out at the land in front of him. Charlette leaned against the banister, staring at the side of his head. She bore into him with an intensity that she didn't understand. The more she looked at him, seeing how calm and serene he was at the moment, the more her face contorted into a scowl.

"Dis why we need to talk," he said without parting his lips. Charlette jumped up. "See! That! That right there, how are you doing that and why do you act like it's not happening," she asked him. Dexter rose from the step, closing the distance between them with slow, intentional strides. Without uttering a single word, he communicated with her.

"Charlie, I got something to tell ya," he said. She looked in his eyes, trying to read them, trying to see if she could find good or evil in them, but all she saw in his eyes was how sorry he felt.

"I seen you floating at the river a few times. I seen you losing yo self and letting the spirit take you over dat day in church too. I gots yo goat and I knows yo secret," he said.

She pushed his hands from her waist, taking an alarmed step backward. "But—how—why—" she couldn't get a sentence out. Her mind was racing a mile a minute, her heart thumping in her chest. *"I can't float, I can't give way to the spirit, but I can read minds. I can send thoughts to 'em too,"* Dexter said to her without speaking.

"So, they wasn't lying," she asked. "They were telling the truth all along, huh?" Burdened by the weight of his betrayal, Charlette leaned over the porch railing for stability. Her fingers tangled frantically through her hair, grasping for a tangible anchor as the overwhelming reality began to crash around her. Memories flooded her mind as she replayed every accusing word said against Dexter: Shelly's horrible story, the disturbing vision at the church, Fred's ominous warning about Dexter. It all flashed before her.

"You get out of my house. Get the hell outta my mama's house," she shouted. They stared at each other.

"Charlie, let's just talk about this," Dexter started. River bounced away from him, running off the porch. "Where you goin, Charlette," he called from the house. She threw up her hand and kept walking. River heard the screen door slam shut. She didn't know where she was going, but she walked.

And walked, and walked, and walked until she was at the North end of the New George. She wasn't close to the river, but she could hear the water. She could hear birds chirping and fish jumping. She knew that it was the voice of God, directing her to her safe haven, but she was too angry, too scared, too embarrassed to be in the presence of God.

Responding to the unmistakable call, Charlette yielded to the prompting of the Holy Spirit, finding herself drawn to the river's edge. Only then did she notice her bare feet, a detail that slipped her mind entirely when she fled from her home. Rolling up her pants and cuffing them above her calves, she waded into the water, feeling the cool embrace of the riverbed beneath her toes. She felt mud, twigs, and perhaps even worms danced against her skin, grounding her in the earth's raw essence. With closed eyes, she surrendered to the moment, allowing her words to flow freely from her lips to God's listening ear.

"God, did I do something wrong," she asked. "You said one of two men would lead me to my destiny, but Eddie's dead and Dex might actually be a demon. What's going on?" She listened to the call of the birds and the lull of the locust, but nothing spoke to her. She took a determined breath to refocus herself, then spoke again.

"God, am I a fool? Was Eddie the person I was supposed to be with all this time, just for me to kill him with a power that I don't understand? Am I not faithful enough to you," she asked in frustration. "Have I not given enough of myself, enough of my life to serve you? Have I not devoted enough of my time and energy to helping people, bringing them to your Word? Am I not good enough to be Blessed?"

She listened, and again, she heard nothing. River dropped her head. She let out a chuckle, a sure sign of defeat. She turned to walk towards the banks of the river before stopping, giving God another try.

She turned her chin upward, looked to the sky, and focused on a cloud that she could see moving behind the trees. She locked into it. "God, if you can still hear me, gimme a sign," she begged. She waited, nothing. "Lord, if you're up there, sitting on your throne, and listening to my cries, gimme a sign." Still nothing.

She stepped farther into the water, following the cloud and shouted, "God I know you're up there and I want a sign!" She waited, but still she heard nothing. Charlette didn't know what to make of her life at that point. She developed some kind of power, she fell in love, she got hurt, she lost her best friend, and she may have agreed to marrying a literal demon.

All she could do was cry. This was why she asked Dexter to give her space, this was why she wanted to speak to Eddie and clear her conscience; she wanted to avoid feeling like this. But, to no avail, she felt exhausted and abandoned.

As she was approaching town, she ran into her parents. "You been in dat water, ain't you," her father asked. "Wit her feet out too," her mother added. River had been trying to hold it together, but seeing her parents made her crack. She burst into tears, as she ran into her father's arms.

"Honey, I'll walk Letty home, you go on and get tha groceries," her mother said, pulling her away from her father. Cleo kissed her forehead, assuring his daughter that he'd be home soon, then headed up the steps of the store.

"What's eatin you," Cecilia asked her crying daughter. "What's the matter, baby." Charlette's emotions surged, a torrent of tears and words pouring forth as she unburdened herself to her mother. She told her mother about the day she met Dexter and when she first fell in love; she told her about the time Eddie tried to kiss her, but she didn't feel a connection; she told her about the fight, she told her about Annie Jones, she even told her about the things Shelly had said.

Through it all, Cecilia remained a silent but attentive listener, offering her daughter the space to release her pent-up emotions without interruption. As they reached the safety of their front yard, Charlette finally asked for her mother's insight, eager to hear what she made of it all.

"Well, baby," she began. "I'm worried about you." River's heart stopped. "Eddie tried to tell me dat Dexter was no good, but I said 'my daughter has a good heart and a sound mind,' only to find out you lost yo mind the day he came into town," Cecilia said frankly.

Charlette couldn't breathe. There she was pouring her heart out, being the most honest and vulnerable she probably had ever been with her mother, just for her to think she was insane.

"And all dis talk about floating and hearing voices–sounds like you might be the one with the demons," Cecilia finished.

"But what about what Fred Jones told daddy," River asked. "I went into they house and saw Annie with my own eyes, mama. She not the same Annie Jones. She's not even a person no more!" Cecilia looked at her daughter concerned. She could tell River really believed what she was saying. She grabbed her daughter's hands, trying to be as gentle as possible before she spoke, so that her daughter processed it without feeling attacked.

"Annie Jones had a nervous breakdown. Fred sent her up to her sisters in Augusta and he thinkin' bout goin' out dere wit her. Miss Annie ain't the same baby, but dat don't have nothin' to do wit Dexter," Cecilia said.

"Got everything to do wit tha devil, though. Satan saw a well-to-do Black woman and took her mind. It's a shame." She pulled her daughter in for a hug and said, "Dat's what he's trying to do to you. But by Christ almighty, we won't let 'em. In Jesus' name, we won't let 'em."

"I told you they was gon' think you was crazy," she heard Dexter say. She looked over her mother's shoulder and saw him staring at them from the living room window. His face was somber but she could sense his vindication.

CHAPTER 22

The next morning, Cecilia walked into her daughter's room with the intention of waking her. To her surprise, Charlette was wide awake.

"How long you been up," she asked.

"I don't know. I didn't get much sleep last night," Charlette replied. "My mind just won't rest."

"Still thinking about all the stuff from yesterday," Cecilia asked, sliding onto the edge of her daughter's bed. "Yeah. I guess I'm just shook from Eddie's death. All the stress from the funeral, ya know?" River sat up in bed, facing her mother. She didn't say anything and neither did Cecilia. They both sat there, thinking, lamenting.

"I want to say sorry, Charlette," Cecilia began. "I haven't been kind to you the last couple of months. I been very hot and cold. Truth is, I feel guilty sometimes. I feel like you and your father look at me for so much, like I'm supposed to know everything, and I don't. For you I have to be yo teacher, yo doctor, yo friend, the discipline, and the one who teaches you how to live in God's Word, so I'm like your pastor and Sunday school teacher. I have to be a lot. For your father, sometimes I have to be all dat and mo'." she grabbed her daughter's face and rubbed it gently.

"I gets jealous sometimes. I gets upset. I want to be able to help you with things, but I can't. I can't do it all. I couldn't help you decide how to feel about E.H. I can't tell you how to feel about Dexter. But I can tell you dat all the foolishness you told me yesterday was scary to hear as a mother."

River longed to connect with her mother, seeking reassurance in her words, but found herself disengaged. All Cecilia was doing at that moment was reaffirming her perceived insanity.

"I can also say dat you don't have to bear dat burden alone. You have a man and a whole town full of people who love you. Let us help you sometime. You hear dat miss saint? Miss Angel," she laughed, hugging her daughter. "Let us be a Blessing to you, tha way you been a blessing to us."

Despite Cecilia's earnest attempt to uplift her daughter, the weight of Charlette's detachment hung heavy in the air, a bitter reminder of their growing disconnect. Frustration simmered beneath Cecilia's surface as she observed her daughter's distant demeanor, her attempts at comfort falling flat against the wall Charlette had built between them. It pissed Cecilia off. "Well," she said with a resigned sigh. Cecilia rose from the bed, her departure marked by an unspoken tension that lingered in the room.

As Cecilia tried to go about her day, her mind was consumed by the image of her daughter's vacant expression-- her blank stare, her cold eyes, she remembered how stiff she felt in her arms when she tried to hug her. Each step away from home as she trekked toward work intensified the ache she felt in her heart. A gut-wrenching mix of anguish and fury threatened to overwhelm her fragile composure. Stumbling over rock, unseen behind the well of tears that formed in her eyes, Cecilia fell helplessly to the ground. "God," she cried out in distress, the magnitude of her sorrow and frustration fully felt.

Kneeling amid genuine despair, Cecilia felt angered by her daughter's unhappiness. Despite all her efforts, doing everything in her power to make sure that her girl was secure, Charlette still needed more. Her daughter was on the verge of becoming a woman and was the most unhappy she had ever been. What more did she need? Charlette had two very handsome men fighting for her at one point, as much education as Cleo and

Cecilia could afford, and a strong spiritual foundation, but it still wasn't enough.

Bitterness gnawed at Cecilia's soul.

At nineteen, Cecilia was married. She was pregnant and alone while Cleo traveled up and down Georgia looking for work, even if just for a week. Cecilia had no one in the world to turn to. By the time she was eleven years old, she was orphaned. Her father left her mother when she was still an infant, gone up north with a woman he met on the plantation where he was born. Her mother died two weeks before Cecilia's eleventh birthday; she bled to death giving birth to the result of her assault. The baby died in CeeCee's arms while her aunt tried to save her mother.

From then, Cecilia was raised by an aunt who had no love to give her. In place of nurturing, she gave Cecilia religion. She wasn't able to teach Cecilia how to read, so she taught her how to work. When Cecilia was fourteen years old and the two of them hadn't eaten in a week, her aunt essentially sold her to an old man who had just come to Freedman the month before. When CeeCee cried to her aunt telling her how painful and scary sleeping with the old man was, she was told to close her eyes and sing hymns until it was over.

When the old man died after dinner one Sunday, his two brothers, their children, his only sister, and her son, came to Freedman to give him a proper burial. That was the day she met Cleo. When Cleo walked through her dead husband's door, Cecilia came alive. Something ignited within her that she never knew existed. From that day on, she and Cleo worked hard to keep grief and sorrow from the home they built with each other. When River was born, Cecilia looked into her eyes and made a promise to her child, herself, and her husband, that Charlette Marie Montgomery would never suffer the way Cecilia had—and then, just over nineteen years later, she was leaving her daughter alone in a room feeling disconnected and hopeless, unreachable by God's Word. CeeCee wiped her eyes and looked to the sky. She stood up, dusted herself off, and said a silent prayer, before walking to work.

Cleo had to leave town at dawn that day to catch a ride into Savannah. He wanted to earn more money so that his daughter could have a nice wedding. He left Charlette a note saying that he may be gone for a while, possibly having to look farther than Savannah for work, but he promised to write to her every chance he got, and if she ever said she needed him, he would leave for home right away. He apologized for not being able to give her away at her wedding, but he wanted to be able to afford for her to buy a beautiful dress and invite the entire town, if her heart desired, so he had to find work that would be able to pay for such an occasion.

Charlette read her father's letter and held it close to her chest. She loved him so much, and he loved her too. She shed a single tear at the thought of disappointing him. "I'll be better soon, daddy," she said with closed eyes. She kissed the envelope before dressing for the day.

With daybreak still sitting on the horizon, Charlette made a silent escape out of her bedroom window, leaving Dexter on the couch asleep. She didn't know where she was going, but she was determined to put distance between herself and him.

Before long, she found herself walking towards the Hicks' home. Going there would give her the chance to tell Shelly about Dexter's abilities, and for her to apologize to Shelly. Her mind wandered as she thought: she should have listened to Shelly that day on the road. From the beginning, Shelly only wanted to help her, and in return, Charlette iced her out– being no better, if not worse, than the people who only saw Shelly for her reputation, not for the tender-hearted, maternal woman she was.

With each step up the long-fenced road, Charlette began to feel comfort in the cadence of her footsteps, the gentle touch of the morning breeze, and the scent of the dewy, wet grass; it all offered her serenity, a sanctuary of familiarity. In an effort to grab hold of the moment and ease her mind, Charlette drew in a long breath, filling her lungs with the tranquility and stillness of nature, but to no avail, heartache and confusion remained.

"What is wrong with me," she asked herself. *"What is going on?"*

She passed by Hop Wilson's shack on her way up the road, and saw Mr. Jenkins was sleeping out front under an old shade tree. Wrapped in nothing but his own arms, Mr. Jenkins' frail body was shivering from the coolness of the morning. She wanted to give him something warm to cover himself with, but she didn't have anything with her to give. She herself was only covered in her nightgown and a light cardigan.

"Hey, Mr. Jenkins. You want me to ask Hop to make you some coffee, warm up dem bones a bit," she asked her friend. "Nah, River gal, don't bother him none. I'll get up and move around in a minute." She helped him to his feet before giving him a hug. As always, he looked to take in her beauty, but that time he read her like a book.

"What's eatin' you up, gal," he asked. "And don't lie and say nuthin'." Charlette gave a weak smile, her mind racing to find an answer to give. "Out wit it nie, I ain't for long on this earth," he said rushing her.

"Mr. Jenkins, I don't even know myself how to explain it to ya. I feel crazy. I feel like I'm losin' my mind and everyone around me thinks so too. I can't put it in words," she said to him. They walked up to Hop's porch and sat in the chairs he kept outside. Mr. Jenkins' face was twisted up, wrinkled and bronzed. He tried to find something to say to his young companion, careful not to rattle out something that could be chalked up to an old man's rambling.

"Well, River, have you tried talkin' to ya ol' man? Surely, he don't think you no kinda crazy," he said. "He the one drivin' me crazy," she answered. Mr. Jenkins replied with a simple, "hmm."

She told him that she tried talking to her mother, visiting the river, she even told him that she was on her way to Shelly Hicks house to talk to her since she was the first person to open her eyes to who Dexter really was.

"She told me about what he did to her and how she been scared of him, but I wouldn't listen. I loved him, I — I love him still. Is that wrong?"

Charlette didn't tell him exactly what Shelly had warned her about, or what he had done to scare the both of them, but she felt like she gave him enough to form an opinion. In truth, she didn't care too much about what he had to say because Mr. Jenkins was old, and not a woman, and not the smartest man she knew, but she was so very desperate for help; she was desperate for someone to listen, really listen, and lead her in a way that will get her back to herself, even if that person was old Mr. Jenkins.

"I'm hearin' you say you talked to dis person and dat person and you up at daybreak tryin' to talk to someone else, but there's someone more important I ain't heard you say yet," Mr. Jenkins began.

"I tried talkin' to Dex, Mr. Jenkins, but dat didn't go well. It made things worse, if I'm bein' honest," she replied.

"Dex ain't none of who I'm talkin' bout neither," he said. He stared at her, looking her square in the eyes. Charlette studied his face looking for something that she could make sense of. His eyes were glassy, and a gray cloud had started to form around the iris, but even so she saw his sincerity, she saw his wisdom.

Neither of them spoke as they studied each other's faces. Charlette had parted her lips to ask who Mr. Jenkins who he was talking about when the door swung up and Hop Wilson stepped out.

"Y'all niggas better be happy I can reckon who voice belong to who cuz I was finna blow some folks' brains out," he said sitting on the bottom step of his porch. "What's dis about Dex scarin' Shelly Hicks and what dat got to do wit you," he asked Charlette.

She looked down at Hop sitting on the bottom step, then back up to Mr. Jenkins. She was trying to decide whether she should add another to the roster of folks who thought she had lost her mind before giving Hop an answer.

"Well, I mean, I think I'm scared of 'em too now, Hop, and I just want to make sure I ain't crazy for feelin' that way," she answered. Hop stood up and walked back into his house. He threw his hand in a disregarding motion before yelling to her from inside the house.

"She ain't nuthin but a hoe who mad because you finna be a wife," he said before emerging with three mugs and a warm pot.

"Dis some reheated coffee, y'all," he started. "She puttin stuff in yo head because you bouta be a kept woman and she ain't ever gon' find a husband runnin' behind nasty niggas like me."

River slouched in her chair. *"I wasn't even engaged yet, when she told me,"* she thought to herself. She didn't say anything out loud because she was tired of being dismissed. Hop turned around to look at her. She noticed him noticing her and asked "what is it?" He shrugged his shoulders and said "you tell me."

Charlette didn't have anything else to say. It was as if her brain was so crowded she couldn't hear her thoughts over how loud they were being. She shook her head and said, "maybe you're right Hop. I guess I ought to leave it alone."

She stood up before walking down the stairs, past Hop and into his yard. She was about to walk away but turned to look at Mr. Jenkins. She opened her mouth to ask him about their conversation earlier, but before she could get a word out before he said, "God. You ain't said you talked about it with God."

River didn't go to Shelly's house because she didn't want Hop to see her walk that direction. She went home instead and made breakfast for herself and Dexter. When she got there Dexter was awake, getting dressed. She told him that she couldn't sleep and was going to go to the river but decided to turn around when she realized she hadn't left him a note.

"Look, Charlie, baby, I didn't mean to scare you. I think now is as good a time as ever to try and talk 'bout this again since yo Ma and Pa are gone. I want you to understand dis gift we both have and how we can use it to be a powerful Christian couple," he said to her. Charlette told him she was too tired to talk, but she would make him breakfast before laying back down.

"Ion want you in bed all day, Charlie, dats a bad habit for a first lady. I know I ain't tell you first, but we got stuff to do today, so I need you at yo best." Dexter spoke to her differently now. All summer his tone was very calm, very smooth, but lately he had been demanding of her. His voice had a sternness to it that she wasn't used to. River nodded her head in obedience and rolled her eyes as she walked away.

"We need to go into Savannah to the courthouse and get a proper marriage license, den I need you to go talk to Ol' Hendricks Johnson, see if he won't marry us."

Breakfast was stiff. Neither of them spoke much after Dexter announced their plans for the day. Finally, Dexter left through the kitchen door to "tend to business," which left Charlette with more questions than a few, but she was too exhausted to ask any of them. More than anything, she just wanted to be alone, relieved from the weight of the tension that hung between them.

Back in her room, Charlette sat in the center of her bed, legs folded beneath her, surrendered to the tide of thoughts that came to her. She imagined her mind being a tropical forest in a jungle somewhere yet discovered, where her thoughts poured from a raging waterfall into a pool that led to a steady stream—this cleared her mind.

As time blurred, she found herself enveloped in a rare state of peacefulness. Her body felt weightless, unburdened by the chaos that once clouded her thoughts. In the stillness of her room, a warmth filled within her as her heart pumped hot blood through her body, igniting inner peace. Floating above her bed, suspended in bliss, Charlette rebuked anything that would keep her from experiencing this moment.

"Dear heavenly father, thank You. Thank You for never forsaking me or abandoning me, even when I convinced myself that you had," she prayed.

"Thank you for giving me the notion to just be still. Thank You for even just a second of temporary sanity to sit back and let You be You. When everything around me is moving like a bat out of hell, you gave me the thought to sit and wait, and for that, God, I thank you," she spoke with conviction and belief, allowing herself to be fully open and vulnerable to God's grace.

"I thank You for helping me. I thank You for being exactly who you are."

The air around her moved in a circle as if it were surrounding her like a protective shield. It was cold but comforting. It was forceful but not harsh. She felt safe.

"God, I need you," she continued. "I need you to speak to me clearly, Lord. Is Dexter not who I think he is? Did I misunderstand the assignment to either marry him or Eddie? Because Eddie is dead now and Dexter can read minds, and God I'm afraid that I made the wrong choice."

She thought about the day E.H. called her a whore, the time he struck her on her birthday. She frowned as she pictured it and asked "God, was I really supposed to marry him?"

"One would bring you a life of respect and honor, but very little happiness," she heard. "And the other will lead you to your destiny."

"Is Dexter going to make something of this church? Are we really going to be some spiritual power couple that leads this town to salvation before bringing your Word to the world?"

She couldn't hear anything but the chaotic buzz of her own thoughts, swarming like ants in her mind. River collapsed onto her bed, staring blankly at the ceiling. Her breaths came in short gasps, her head throbbing with frustration. Clenching her fists, she tugged at her comforter, seeking solace in its soft embrace. Then, Dexter's voice pierced the silence, calling out to her from the living room, "Charlie, you ready baby?" he asked. Despite her inner turmoil, Charlette remained silent, her scream stifled in her throat.

Suppressing the tears threatening to spill, she rose to her feet and composed herself, hastily dressing as Dex knocked on her door. "You good?" he asked, concerned that she may have left through the window again. "As good as God is great," she replied. With a forceful gesture, she tucked her shirt into her skirt and gathered her hair into a messy ponytail, a silent declaration of her defiance. "Let's go," she declared, striding past him, out into the world, a facade of composure masking the storm raging within.

CHAPTER 23

"Would you looka der," Cecilia rejoiced as she held her daughter's and Dexter's marriage license up for all to see. There was no one in the room but the three of them, but nonetheless, she wanted to show it off.

"Cleo and I are not really married by law, "she announced, looking at Dexter. "We just went out back and jumped the broom like they did in slave times." She turned her attention to her daughter, who was sitting next to her with a nervous expression. "Oh, Charlette, baby, I kept that broom too. I always wanted to pass it down to my child, and finally, O God, I can give it to you." Cecilia's cinnamon-colored hand cupped her daughter's cheek as she shed a tear blissfully.

Charlette grabbed her mother's hand, placing a soft kiss on the back of it. She wanted to be excited with her mother, but she couldn't shake how uneasy Dexter had been making her feel. He wasn't the same man she met that day in town. His demeanor was different. His aurora had changed. The smile that once warmed her heart now sent a shiver down her spine.

"Are you ready, baby," Cecilia asked. River gave a weak smile, holding back tears. She knew what this day would mean to her mother. She remembered what it was supposed to mean to her. It's a woman's duty to be a wife and serve as a helpmate to her husband. She was to support her man and maintain her home. This has been Charlette's dream — to fulfill her Christian duties. She never really cared about the romance or companionship of marriage, she just wanted to do her job as a woman of Christ to honor the sanctity of marriage and raise children who believe in the gospel of Christ Jesus.

But now that she has loved and lost, and possibly been

deceived by someone her heart aches for, the covenant between two people, bound by the promise to God and one another, to be close in every possible way, for the rest of their lives, marriage sounded like something she should be serious about.

"What is it?" her mother asked. "You look upset, River, girl, what's the matter?" Charlette started to speak – and intended to speak candidly – but the stares from her mother and Dexter rendered her speechless. Speaking about her doubts would break her mother's heart and would likely cause Dexter to chastise her somehow. Sensing her desire to unveil the truth, Dexter walked over to his bride, placing his large, intimidating hands on her shoulders. "She was probably thinking about how amazing our wedding is 'bout to be," he answered on River's behalf.

Cecilia blushed. She laughed, tearing up again, just thinking of the splendor of her only daughter's wedding. "Oh Miss Montgomery, we finna have a grand ol' time. We finna cut up," he boasted, beaming with excitement.

Cecilia's eyes glowed with anticipation. She was smitten by the thought of her Charlette marrying Dexter—a young, handsome Pastor. She really liked Dexter. She didn't think she ever really would, especially after all the turmoil between him and Eddie, but at the end of the day, she fell victim to his lure, just like the rest of Freedman.

"If y'all don't mind, I think I'm gonna go to the New George," Charlette said as she stood up from the couch. She turned to her husband-to-be and placed a kiss on his forehead. Her lips tingled from touching his dark, brown skin. He looked up at her and winked.

River walked out of her home and onto the road, relieved that she made it out without Dexter interjecting. He had been asking her to visit Pastor Johnson for the last few days but she had been putting it off as much as possible. She wasn't ready to see Pastor Johnson. She wasn't ready to be in the house *he* grew up in; she wasn't ready to be in the church that they worshiped together in. She wasn't ready to accept that Eddie was dead.

Making it to the edge of the town square, she stopped just before the pasture that led to the dirt road to the river. *"What's keeping me here,"* she asked herself. *"Really. What's keeping me from breaking and running?"*

She turned her head, looking at the small patch of trees, the small fence of protection around Freedman. She wanted, so badly at that moment, to run through the patch of bare trees and head North until she found a new home, where she could be called by a new name. She paused. What would life be like with no River, no Charlette? Who could she be if not Letty or Charlie?

The next few days were a blur. She spoke to Pastor Johnson about ordaining their marriage, to which he obliged. Her mother and Miss Tolbert worked together to make her a lovely white dress, though they both agreed Miss Annie would have done better. By the end of the week, she was in front of the church, standing before Dexter, Pastor Johnson, and God, vowing to love, honor and obey Dexter Alexander for the rest of her life.

Just like Dexter said, the party they threw after the wedding was spectacular. Nearly the entire town showed up. Hop had ordered whiskey weeks ago for the occasion in addition to the batch of his famous hootch too. Every woman over thirty had agreed to cook for the event, and anyone who knew how to play an instrument all banded together to turn the small patch of field between their town square and the river, into a sho'nuff juke joint.

Charlette didn't remember much from that night. Dexter kept sneaking her drinks, telling her to relax. By the time the sun started to set, Charlette "River" Alexander, formally

Montgomery, was as drunk as Cooter Brown. She had hardly eaten, and had never drunk before, but Dexter said that it would ease her nerves. So, she drank, and she drank, and she drank some more. He had to carry her home that night.

"I wrote Cleo and told him to send for me, so y'all will have the house to yourselves after Friday," Cecilia said to the young couple. Charlette looked at her mother pleadingly, asking her silently not to leave her alone with Dexter any time soon. Her mother responded by giving her a wink, thinking her daughter was only nervous about fulfilling her marital duty as a wife for the first time.

"Won't be necessary, Ma," Dexter said to Cecilia. Dexter said, with a wide, broad smile gracing his face as he spoke to his new mother-in-law, before winking at his new wife. "Me and Charlie here are moving into our own place," he announced. "I bought us a house."

River wanted to throw up right then and there. She felt like the world had just caved in on itself, swallowing her whole in the process. Cecilia on the other had thought she would faint from sheer excitement. Her daughter — *her* daughter — was beautiful, educated, married to the most handsome man anyone had ever seen, and he bought her a house. The little orphan girl, who no one loved, grew up to raise the prettiest girl, married her to the most handsome man, and taught her how to be humble and submissive to God's will. Cecilia wanted to cry.

"What house did you buy? Where is it?" Cecilia asked her new son. Dexter stood proud before his wife and mother-in-law, telling them that he visited Fred Jones to make amends, but when he got to their house, he found Fred packing up his home and putting all his and Miss Annie's belongings in the bed of some light-skinned man's truck. "Fred Jones is a good man, hardworking, God-fearing. So, he said he could forgive me if I forgave him."

"Say Miss Annie is gettin worse. He say her sister can't take care of her alone so she asked him to come move in with em. I asked him what he was gon' do wit tha house and he say, 'I reckon I ought to sell it.' So, I told him that I had $200 in cash and could send him another $1200 by the end of two years, if he let me pay him each month," Dexter explained.

Dexter told them that Fred Jones was so desperate to leave Freedman to be with Miss Annie that he agreed to take the cash upfront with the promise of monthly payments over the next six months. Cecilia's joy had finally got the best of her. Cradling her daughter, Cecilia let her tears flow unashamedly. Fred and Annie Jones had such a big, pretty house, and the thought of her daughter living in a home like that with a husband like Dexter made Cecilia surge with emotions.

Charlette, on the other hand, remained suspicious. Fred Jones loved money and hated Dexter. There was no way he would willingly give his home to Dexter-- not the house he built with his own hands, that his beloved wife cherished and filled with love, not to Dexter. She figured Fred would rather die than sell their house to him.

After a couple of days of packing, Dexter and Charlette Alexander finally moved into their new home. River hated it. It didn't feel right. She wasn't supposed to be living in Miss Annie's house. It wasn't her job to make a home out of a place that was never meant for her to live in.

That night, after everyone who had helped them move in left, Charlette asked Dexter how he really was able to acquire this home. She asked if Fred Jones had even known that they were moving in, in the first place.

"He ain't here is he," he asked. "All of his and Annie's stuff is gone, ain't it? And didn't the keys I gave you on our wedding day unlock the doors dis morning when we came?" Charlette shook her head yes, looking up at him. "I can see a storm brewin' in dat pretty little head," he said to her before landing a kiss on her forehead. "I'm not gon' ever let anything happen to you, Charlette. You are the most important thing in my life, believe dat."

The next morning, Charlette awoke determined to rid the house of any lingering traces of the Joneses from her new home. She cleaned every nook and cranny with diligent precision. She dusted, swept, and scrubbed away any memory that the Jones family had left behind. In her cleaning, she stumbled upon Miss Annie's valued collection of buttons– a treasury of buttons in various shapes and hues spread across several baskets and tins. There were gold buttons, ruby buttons, shiny buttons, big buttons, itty bitty, tiny buttons; some were shaped like fruit, others were shaped like insects, but all of them were a testament to Miss Annie's taste for the visually unique.

By the end of the week, Charlette had collected nearly two pounds of buttons, which she stored in a burgundy-colored velour sack that she found in the closet. With purposeful resolve, she dragged an aged tub she found in the attic to the backyard, throwing the weighty sack of buttons into it. Gazing at the wine-colored sack, she paused, deciding whether she wanted to keep this one piece of her home's past.

"Should I burn it," she asked herself. "Do I really want to learn what I already know?"

The day before, after Dexter left to do some work around Mr. Greene's farm, River wrote a letter to Miss Annie's sister, Robertta Bell:

Ms. Bell,

Forgive me if Bell is no longer your name. I'm writing you to check on your sister, Miss Annie Lou Jones. How is she doing? Freedman hasn't been the same since we last saw her beautiful face or ate her good food. The news of her nervous breakdown has really shocked the township of Freedman.

I am covering Miss Annie in prayer. I'm asking that God touches her mind and heals her, both body and soul. I'm praying for you as well, as the work of a caregiver is honorable in the eyes of God. I pray that you are strong enough to bear the burdens of your own life as well as the burden of caring for Miss Annie.

Thank God for the gift of knowing when to ask for help. It's a good thing you did asking Mr. Jones to help you care for your sister. He loves his wife. He will offer whatever support you need.

And lastly, will you please thank Fred Jones for me. Dexter and I love the house and are forever indebted to him for allowing us to live here. I will see to it myself that he receives his monthly payments.

Be Blessed in the eyes of the Lord and covered by his mercies.

Love and Prayers,

Charlette "River" Alexander (formally Montgomery)

She sat, crisscrossed in front of the tub for a while, wary—aware that she had written her letter in vain. She sighed deeply before tossing the letter into the tub with the sack of assorted buttons. She looked at the tables and chairs that were leaning against the house. She smiled at the memory of her and Eddie coming over early Saturday mornings, helping Miss Annie set up her tables to get ready to serve people. She closed her eyes and cried softly. This was her life now.

For the rest of her days, she'd have to sleep with one eye open because she could never tell if her husband was a true man of God or a snake oil salesman, trying to push salvation to the community like it was some kind of new drug. Her life was going to be spent trying to avoid places around town that once brought her comfort, now reminding her of loss. This was who she was. Confused, afraid, and alone.

A gentle breeze whispered through the air, teasing Charlette's free-flowing hair into a chaotic dance. Strands of her hair veiled her face, and she impatiently brushed them away from her right cheek. Her fingers grazed her skin, as she caught a glimpse of the back door. She had left it open. The sight rooted her to the spot, her blood turning to icy sludge within her veins. An unseen force gripped her, rendering her unable to turn her head, to look into the darkness of the doorway. It was as if she had become a statue, petrified by an inexplicable dread.

Her mind churned with the grimness of her past experiences. What if Miss Annie hadn't left? What if she still lurked in the shadows waiting to strike again? And what if Dexter, with his reassuring words, had been lying all along-- which she had suspected, but was too weak to believe? Time seemed to warp and twist around Charlette, leaving her suspended in a chilling limbo. This sensation was not pure fear but a deep sense of skepticism that gnawed at her resolve, threatening to unravel her fragile sanity.

A voice from the road shattered her paralyzing thoughts. "Hey, River," a woman called out, "I'm still not over that wedding, girl." The words yanked Charlette back to reality, and she managed a weak wave in response. She watched the woman and her child pass by, their ordinary presence starkly contrasting her inner turmoil. Once they were out of sight, Charlette reached into the pocket of her apron and pulled out a box of matches. With trembling hands, she set the sack of buttons ablaze. The flames crackled, devouring the remnants of Miss Annie, Fred, and all the haunted memories they embodied. Charlette knew she had to purge these ghosts to claim the house as her own. She loved Miss Annie, but she couldn't live in constant fear of shadows. To move forward, she had to banish the past.

Chapter 24

Charlette couldn't sleep. She laid in bed next to her husband thinking of Miss Annie. She thought of her smile and her voice. She thought of how much Miss Annie loved her and Eddie— and Shelly and her sister, Eliza, and all of the other children of Freedman. The memories of her made Charlette sit up in bed. She couldn't help but let out a chuckle thinking of the time Miss Annie proclaimed: "ain't enough babies in Freedman, now" last summer. Laying in her bed felt strange. It felt wrong.

Charlette gazed at her husband as he slept, wondering what kind of dreams he had if he dreamed at all. She took a deep breath, closing her eyes to imagine being inside his head. She pictured it dark and blank at first, then vast and complex, a maze of thoughts and ideas. She visualized the brilliance and charisma he exuded, wondering where such traits would live in the human mind, and how they must look in physical form. Despite her efforts to enter his mind, she found herself wandering the recesses of her own.

Opening her eyes, Charlette glanced at Dexter, who was still peacefully asleep. Determined, she inhaled sharply, held her breath, and tried again. She pictured him on the day they first met in the middle of the road, his smile, his arms holding her, his fingers gripping her skin. A smile tugged at her lips as she remembered those moments. She pictured him walking her home through the woods after she levitated for the first time, his hands on her thighs, the memory of their first kiss lingering on her lips. She frowned, recalling how delicately he touched inside of her, how cautious and attentive he was before she drifted. This time, she felt herself slipping deeper into the memory, immersing herself in the vivid recollections of their past. She was in.

It was dark and vast. Open. Empty. He didn't dream. She looked to the left and right but saw nothing. She looked up, then straight ahead, but there was nothing. She was about to close her eyes to pull herself out when suddenly she heard singing—she heard herself singing. She turned around and was met with the memory of herself floating, Dexter's memory of her floating. Hovering about the New George River in a white linen dress, her hair in a braid, singing.

"Going to lay down my sword and shield,
Down by the riverside,
Down by the riverside,"

As if every muscle in her body had been frozen solid, Charlette's blood flushed cold, her heart plummeting into the pit of her stomach, which felt as though it had sunk down to her feet in a paralyzing wave of dread.

"He saw me," she whispered. *"He was there."* Charlette couldn't breathe. She couldn't move. Her thoughts were racing, and she was afraid. Was he controlling her the whole time? Were these *gifts* really gifts at all? Was he the one making her black out? Was he there that day at the church? Was she really the one who killed Eddie?

"Charlie," she heard him say. She turned to find him, but there was nothingness all around her. "Charlie," he said again, angrier, more forcefully. She strained her eyes to see in the blackness that had engulfed her, but she couldn't see a thing. "CHARLETTE," he shouted.

With a gasp, Charlette woke up to the morning sun creeping into her bedroom window. She turned her head to find that Dexter was not in bed with her. She sat up, peering into the closet. He wasn't there either. She stood up and walked to the bathroom. It was empty. River grabbed her housecoat from the back of the chair at Miss Annie's vanity and rushed out of the door. She snuck quietly and intentionally into every room upstairs before looking downstairs, but Dexter was nowhere to be found.

She sat down at the kitchen table and placed her face into her hands. She forced her palms into her eye sockets, rubbing them roughly. "You're losin' it, girl" she said to herself. "Get it together." She opened her eyes and looked at the house around her. The house felt lifeless, it felt sullen.

She had only been inside the Jones home a couple of times growing up, but it didn't feel this way. Miss Annie was always cooking or sewing. She was always talking to someone, making them laugh. The house was always filled with people who were staying there for the week, or stopping by to pick up a plate, or to just sit and gossip with Miss Annie. The house was so full of life, but now it felt barren.

Charlette sulked around the kitchen for a while longer, before finally dressing and preparing for the day. Upstairs, she sat in front of the mirror, staring at her reflection. Her skin seemed ghastly; her eyes shadowed by dark rings that had recently appeared. Her face looked thinner, the lines around her mouth pulling downwards. She traced them with her fingers. "Means you laugh too much," she remembered Eddie saying. Now, she wondered if their new shape meant she had been frowning too often. The thought settled heavily in her mind, a silent testament to the unseen burdens she carried.

"Beautiful, right," she heard Dexter say from the doorway. He was wearing a pair of blue jeans, a white under shirt, and a pair of thick, black boots. "Looks like you been workin'," Charlette responded. "Well, we got to open the church doors soon, so I woke up early and went down to clean it up some. Thinkin' bout hirin' Henry Stitts to help me rebuild a bit too," he said. "Just gotta pay 'em enough to keep his mouth shut 'bout the place for a while."

He leaned down to kiss River on the forehead, but she turned and grabbed a brush. They looked at one another in the mirror, not saying a word. Finally, Dexter chuckled before walking into the bathroom. River started to brush her hair, aimlessly, with no particular style or goal in mind. She saw Dexter walk back into the room half dressed. He sat on the bed and watched her.

"It's the middle of the day, Dex, whatchu doin'," she asked. He lowered his head, laughing at the naivety of his young wife. She turned in her chair to face him. "It's been a week, Charlette," he announced. They stared at each other in silence again, waiting for the other to say something. "It's been a week since we married, Charlie. Don't you think we need to make it official," he asked. Charlette's throat closed.

She turned back towards the mirror and started to brush the other side of her hair. "Naw, naw, naw, put that brush down and speak to me," he said. "What are you afraid of," he asked.

Charlette ignored him, carefully opening bottles of oils and lotions, taking in their scents as if selecting the wrong fragrance would be fatal. She grabbed a tube of lipstick and began to apply it, her disregard for Dexter growing with each stroke. He walked toward her, calling her name. But she pressed her lips together tightly, focusing intently on her reflection, trying to block out her husband's insistent demands. "River," he shouted. She jumped from the sound of his boisterous voice before seizing the large, brushed-out bush of hair resting on her shoulder, twisting it, desperately clinging to the act to avoid the situation. "River!" Dexter's voice rose sharply, punctuated by the slap of his hand on the vanity.

"Get in the bed," he demanded. She didn't know what to do. She could tell that he wasn't in a mood to be tested, so she stood up. "Gon nie," he said. "God Blessed you wit some beautiful legs, gon' on and use em nie."

River walked over to the bed, staring at her husband who

stood on the other side of it. He took off his shirt and sat in the bed. "Come walk 'round to this side," he said. She did as she was told and stood before him. He grabbed her hand, placing a sweet kiss on it. He moved up to her wrist, then the inside of her forearm, laying soft, delicate kisses on his blushing bride. "Take dis off," he said, pulling at the skirt she was wearing. Charleltte reached behind herself and started to unfasten her skirt. "Dis too," he said, yanking her closer to him by her shirt.

Charlette's skirt rested around her ankles as she bent over besides her husband, kissing him. He cuffed his hand around her thigh before squeezing it gently. "Come here," he said softly, pulling her on top of him. Charlette sat in her husband's lap and pulled her shirt over her head. The two of them looked at each other, silently. She saw him looking at her, examining her. She felt the urge to cover herself with her arms, but she figured it would be pointless. He was her husband and she was his wife—and he was right, they had been married for just over a week but had yet to consummate their marriage. It was easy to say she didn't feel comfortable doing it when her mother was asleep across the hall, but they had been in "their" own house for three nights now. If she was going to be married to him, she had to commit to really being married to him.

Her heart was racing and her skin was hot. Her mind was yelling at her to grab her robe on the way out, and run home to her mother. But her body was curious. Dexter leaned forward, kissing her square in the center of her chest. He looked up at her eyes and smiled. She blushed.

"Look at all that damn hair," he said through a chuckle. River blushed some more, biting her lip both in embarrassment and anticipation. He kissed her. He wrapped his arm around her waist and pulled her closer. He pushed her back gently, laying her on the bed, then mounted her. She wrapped her arms around his neck and stared at him. *"Charlette,"* she said to herself. *"Please don't do anything you'd be ashamed of later. Get up girl,"* she thought to herself. *"Run!"*

But it was too late. She was biting his bottom lip while he was fully entrapped in every inch of her. Soon, her mind had caught up to what her body was experiencing. She wanted to be disgusted by him. She wanted to be upset and anxious, but the more attention he put into making sure she was satisfied, the more comfortable she felt beneath him. Her mind kept trying to snap out of the spell pleasure had placed on her, but with each thrust, and every kiss, Charletted tightened her grip around him.

"Dexter, please," she called out. She didn't even know what she was pleading for. Her hair was hanging off the foot of the bed, and her body was pinned under his. She had fully submitted to gratification. She thought about the day they were in Hop's house, so close to being in the exact position they were in now. She thought about that time they were in the woods with her sitting on top of him. Nothing she could have imagined was anything like reality. She felt safe in his arms again, she felt loved by his embrace. His determination to make her climax made her feel like she was his only priority.

All of the doubt she had been feeling in the weeks before were suddenly washed away by the sweat they shared between them. Each breath she let out was a release of apprehension. Charlette was stuck. There are no words to describe how mesmerized she was by her husband at that moment. If Dexter had done to Shelly even half of what he was doing to Charlette at that moment, she figured she may have gone around calling him a demon too. And if Eddie had truly caught the two of them in the act that day in the store, it made perfect sense that he would want to keep her away from Dex, for surely no other man could do what Dexter had just done with such disturbing skill.

When they were done and the acid in Charlette's stomach had finally settled, she turned to her husband and stared at him, examining him like he had done to her earlier. She was searching for something, looking for anything that would prove she wasn't crazy. Surely, this man was, in fact, human.

There were no blemishes on his smooth, brown skin. There were no fangs in his gorgeous smile. His fingernails were short and relatively clean, they weren't long and yellow like you would imagine a demon's to be. All that she had known of a monster was unlike the man she was lying next to.

"You scared of me now," he asked her. "You think kinda loud when you focusin'," he followed. "Sound like you think I'm supposed to be scary."

Charlette pulled her hair around her shoulder to twist it around her finger. She kept trying to speak but she was embarrassed. Here she was trying to prove to herself that he was just a man, no different than any other. And yet, he announced that he knew what she was thinking without her parting her lips. What was it? What did she believe? Was he just a man with a gift, like she was a woman who could float, or was he all the things Fred Jones and Shelly Hicks warned her about?

"Spit it out, now, gal," he said to her. "Ion feel like diggin' around in dere." Still, she had no words.

"Do you trust him or not," she asked herself. *"You can't sleep with a man you're afraid of. You don't share a bed with your enemy. Is this marriage going to be a testament of God's divine power or a testimony of surviving by clinging to his Word? If he is evil, can you defeat him and leave this situation unharmed and with your faith unbroken?"*

Charlette looked at her husband. She placed her lips at his temple, kissing him. He laughed. "What was dat fo, Miss River," he asked. "For making me your wife," she answered honestly.

CHAPTER 25

The next day, Charlette and Dexter were up early. Charlette still couldn't sleep in Miss Annie's bed. She also couldn't shake how strange it seemed that Fred Jones allowed Dexter to buy their house. He hated Dexter. She could understand being in a bind and desperately wanting to leave a situation, but she heard Fred Jones in town telling people how trusting Dexter would be the downfall of the town.

She had only slept a few hours, so when Dexter woke up, she was already downstairs, reheating chicken and making eggs and flapjacks to go with it.

"You still love me, Charlie, or you think I'm some kind of monster again," he asked as he moved her hair to one side, before placing a soft kiss on the nape of her neck. Charlette's stomach knotted and tightened, just like it used to when they first met. She turned to him smiling. "Ion know yet, Alexander," she said. "Maybe you ought to remind me again what it is I like so much about you."

He picked her up, threw her over his shoulder before going from the kitchen to the stairs. "Dexter, don't drop me," she shouted. "I was just playin'," she said unconvincingly. Dexter placed her on the landing of the step and kissed her sweetly. "I don't have no time to be playin' wit you anyway. I got to meet Ol' Henry this morning anyway." Charlette insisted on going with him to the church that day, offering to help clean things up while he and Henry did the heavy work. After pouting at her husband, batting her big doe eyes, he agreed to Charlette visiting the church with him.

The three of them–Henry Stitts and the Alexanders–crossed the New George, carrying wood and tools with them. Charlette had said to Henry on their walk that she was thinking of catching a ride to Savannah to buy velvet to reupholster the pews of the church. She even thought about planting a garden for the members of the congregation to tend to. She spoke of her ideas and hopes for the church the entire walk there. "Wow, Miss First Lady. Sound like you plan on bein' more of a Blessing to Freedman, than you already was," he said to Charlette.

Charlette blushed, but she noticed Dexter's jaw clench from frustration. He always called it their church, but she knew that it was his vision to be a leader among the community. "Aw, Henry, I only plan to aid in making my husband's dream come true. He's the Blessing here, I'm just his helpmate," she said bashfully, glancing at Dexter to make sure his tension had eased.

They approached the church and stood at its steps in admiration. "My God," Henry said. "Has this building always been here?" he asked.

"I can't say, I never crossed the North end of the river befo'. Sho'll ain't ever thought to walk this deep into the woods," Charlette replied. Dexter walked up the steps before standing in front of the doors with his chest stuck out and his back straightened. "I likes to think the Lord hid dis church from you good folks and waited for a worthy man to find it. And I happen to be the man, worthy, bold, and brave enough to bring salvation back to Freedman, Georgia."

They entered the church and got to work. Henry and Dexter began to knock down cobwebs before scraping years of dust and dirt from windows. Charlette went behind them, sweeping the ground as they worked.

"Ain't no sense in cleanin' and sweepin', Miss Alexander," Henry said. "Things gon get a whole lot dirtier from here. We a ways away from gettin this place cleaned for service." Dexter agreed with the handyman and told Charlette to go into town to ask about having a poster made in the post office. "Bout time we start tellin' folk of the work we doin," he said. "But for now, let's just say we'll hold a weekly sermon in front of the Brooks' sto while the sanctified folk is down at First Baptist."

Dexter told Charlette exactly what he wanted the poster to say and where he wanted them to hang it. He sent her off with a kiss and Charlette was on her way. She walked into town and thought about the night before.

Charlette's mind raced with doubts as she grappled with the unsettling truth gnawing at her sanity. Surely, she had been driving herself crazy for no reason, she thought. There was no way she would fall in love with a man capable of doing such wicked things. Despite her attempts to bury her suspicions, the nagging feeling persisted. She wasn't feeling this way for no reason. This consistent pattern of unease had to be more than just paranoia.

Dexter, with his vague demeanor and veiled intentions, was an intimidating presence that both captivated and terrified her. Each passing moment in his company felt like a tightrope walk between pure bliss and dread. Yet, despite her better judgment screaming for her to flee, Charlette found herself bound to him by the chains of love and fear, trapped in a twist of devotion and deception. She was married to him now, tangled in a web of uncertainty from which seemed impossible to escape. How was she going to get out of this situation with her faith and reputation intact?

Just as the thought passed, Charlette looked up and saw Shelly Hicks approaching. She was thinner than the last time they had seen each other, and her hair was almost entirely gray.

"Shelly," Charlette called to her. "Are you okay?" Shelly stopped and rolled her eyes. She turned the other way and kept walking. Charlette called out to her and followed her until she finally stopped.

"Nah, River, I'm not okay. I'm doin' bad," she said angrily. Shelly looked completely different. Her hair was brittle and dry; her once shapely body was just a small frame of skin and bones. Charlette could hardly look at her. "Things with your Ma not goin' well?" she asked with concern.

Shelly sucked in air through her nostrils. She held her breath for a while before forcefully exhaling, again, from her nose. Charlette could sense the disdain radiating from Shelly. She felt her betrayal, the disappointment and heartbreak she was experiencing because of Charlette. Without saying a word, Charlette looked down and started twisting the ends of her hair as she waited for Shelly to respond.

"If you must know, if you just gotta be all in my damn business," Shelly began. "My Ma is gettin' worse, by the damn second, it seems. It's me. I'm killin her," she said. Charlette reached for Shelly's hand to console her. She wanted to say that nothing she has ever done or is currently doing is killing her mother, but Shelly jumped back and began to speak.

"It's your man! He done something to me and it's killing me, and it's killing my mama! Every night I go to bed, I have the same dream. We're in the woods, it's late at night, and Dexter has candles sat out in a circle. My Ma is laid up in the middle of it, sick and dying. He has all these bones round his neck, a snake crawling all up his arm, and his eyes is gray." Charlette wanted desperately not to hear the story she was sharing. She didn't want to imagine such a horrible scene. She wanted to drag Shelly to the ground, telling her to shut up, but she was curious. She was interested in everything she was saying, and as much as she hated hearing it, she wanted to know more.

"He looks like a dead man again. The glow from the flames of the candles is casting dis red light onto his swollen skin and you can see that he's really the living dead. It's satanic, River.

It's disgusting."

"Anyway, my Ma is on the ground groanin' and cryin', beggin for her life. And every single night, Dexter cuts her, makes her bleed, then he reaches out and I take his hand, and he kneels me down besides my mother and he makes me drink her blood." River turned away and started to walk off. "Nah," Shelly yelled. "Come back and listen! Listen to what your *husband* is doing to me!"

Charlette shook her head in disbelief. She covered her ears, beginning to pray. She asked God to remove the demon that had taken hold of Shelly and the rest of Freedman. She prayed that God would shed the blood of Jesus upon her small town, cleansing it of the evil that had been casted down upon it. Shelly grabbed Charlette's shoulder, spinning her around.

She mocked her. She copied her, and laughed at her. "Oh, you think God is goin to save you from your sin? Nah, sister, you married the enemy." Shelly smirked at Charlette. She enjoyed seeing her bothered this way.

She trusted Charlette. She expected her to do her thing and run the evilness that Dexter had brought to their home right out of town. But instead, she had married him. She was endorsing him. She stood next to him while he committed blasphemy and falsely called upon God in front of the people outside of Mr. Brooks' store.

"I'm goin' to the New George and I'm drowning myself. I'm walking to the south end of the water where its deep, and wide, and dark, and I'm gonna take this letter, and leave it under a heavy rock, and I'ma tie another one to myself, and I'm gonna drown in that river to be cleansed of my sins." Charlette saw the seriousness in Shelly's eyes. She saw excitement and hope. Shelly was convinced that she was going to right all her wrongs and be free of Dexter if she died. Shelly was beyond saving. Charlette had to stop her.

"Shelly, you not thinkin' clearly, honey, come wit me," she

said.

"Talk to me some more, pray with me for a spell, just don't do anything crazy." Charlette was able to grab both of Shelly's wrists. She pulled her in the direction towards the woods, speaking to her calmly. Shelly moved slowly with her. She still trusted her. She still saw Charlette as the woman whose prayers moved mountains. She wanted to believe that she was finally on her side.

"I wrote it all down, I told the Lord about everything I been too ashamed to say out loud. I bared my soul to God. I asked for forgiveness, and I wrote one page specifically about the sins I've committed at the hands of your Dexter." Charlette stopped and looked at Shelly again. What sins had she committed because of Dexter? What did he make her do? "Oh, you don't know," Shelly said. "You think dis starts and stops at my dreams? No, sometimes, I'll be at home cookin or dressin Mama, den suddenly I'm not myself no more, suddenly I'm not even human. I killed a boy, River. One of dem young boys, Dr. Bailey's nephews dat was visitin; I caught him walkin out of town wit out his brothers and asked him if he ever kissed a woman. Got em all hot and bothered, told him that I'd teach him what to do with his wife someday.

He was so nervous, but so excited. He was scared to touch me, but he couldn't take his lil hands off me. I laid him down, I kissed his head, his mouth. I kissed his lil ol nose, then I kissed his neck. I bit it a little bit. He liked it, it made his body jump. He kissed me. It made him real confident. So, I bit his neck again, but harder. He flinched, tried to hit me. But I grabbed his wrist and kissed that too. Then, and I don't know why, River, I bit his wrists so hard that it ripped through his skin. I yanked out his veins with my teeth. His blood was flying everywhere. I didn't even know that much blood could be in one person."

"It made me think, 'if all dat just come from his wrist, how much more is in his neck?' So I ripped out his throat with just my teeth. I used my nails to dig into his chest and scratch the skin and get it under my nails. It felt so good. I felt so alive. His blood was hot and thick. It was sticky, but smooth. I covered myself in it. I even laid next to the boy's body and used his blood to please myself."

"I had no control over what I was doing, but I could feel the joy of it all. Then just as I was getting close, just as my toes started to curl and my back started to bend, I opened my eyes and looked up, and your man was standing there. Your man was over me. Smiling, beaming. Oh, he was lovin it. And my body tightened, my nipples hardened, and I came harder than I ever have in my life."

"That was yesterday. I stood up and looked at Dexter and he looked at me. He walked over and kissed me on my forehead and told me to go bury the boy's body behind some church. And I did. Then he told me to go to the south end of the river and bathe. He told me to come back today in all white and wait for him. I asked him what time he wanted me to be there, and he said to get there early and wait. So dats what I'm doin. I'm wearing my white, I'm takin' my letter and my rocks, and I'm going to throw myself in the river before he can get to me.

I can't do dis no more, so I won't do it no more. I'm killin myself."

Charlette stood for a while, staring at her. She didn't know what to say. "No, Shelly, it couldn't have been yesterday," she said. "I was with him. He came home early, just befo' afternoon, and never left again." Shelly was mistaken, she thought. She had to be. Dexter stayed home with her all day after they made love. They even did it again before nightfall, and when they were apart while she was making dinner, Dexter was outside sitting with Hop Wilson, singing and drinking hooch. Yeah, Shelly was losing her mind, like Cecilia said; that's what Charlette told herself.

"But what was he doin' that mornin', River," Shelly asked. "You said 'he came home,' meaning he was gone at some point." Shelly was right. He told her that he was at the church, but how did she know that was true.

"Bet he came home all riled up and ready. I bet he came home and made this pretty little saint do dirty, nasty things." Charlette's ears were hot. Her cheeks were red. She was embarrassed and angry. "Why you think he wanted you so bad? What you think turned him on? It wasn't me; it was the blood. It was the death. He loved it. He couldn't take his eyes off of how vile and disgusted and ashamed I felt. Bet you felt that way too." Charlette turned her head, balling her fist, clenched her jaw.

"Oh," Shelly sang in shock. "You liked it. You liked doing those dirty, nasty things. You liked being his filthy little whore." Charlette lunged at Shelly, but she moved out of the way. "Who knew Miss 'holier than thou' was really just a ol' nasty freak all along." Charlette jumped at her again but fell.

Shelly laughed. She laughed until she started to choke. She coughed and doubled over, trying to catch her breath in between laughing, when suddenly she looked to Charlette for help. Her eyes were bulging, her mouth was wide, and she was clawing at her neck and chest. She was suffocating. Charlette sat on the ground, watching her. Shelly reached out to Charlette, begging with her eyes, pleading for help.

Charlette looked at her dispassionately. She was sick of Shelly. She was annoyed with her. Charlette had been trying to be a friend to her even when the rest of the women and girls treated her like a Leper. Charlette always told herself that she was no different from Shelly and that Shelly deserved grace, but truthfully, she always hated Shelly. She wouldn't help herself. She couldn't stop herself from being a degenerate. All Charlette could ever do was pray Shelly would wake up someday and realize that she was the problem. But sadly, that day would never come. Shelly was going to die right here in the woods, choking on Charlette's spite.

Finally, the corners of Shelly's mouth turned a dark blue, they were almost purple. Her eyes were bloodshot. She had fallen over, hitting the ground. She didn't really want to die. All that talk of suicide was a bluff, just dramatics. She drew her last breath while looking up at Charlette. She looked down at her in silence. She felt no guilt, she felt no shame. She didn't feel anything at all.

Then suddenly, without any apparent reason to do so, she felt the urge to run. This sudden sense of urgency struck her like a bolt of lightning, telling her to get away. It was as if her decision to stay there or run away was a matter of life and death. As she crossed back over the field, she realized that her instinct led her to the river. It didn't seem like the best hiding spot, considering she went there so often she had a nickname behind it. She made it to the bank of the New George and stopped. The water covered her ankles as she thought. What to do, where to go?

Without warning, Charlette suddenly felt small. The atmosphere behind her felt heavy and malevolent. She couldn't move an inch. She wanted to turn her head or trudge across the water, but she absolutely petrified where she stood. Charlette was scared. She felt fear. She had been spooked a few times in the last few weeks, but this was real fear.

And just as suddenly as it struck her, she was urged to move forward. The tension in the air subsided and her vision tunneled. River sprung forward into the middle of the water and trekked a few feet to the other side. She ran into the woods and kept running ahead. She didn't know where she was going, but she knew that whatever was following her was full of wickedness and intended on terrorizing her.

The earth seemed to have been whipping around her as if she were running at the speed of a cheetah. Her body felt heavy, and even though she was running as fast as she could, it felt to her like something was weighing her down. Charlette could feel the veins in her forehead pulsating, throbbing, as she ran. Her head started hurting.

"Letty," she heard someone call from a distance. She stopped. "Eddie?" she called out. She felt a rush of warm air blow past her, and her head began to pound. "Letty," she heard the voice say again. Charlette knew better than to follow the sound of a dead man's voice and started to run in the opposite direction.

It was the end of July, and August was just around the corner, so being hot was not an unusual sensation, especially if you had been running aimlessly through the woods; but Charlette was burning up. She felt as if she was boiling from the inside. She was trying her best to keep moving, but her body was betraying her. The skin around her head felt tight and her brain seemed to have been pulsating, hard pressed, against her skull. Physically, she couldn't go on because lifting her legs was like trying to pull them out of quicksand.

She fell to her knees before trying to call for help, but her voice was weak. She knew that even if she could yell, no one would be around to hear it. She looked up around her and saw the trees still spinning. Her vision was blurred, her breath was short. "Letty, I'm right here," she heard Eddie say from above. She looked up and saw a figure of a man with his hand outstretched. The earth was still moving around her, whooshing with speed and force. It was overwhelming.

"Follow me, Charlette," he said. "Let me save you." She attempted to grab his hand, but hers went straight through his, slapping the twigs and dry grass that covered the ground. She squinted her eyes to try to see through her blurred vision but could not make out anything other than the shape of a man. She tried to stand but couldn't make it off her knees. "He can't save you now," she heard Dexter say.

Charlette didn't know what was going on. She tried to open

her eyes again, but her sight was weakening more and more as time passed. "You shoulda listened to Ol' Shelly Hicks," she heard him say. "You mine now," he said through a laugh. "Til death do us part."

CHAPTER 26

Dexter busted through the front door of the Montgomery home carrying his betrothed in his arms. River's body lay limply in his arms. She was drenched in sweat and completely unconscious. "Miss Montgomery," Dexter shouted. "Miss CeeCee!"

Cecilia flew out of her room, running into the living room. "Sweet Jesus, please say it ain't so," she cried. "She's alive. I found her in the woods like this. She was on the other side of the north end of the river. Dis is my fault," he cried. "We found a church out there and she was lookin' for it. I don't know what happened, but she won't wake up. She won't move." Dexter cried. He broke down in Cecilia's living room.

Cecilia instructed Dexter to take Charlette into her room and lay her on her bed. He gently laid her down before kneeling on the side of the bed, whispering softly into her ear. Cecilia knelt beside Dexter, whose vague demeanor and veiled intentions left her uncertain, as she offered comfort to her distraught soon-to-be son-in-law. She rubbed his back, assuring him that everything would be okay, despite Charlette's condition hanging heavy in the air. She glanced into Dexter's eyes; a shiver rippled through her that kept her heart from beating for a moment. There was something unsettling about him. a flicker of unfamiliarity that pricked at her senses. She pushed the sensation aside, her focus fixed on her daughter's wellbeing.

Checking her daughter's symptoms, Cecilia attempted to gauge Charlette's temperature, but her hand recoiled as if scorched by fire. She shot a glance at Dexter, her mind racing with suspicion. How could he have carried River all this way without noticing her how hot she felt? Her heart pounded as she inspected her daughter's pupils, a stark contrast to their usual appearance. There was no light, no color, no life in them. They were empty black orbs that sat in Charlette's skull. The sight sent a chill down her spine, and without a second thought, she bolted from the room.

Dexter's continued murmurs, barely audible, stirred an unease within Cecilia. His words were a whisper, sharp with intent, but their meaning eluded her grasp. Was he invoking some higher power or something more sinister? Cecilia's gut churned with uncertainty, her maternal instincts alert.

Ignoring her rising suspicions, Cecilia hyper-focused on her daughter's needs. With determination, she enveloped River in warmth, her hands moving with practiced urgency. She ordered Dexter to assist, his aid unsettling yet necessary in this moment of crisis.

As she tended to Charlette, Cecilia couldn't shake the feeling that Dexter harbored secrets darker than she dared to imagine. But in the midst of the turmoil, her priority remained clear: saving her daughter's life at any cost, even if it meant burying her suspicions deep within.

"What you doin', Ma'" he asked.

"I'm sweating this demon out. Look under the bed," she demanded.

Dexter kneeled down and saw nothing.

"There's a loose floorboard under there; right in the middle. Slap it hard and pull out one of dem bottles."

Dexter obeyed, slamming the floorboard with a thud that echoed through the small bedroom. The sudden jolt sent the opposite end flying upwards, revealing a dusty crate filled with small crystal valves. His pulse quickened as he reached out, but a paralyzing dread gripped him, making his hands unable to make contact with the mysterious objects.

"What's this," he asked.

"Blessed oil, holy water, weapons against the enemy. Gon' on and grab one," she answered and instructed.

"Now, why you so convinced this is possession," he inquired. Trying to avoid reaching for the bottles again.

"Dexter, look at her! She look half dead and her eyes is pitch black! If dat ain't satan trying to take hold den what is?"

Cecilia stopped molding the covers and quilts around her daughter to grab a bottle. She placed four dots of holy water on her daughter's forehead, forming a cross. She stood up reciting Psalms 23 over her daughter. Dexter rose to his feet to "pray" as well.

Charlette started to shake. Her body convulsed and seized. Her eyes shot open, and her mouth was agape. Something was trying to be released from her, but it was stifled. Cecilia grabbed her daughter's hand and spoke over her, declaring that the enemy would not take her soul. She prayed that her body would be spared, but that her spirit goes on with God.

Dexter grabbed Cecilia's hand and joined her in prayer. Charlette sat up and turned to her mother. Her eyes were still black, but they were pleading. They called to her mother. "Help me," Cecilia heard River say. She was in her mind. "Get away from him, Mama," she cried. "Don't let him take you like he's trying to take me."

With a gasp, Cecilia released Dexter's hand, her eyes wide with panic. She darted beneath the bed, her movements frantic as she clawed at the crate, pulling out bottles with shaking hands. With a savage determination, she tore off their tops, the pungent scent of anointed oils filling the air as she drenched herself and her daughter in the sacred liquids. With trembling fingers, she reached for the vial of holy water, pouring it over their heads in a desperate bid for salvation against the threatening darkness.

Dexter stepped back. "Dex, I don't know what's going on, but she is not leaving. She is staying here with me. I think it's best you gon' home. I got her." Her breathing was short, and her chest was heaving. She was standing firm in her faith, but her body was quivering.

"If you think that's best, den I'll be on my way."

CHAPTER 27

She didn't wake up, she didn't eat, she didn't move an inch. She just slept. Cecilia couldn't shake what she thought she heard Charlette saying to her. She was looking at her daughter, and she never said a word. But she couldn't stop imagining her voice begging for help.

Dexter came over every day to check on his wife. Cecilia always stood watch though. She didn't trust him anymore, but she didn't want to assume the worst either. He would hold her hand and tell her about his day. He told her about the sermons he would give in the town square. He'd tell her about the jobs he worked and the people he spoke to.

"We built a bridge, Charlie," he told her. "Right over your river; that way folks can get to tha church easily," he said to her one day. "I think I'm 'bout ready to open the doors. It's not pretty like you want it, but it's clean and it's safe. I'm just waiting for you to wake up, baby."

Charlette never felt like she was asleep. She was present in her mind the whole time. She could hear her mother crying. She could hear her praying. She learned secrets about her mother too. She drank, she cussed, and she didn't always like River.

Charlette heard it when Pastor Johnson came over and prayed for her, she heard when Dr. Bailey gave her a checkup. Everyone told her mother to prepare for the worst. "There isn't any way she could sleep this long and still have a pulse," Dr. Bailey said. "Certainly, can't go this long without eating and drinking. Write your husband and tell him to come say his goodbyes."

Charlette heard her father too. He came in with Dexter one day. They sat in silence for a long time. Her father just held her hand. Finally, Dexter kissed her forehead and went home, so Cleo took that time to kneel by her bed and sob. She wanted to cry too. She wanted to wake up and tell her daddy about everything that had happened, but she couldn't move. She couldn't scream. She was trapped.

Then, one night, *he* came to see her. Things were quiet in her mind. It was dark and dreary. Charlette had assumed that it was night because the house was quiet, and crickets were chirping. "You miss me," she heard him say. Dexter was fully and physically inside of her mind. He reached out for a hug, but she stepped back. "Where you gon' run," he asked. He had a point.

"What do you want from me, Dexter?" She knew he did this to her. She knew he placed her in her own, personal hell— where she could not escape or speak or even rest. He did this to her.

Dexter didn't answer. He just looked at her. "What do you want," she repeated, but still Dexter would not speak. "What do you want from me, dammit," Charlette screamed, and at that moment she and Dexter were at the New George.

She didn't know what was happening. She didn't know what to think. Was all of this in her mind or were they actually at the river. What all was Dexter capable of? "What's goin' on, Dex," she asked her husband. "What's goin' on, honey, just tell me," she begged.

Dexter laughed. Charlette asked him why they were there and what he was going to do, but still he laughed.

"God, please protect me. Please cover me in the blood of Jesus and bind any evilness that has taken hold of my life," she prayed.

"Dats right, dats right. Call on the Lord, our God. See if he can get you out of this," he taunted. Charlette felt her throat tighten as if she were about to cry, but she continued to pray. Dexter was annoyed. She opened her eyes and continued to pray.

"Look, Charlie, I love you. I'd never hurt you, but I'm gettin sick of dis. I was hopin we could just talk, and you'd decide to work wit me instead of against me, but you not lettin dat happen," he said candidly.

She stared at him but continued to pray. She gazed into his eyes, searching for his soul, and prayed with all the conviction in the world. Dex started to step away, but she grabbed his wrist and followed his eyes. They stared at one another. She saw *him*. She could see him, but she could tell that he was hiding.

Dexter felt Charlette piercing his soul and yanked himself from the firm grasp she had on his wrists. "You goin' round askin' Shelly Hicks questions and killed the bitch. You searchin' for Annie and Fred Jones like you don't know they dead, and then you tried to snoop around in my mind." Charlette stopped praying and listened.

"Dis shit is gettin old, you want to know the truth, I'll tell it to you." River stood still. She didn't move, she breathed softly. Her eyes followed her husband as he moved around the room.

"I came to this town for a reason. Something I couldn't explain called me here. Something told me dis place was special," he began.

"There's power in Freedman, Georgia, gal, and y'all niggas don't even know it. Dem woods is cursed, or blessed dependin' who you ask. Dem trees hold power."

Charlette was genuinely unaware of what Dexter was

talking about, yet she sensed that she had felt the exact presence he was talking about. There was something about the water that drew her near it; there was something about nature that made her feel a connection to the Most High God, but Dexter's talk of blessings and curses left her feeling torn between confusion and a thirst to understand – curious, wanting to know more.

"Why y'all think white folks ain't burn dis place down? Why you think they ain't ran y'all out of here? Y'all don't think they ever tried? Y'all think it's prayer? Nah, it's blood. Not da blood of Jesus either." Dexter was beside himself as he spoke to Charlette. He was speaking to her with confidence in his voice and a gleaming light in his eyes. She had only seen him this enthusiastic when he was preaching, so she knew that there was truth in what he was saying.

"See, at first, I didn't get it. I didn't know what made this place so special. I mean besides a bunch of Black folk runnin they own business, and building they own houses, and not having nothing to do with the rest of the world. But that couldn't be the thing dat was keepin' me up at night. Dat couldn't be what was calling me to this little town in this stretch of woods. But I got to know er'body. I got to stick around and speak to folks and it hit me by tha end of my second week: you niggas is under a spell."

Dexter and Charlette were face to face again, Dexter flashing his infamous left-sided smile. *"Under a spell:"* rang in her head. *Under a spell…*

"Y'all walkin' round here, happy and smiling and livin' life wit no real problems. Yeah, people might be po and Black, I get it. It ain't nobody in Freedman that got it as good as a white man in Savannah with three kids, a wife, and a big nice house to sleep in, but y'all ain't got no real problems, Charlie."

"It's in the way y'all speak, the way y'all smile, y'all ain't like everybody else. Y'all different. Shelly got left fo a yella bone, Eddie's mama died young, people done fell sick and died who ain't ever died befo, but y'all don't got folks being lynched. Y'all don't got kids being kidnapped. Ain't shit happenin' round here for real. And it's because them woods is powerful and got all you happy people under a spell dats something serious."

Charlette was staring at him, taking it all in. She had questions but she wasn't sure she wanted answers. Dexter was talking about things she never thought to ask about. Were the people of Freedman different? Was there something special about their land? "We just a peop—," Charlette began, but Dexter shut her mouth before she could finish her thought.

"Y'all not no special people of faith who protected by God. Y'all a special people protected by rootwork, by blood magic."

Charlette turned her head, casting her gaze over the water, her senses keenly attuned to the rustle of the breeze over each blade of grass. The familiar scenery mirrored the sanctuary she once found solace in, yet a chilling realization crept over her. This serene facade, so similar to her safe haven, now felt like the eerie setting of a nightmare. As she stared up at the sky, a shiver raced down her spine. It was as if they were standing by the river, by her river. Yet, she knew deep down it was all a sinister illusion crafted by Dexter. His presence behind her sent a wave of dread coursing through her veins, for she knew he held her captive within his spell, but she felt a sense of pity from him– like he felt sorry to be the person crushing her naivete.

"Even after I realized what was going on I still didn't understand what drew me here," Dexter started. "I gotta be honest, baby, I ain't no good man. I know Ion deserve to be in no negro paradise." He turned Charlette to face him, they bore into one another. This time he was looking at *her*. She was curious, but frightened. He saw that she needed to know more.

"It's like dis, Charlie: the people who founded dis town was sleepin' in the middle of da wilderness, with animals, catchers, hounds, and spirits all around 'em. Some people didn't make it. People were eaten, children were stolen, dis place was hell on earth for weeks. Den, Hendricks Johnson's daddy had tha good sense to make a sacrifice to this earth." Charlette didn't believe him. Pastor Johnson would never do a thing like that, so it was hard to believe that he would be raised by a man who could kill. All the desire she had to believe the things Dexter had been saying left her. She was angry for being so gullible, for being so blinded by a handsome smile that she threw caution to the wind. Dexter was torturing her and this was just another means to hurt her.

"Oh, you think I'm bullshittin' huh? Ask Mr. Jenkins, he knows da story! I talked to him bout it and he told it to me one night! He drank some old hooch that had turned and was sayin' anything to anybody. He say dere was a young girl in the group of slaves dat came here; she was carryin' a child, half white. Chester Johnson, yo pastor's daddy, had planned what he was gon' do for a week. He found a tree stump in the woods, just cross the river, and made a altar out of it. He had been trappin' rabbits and killin' 'em, keeping their bones and drying 'em. He collected snakeskin and grounded them. Got herbs from tha women and made sure they told 'em what all they did besides goin on food."

Charlette didn't want to hear anything else. This was all too much for her to handle. She had to get away, distance herself from Dexter's evil. She started to walk towards home, and Dexter let her go. But as soon as she made it over through the pasture, she walked right into Dexter's back, falling to the ground as he continued talking.

"He got it all together. Den, early one mornin' he woke up da girl, took her cross that New George, and gave her some herbs to make her sleep. He laid her on the altar and cut her wide open."

"Da gal was still alive, but she was asleep. She couldn't move, she couldn't scream, all she could do was cry. Chester pulled the baby from her and prayed over it. He offered it to God, to the land, and to the spirits dat lived in the woods. He cut and bleed the boy and mixed his blood with water that he boiled the bones and snakeskin in. He placed the boy's body back in his mother and pushed their bodies in dat river *you* named for."

Charlette shook her head and started to pound her fists into her ears, repeatedly rebuking evilness in the name of Christ Jesus, but still, Dexter's voice broke through. She didn't want to hear what he was saying but she knew that if she tried to walk away, she would walk right back to the spot she had just left from. She could not escape.

"He prayed over the blood and water and poured it all around the land. He declared that white folks and their evil would never make it cross dem trees. He prayed dat dis land would always have a protector. He said dat once every three generations, dis land would have a powerful protector. Someone whose prayers could move mountains; one who could speak to da deaf and mute; one who could walk on air as they do on Earth. You know who was born in the third generation of people living in Freedman, Georgia—who can speak without her mouth, whose prayers can move mountains, who can walk on air just like she do on Earth?"

She had heard enough. "No," River said quietly as she shook her head. "No," she repeated just a little louder. "No!" she shouted at the top of her lungs when she walked past Dexter, putting at least ten feet of distance between them.

"Oh yeah, you dat protector. You keepin evil out of Freedman, Charlie." Dexter was trying to be gentle, but he wanted to break her too. He wanted to pull Charlette out of her cloud of safety, bringing her to the real world. She was so convinced that she had a strong, radical sense of faith, but couldn't handle the existence of the supernatural right in front of her. He loved his wife, but it was time for her to wake up, and if waking her up meant shattering her sense of reality, crushing her false sense of security, then so be it.

Charlette's mind was in a frenzy. On one hand, everything that Dexter was saying sounded like a fireside story to scare children, but after all that she had seen this summer, how could she not think any of it was true?

Not knowing what else to do, Charlette turned to prayer. Dexter gritted his teeth, enraged by Charlette's feigned peace in the power of prayer. He rolled his eyes and let out a sigh, before grabbing his wife to shake her. When Charlette opened her eyes, she saw him. She saw the gray decaying skin, she saw the green undertones, the swollen flesh, the dead eyes. She saw him for *what* he was.

"How did you make it here," she asked. "How did you make it into Freedman if me or the woods or whatever supposed to keep out evil?" Dexter turned and sat on the bank of the river. He motioned for her to sit with him. Charlette was weary, but she followed.

They sat by the water's edge, gazing out at the world before them. The river surged; its flow rushed with fury. Waves clashed violently, assaulting the shore with relentless force. Yet, amid the chaos, they remained untouched and dry.

Dexter stayed silent; his focus fixed on the rough waters. Beside him, she studied the features of his face, recognizing traces of the man she once knew in his profile. His lips, once warm and inviting, now seemed cold and lifeless. He looked so much like Dexter, just a version of him who had died and come back to life again.

"Dexter, how did you make it into Freedman," she asked. "Well, Charlie, that's the thang," he looked into her eyes. Charlette's gaze met glassed over gray orbs, but she could see his sincerity.

"You brought me here." He smiled at her as he spoke. He delighted in her terror. How did she bring him there? Why would she bring evilness to her home?

"Now dat you know dat we supposed to be in dis together, I guess I'll tell you tha plan."

The water calmed, and the sun shined, his color slowly started to return. "Lay back dere, Charlie, this gon' be a while."

CHAPTER 28

THE LIFE AND DEATH OF DEXTER ALEXANDER

He started to tell her about his childhood. He told her that he was raised by his mother and father who were two of the most beautiful people he had ever seen. His father was a Pastor and his mother was a maid. His father did handiwork around the community for extra money here and there. He told her that he had a little brother named Donovan, and a baby sister named Deborah. Deborah died when she was three years old from pneumonia, and Donovan was killed one day walking home.

"I wanted to go crazy, Charlie. I wanted to just die. But my father told me that I had to live. Had to live in order to prove dem people wrong," he said to Charlette. He looked up to the sky and chuckled before dropping his head again. "He said, 'you gotta show em dat dey can't kill us all, and dey can't take our minds.'"

Dexter continued by telling her how his father was never one to lie or sugarcoat the truth for kids. He would give it to him straight about anything and everything. His father was his hero. He wanted to be just like him. When Dexter would imagine himself as an adult, he'd picture himself in his father's suit, standing in front of his father's church. That's why Dexter wanted to be a Pastor desperately.

Charlette had known a lot of this already—about his father, why he wanted to be a Pastor, where he grew up—but some of this was new to her too. "My mama, God bless her soul, was a saint. She wasn't like you doe, she cussed and she drank a little, but her heart was just as big." Dexter smiled as he spoke, gazing upward in his delight.

"She lost two kids and she still kept her joy. God was good to my Ma and Pa. God's good grace touched them and they truly had dat peace that surpasses all understandin. Dat is til the day His favor dried up."

Charlette looked upward towards the sky as Dexter lowered his head, facing the ground. The clouds were gray and the atmosphere was dark. She could see something playing out in the sky, but it felt distant. She looked at Dexter who was still looking down. She saw a softness to him, a vulnerability that she only just realized she'd never seen in him. She wanted to comfort him, she wanted to understand him. How could the man she loved, this beautiful man of God, be a demon amongst saints?

Charlette looked up from Dexter to set her focus on the sky again. She could see a child and his parents at a dinner table. They were happy, laughing with one another as they prepared the table. The father stood up to grab the mother and son's hands. They bowed their heads, and he began to pray. The father — Dexter's father — was tall, taller than Dexter, and just as handsome. He turned to his son and smiled. The mother, prettier than anyone else Charlette had ever seen, had her head bowed, nodding in agreement to her husband's prayer.

There was no sound to the scene that played in front of them but the images were crystal clear. They looked so happy, so in love with one another. Dexter's smile started to make sense to her. His heart, his hospitality. He was raised well. He was loved.

She looked over at her husband, whose head was still bowed. Then suddenly she heard a loud bang. Charlette jumped as she looked back towards the sky. She could hear everything now. It was all so vivid and real. It was as if she were standing in the corner watching it all unfold.

"No, no, no, no, no, no," she heard Dexter's mother cry. She leaned over her husband who was slouched over the table, bleeding from his stomach. "Mama," she heard young Dexter cry. "No," she shouted as her husband bled out. The desperate woman looked up to her son and told him to run, but she was shot as soon as she said it.

Dexter dropped to the ground, seeking refuge under the table as his parents' blood dripped around him like a thick, scarlet rain. He heard the front door open and three men walked in and stood around the kitchen table. Dexter slowly, quietly, tucked his knees into his chest and held his breath. His eyes were wide and red looking from knee to knee of the men standing around him.

Charlette tried to close her eyes, but Dexter grabbed her chin, forcing her to her look up. "Nah, Charlie, you can't miss dis," he said. She and Dexter were sitting by the stove in the kitchen, their backs against the wall, watching as the men began to stomp, yell, and hit the top of the table to scare the little boy.

"Don't miss dis," Dexter said.

Charlette watched as the boy closed his eyes and prayed. As he was praying, some reached under the table and drugged him from underneath it. The men strapped him into a chair with their belts, laughing as the boy called out to God. Charlette tried to divert her eyes as the men who had broken into the home took turns pissing, spitting, and raping the corpse of his parents, but Dexter would force her eyes open every time she shut them.

One man, the ringleader, turned to the boy and spat on him. The boy balled his fist and gritted his teeth. The man laughed at Dexter's rage. Then he bent over and told the boy to hit him. "Go on, take your best shot," he said. So, the little boy, with all the power in his small body, balled his fist and punched the man in his nose.

The man fell backwards and did not get up. The other men began to beat the little boy. They hit him, they stomped on him, they even cut him and burned him with a knife they placed over a flame first. When they were done and the ringleader was satisfied, they threw the boy in a burlap sack and took him from his home.

"They sold me to a white woman in New Orleans," Dexter said as the bank of the New Gorge began to form around them.

"There was a woman who worked in the house that did Voodoo. She was the lady's handmaid. I told her I ain't want nothing to do with Voodoo. Told her I had a God."

"She told me that she had no desire to take God out of my life, but wanted to introduce me to something that would move a little quicker than He did." Dexter told Charlette about how he spent his life going back and forth between learning the Word of God and learning Voodoo from the mistress's maid. The white woman in New Orleans taught him how to read, but only let him read the bible. The maid taught him how to write by having him write down recipes and spells.

After two years in New Orleans, Dexter finally was able to run away. He didn't know where he was going, but he wasn't going back there. He was always moving; he kept moving, for the rest of his life. Every day, he woke up and walked. He used his faith in God to keep him sane, keep him grounded, but he used Voodoo to keep himself protected.

One day, maybe four years after leaving Louisiana, he made it to a small town in Florida: Eatonville. Dexter lived down in Eatonville, Florida for a while where he met a beautiful young woman. He was seventeen years old, she was eighteen. They fell head-over-heels in love almost instantly. Even quicker than he and Charlette fell in love. She was the seventh of nine children. She had two nieces and four nephews, and her mother and father were still alive and well.

Her family was huge. Full of people, full of love, and they

were all willing to take young Dexter in. Their community was prideful and full of support. People looked out for one another and leaned on each other when they needed it. Just like Freedman, it was entirely Black. He heard about Freedman there in Eatonville.

Dexter had been living there for eight months before he died. He lived with his lady love and her family, while working as a carpenter, serving as a protégée for a local expert. Dexter's mentor was a great man who was adored by many people in town. Everyone knew and loved him. Kids looked up to Dex's mentor, men respected him. And what was vital to know about this great man, was that most women wanted to sleep with him—so they did.

One day, Dexter went to visit his teacher after not seeing him for a while. To the boy's surprise, he found the man lying in a pool of blood, dead in his living room. His throat had been slit. The man who killed the mentor was still in the room. "Bastard fucked my wife," he said to Dexter.

Dexter rushed to his mentor's side. His body and blood were still warm. "Get out of here," Dexter said to the man.

"If I go, you gon' tell someone bout dis?" the husband asked.

"Nah man, just leave," Dexter replied.

"I can't have nobody comin' after me man, I got a son, he just a babe," the man sobbed frantically.

"Look, less you want to see things you ain't meant to understand, I 'gest you get from 'round here," Dexter said to the man. He stood up and walked over to the door. He held it open, instructing the husband to leave.

The man lunged at Dexter with his knife but missed. Dexter grabbed the knife, stabbing the man in his spleen. Dex dragged him over to where his mentor was laying. He took chalk from his pocket and began to draw symbols around them. He went through his mentor's belongings and found a bottle of homemade peach wine. He poured the alcohol over both men's bodies.

He stood in the middle of the both of them and repeated words to himself before finally slitting his own wrists. He combined his own blood with theirs. He bled. He died. And his mentor drew a breath of life again. And there, in a pool of the blood of three men, Dexter lay dead.

He was dead for six weeks before waking up in a grave. He went to visit his lady love, but she refused him. Her family shunned him. The entire town of Eatonville rebuked him in the name of the Lord.

So, for six years Dexter walked around the South looking for belonging, looking for mercy, and looking for love. Then, came the day he made it to Georgia. As soon as he crossed over state lines, he felt a pull. He followed that energy until he reached Freedman. Upon arrival, he didn't know that there would be an assignment waiting for him there, but he knew he was being called to the state of a greater purpose. Dexter figured it was God leading him to a place as close to Eatonville, if not better, as possible.

Then, just before he ran into Charlette in the road that day, he heard his name being called. He followed the calling to the middle of the woods and found a woman who reminded him of the maid in New Orleans. "My sister told me to find you," she said to him. "She heard you was dead." Dexter told her that he had been; he told her how he sacrificed his life and that of a stranger's to save a man he admired. He confessed though, that he didn't know how or why he was living again.

"It's cuz my sister got a job fo' you," she said to him. "She heard a story about some gal and her child being sacrificed in exchange for protection. The spirit of dat woman lives in a young gal today, but da spirit don't know dat she's angry. Dat spirit been calling out to people looking fo some help. Go release that spirit, show her dat anger. If you do, my sister will give you life, a real life. Fail her and she'll make sure you never know love, joy, or life again."

This, Dexter said, was why and how River called him to Freedman, Georgia.

CHAPTER 29

Charlette woke up in her mother's home feeling something in her that she had only felt once before. The same spite and disgust she felt when Shelly mocked her, surged through her veins.

She tried to rebuke the spirit of spitefulness, she rejected the spirit of disdain, but that thing held onto her like an infant to its mother. Dexter walked in the room with a smile. "You up now, Charlie," he said. "Dat spirit don awakened in you."

Charlette tried to run out of the room, but her father stepped in the doorway grabbing her. He held her, hugged her, and sobbed into her hair. He praised God and thanked Him for his goodness and favor. Cecilia came around the corner and fell to her knees at the sight of her daughter finally out of bed. She threw her hands up and thanked God for answering prayers.

Charlette's parents praised God and worshiped in their home, touching and covering their child in their rejoicing. Thank God for the power of borrowed prayers. Her parent's praise, her parent's anointing, them touching and agreeing, decreeing and declaring, and speaking over their daughter renewed her soul. Despite her desperation to flee or the rage that burned within her, she couldn't help but cry, joining them in their worship.

When all they had to say had been said, when all the celebrating had been done, Charlette asked her parents if she could stay with them. Dexter came behind her saying that he wanted her to come home.

"Ma, I can't be in that big house tending to myself, and

Dexter has so much work to do. Please, can I stay home with you and daddy?" she begged. Her mother explained that their job as parents had been done. They raised her and prepared her for life as a woman and a wife. Her father said that she could stay until Sunday, but that she couldn't be away from her husband for long.

Dexter agreed, saying that he would come see her every day. Before he left, he went to kiss his wife, but she turned away. He grabbed her softly before yanking her close. He whispered in her ear, "you can ignore her all you want, but she in ya now. Come hell or high water, she gon' find her way out."

Charlette spent the week with her parents trying to tell them all that had happened that summer. She told them about her divinity, about what Dexter had done to Shelly, and how he killed Eddie. She bared her soul to them. They listened in horror, nearly crying as she spoke. They told her to rest. They sent her to her room encouraging her to recover. But later one evening, Pastor Johnson came by, along with Dexter. They performed an exorcism, and for hours, they had her strapped to a chair, throwing water and Blessed oil on her. They shouted prayers at her, they held her, grabbed her, pulled and yanked at her.

This lasted from late in the evening until early the next morning. Charlette was exhausted. They released her to Dexter and sent them home. Dexter couldn't touch her for a while, but he could get in her mind. Every night he'd enter, and every night he'd torment her. He would tell her the story of the young woman and her child. He'd talk to her about the pain the woman felt, not being able to move or scream while Chester Johnson cut through eight layers of flesh and muscle. He'd ask her to remember what it felt like to carry her son's corpse inside her body as she drowned in the river. And every day Charlette woke up, she woke up praying.

For weeks, Charlette stopped leaving home. She didn't go with him when he ministered in the town square. She didn't visit her parents. She didn't go to church. She stayed home and prayed. Finally, her mother came over to speak to her.

"Letty, baby? How are you feeling?" Cecilia asked, sitting a cup of coffee in front of her daughter as she spoke.

"I'm fine," Charlette answered dryly. She had no intentions of opening up to her mother. She had tried time and time again, and each time Cecilia let her down.

"I ain't seen you at church in a while. You ain't even been by tha house either," CeeCee said.

"I've been busy, mama," Charlette replied.

"So busy you can't praise the Lord?"

River rolled her eyes before leaving the table. She walked to the kitchen sink, dropping her head to shake it.

"Dex say you ain't even been by tha New George, is eve—," Charlette interrupted her.

"Mama, I'm alright," she interjected. "I'm just trying to recover. I spent weeks, months almost, sleep. I woke up talking 'bout dead babies and seeing things. I need to rest," she said, hoping to keep her mother's questions at bay. Cecilia shook her head as she sipped her coffee. "Well then," she began. "I guess I don't need to ask you anything else. But I will say that as your mother, it is my place to teach you how to be a good wife." Charlette stopped picking around the kitchen and turned towards her mother.

She rested a balled fist on her side and leaned on the stove for support. She looked at her mother, annoyed, and anticipating what she had to say next. "Now, Dexter been building dis church and promised everyone you would sing in dere every Sunday. I expect to see you in dere when it opens tomorrow, you hear?" Charlette pulled a towel from her apron, turning the other direction to wipe down her countertop, an intentional display of her disregard for Cecilia's advice.

"God done blessed you with this handsome preacher and you don't appreciate it," her mother said as she stood up. She stomped out of the kitchen and into the foyer, lingering before opening the door. "Like everything else we've ever given you in dis world, you takin' that fine man for granted. Better hope he don't let nobody steal em from you," she said angrily through gritted teeth. Cecilia opened the door and slammed it shut behind her. Charlette stood over her stove weary. Exhausted by the weight of just existing in the midst of so much physical and spiritual turmoil.

CHAPTER 30

The next morning, for the first time in months, Charlette decided to visit the river. She woke up before Dexter that day, and left the house early. She looked at the place she once felt the safest and realized that it seemed entirely new to her. There was a new bridge over the water that led to a new path that had been made for people to find the church, and the air even seemed different.

She lifted the hem of her dress, her heart pounding as she teetered on the edge of the bridge. Peering into the murky depths below, she stared at her reflection, but the person who stared back at her was not herself. The woman in the water seemed like a distorted version of her own image, a manifestation of all that she had been through over the summer. But, as she continued to gaze, a flicker of recognition sparked within her. There she was—the young woman Dexter had spoken of—staring back at her with haunting familiarity. Instead of fear, Charlette felt a strange sense of calm wash over her. Questions flooded her mind: Who was this woman? What secrets did she hold? And in that fleeting moment, as quickly as the apparition had appeared, it vanished, leaving Charlette with a newfound clarity. She knew, without a doubt, exactly what she must do next.

With a welcoming smile and warm hugs, Charlette Alexander stood out front of the New Hope Church of God in Christ. She blushed when people mentioned how proud she must be of Dexter. She touched her heart when people said they prayed for her. She put on a performance. "If only Eddie could be here now," she heard someone say. And when the doors closed and everyone had found their seats, Charlette stood at the altar and sang, *"Blessed Assurance, Jesus is mine."*

By the end of the song the entire congregation was on their feet, giving God praise. She filled the room with the presence of the Holy Ghost. She sang with intention, with a devoted sense of purpose. She called upon the Lord, our God, and asked that he made his presence known. Surely, she thought, that if a true believer could anoint the minds and souls of the people in the church, they would not be harmed by Dexter's blasphemy. This went on every week, and every week, Charlette evoked the spirit of our living God.

Charlette prepared herself for warfare. Her husband, for months, had been trying to submit her body and soul to the will of a vengeful spirit. Charlette wasn't going to let go of her salvation that easily. If he wanted her soul, he was going to have to fight for it.

So, she turned their closet into a place of worship—she made it into a war room. She spent her days fulfilling her duties as a wife—cooking, cleaning, obeying Dexter's commands—but she'd spend her free time in their closet praying and planning. If she couldn't leave this evilness, if she couldn't do it with the help of her community, she was going to kill it. With God on her side, Charlette Alexander planned to kill her husband.

For months, Charlette and Dexter engaged in a silent struggle for control over her thoughts. By January, Charlette found herself consumed by a singular activity: prayer. Every waking moment she found herself engaged in active prayer. Whether in the solitude of her room or amidst the hustle and bustle of the life of a First Lady, Charlette sought solace in silent pleas to a higher power. She hadn't realized it, but Dexter had gained a foothold in his battle for dominance, he had won part of their battle. In her relentless pursuit to safeguard her mind, Charlette unwittingly surrendered her body to his will, a give-in made in the desperate hope of preserving her sanity.

"Wear dis dress, it goes wit my suit," he demanded, and without question, she would oblige. "Ion like it when you braid yo hair like that, leave it loose so I can run my fingers through it when I please," and Charlette would only comb it out and part it to the left side, matching his smile. He had her body. His wish was her command. But despite all his efforts, he could not take her soul.

Finally, Dexter stopped focusing on her. He put all his effort into listening to the voice of the woman in his head. *"Dat gal is only part of tha plan,"* he heard the voice say. *"Get into the minds of these people."*

With Charlette fully distracted, Dexter found it effortless to win over the people of Freedman. Most of them already liked him, but they became utterly captivated when he began preaching. The fiftieth anniversary of the First Baptist Church in March 1920, nearly two years after Dexter's arrival, was once one of the biggest celebrations in Freedman. That year, however, the event was sparse. Nearly everyone in town had joined New Hope.

Dexter had become the unofficial mayor of Freedman, Georgia. The townspeople adored him. Charlette, on the other hand, had started to frighten them. Where once people greeted her warmly in the streets, they now turned away. Her prayers, once a source of comfort, now filled them with unease. The jewel of Freedman had become a pariah.

Dexter initially used Charlette to boost his popularity. She would sing in church and pray on command. Reverend Dex rented her spiritual services to the highest bidder. Charlette could no longer distinguish her prayers from Dexter's. She didn't know where her prayers for profit ended and those for protection began. They all blended together, just like her days. She'd wake, walk to the river, walk home, and do it again. People no longer spoke to her; they just let her pass by. Meanwhile, Dexter whispered his convictions into every ear. He had every man, woman, and child eating out of the palm of his hand. He'd tell someone to jump, and they'd ask how high. He had won.

As the first rays of dawn crept through the curtains, Charlette awoke to a world spinning out of control. Gripped by dizziness, she struggled to lift herself from the bed, her head pounding with each movement. Silence hung heavy in the air, her voice stolen by years of unrelenting turmoil. The memory of that fateful night in town clawed at her mind, the haunting echo of a midnight service where she was called upon to intercede for a grieving couple whose son drowned in the New George.

In their eyes, Charlette was tainted by madness. They didn't want a word of prayer from a woman who lost her sanity because of the river. It didn't feel right to accept the prayers of a woman who worshiped God's creation, rather than God, the Creator. They turned to Dexter, dismissing her as a vessel of God's creation, forsaken by the divine himself.

"My wife's a prayer warrior, y'all know dat right," Dexter said to the congregation, more specifically to the hesitant young couple.

"Y'all been knowin her her whole life. Is she not tha same River whose faith turned your mountain sized problems into molehill bothers? Is she not the same River whose voice Blessed your soul every Sunday back at First Baptist? Is she not the same saint who jumped into flood waters, to save the life of her very best friend? Is dat not her?" The congregation fell silent. "Don't cast judgment on a child of God's. For you know not, what spiritual gifts his children possess for the greatness of you, his people."

Charlette stood tall, her arms outstretched. She touched the head of each parent of the child who died, and called upon the spirit of the Lord.

"Father, we come to you as humbly and openly as we can. Our hearts are wide and yielding to your word. Make way for

your presence, God, and let our spirits, bodies, and mind bare witness to the power that is You.

God, I call upon Your holiness into this place. Bare before us your glory. We lift up this mother and this father as they grieve the death of their only child. Their boy, Henry, was their only son, O Lord, to a world that was not ready for his life.

God, You giveth and You taketh, and you leave us here to weep. For it is in those dark moments that our faith is truly tested. In the midst of our darkest hour, is when we are called to show just how faithful we are.

Lord, Bless this mother and this father as they hurt. Bless this mother and this father as they mourn. Their son, their Henry, just three years old, drew his last breath and they do not know how to go on.

And, O God, as they may curse your name and question your goodness during this time of grief, God I ask that you never leave their side. As anger fills their hearts and rage fuels their souls, I ask that you never forsake them. For that is the kind of God You are. You love us even when we are undeserving.

And God, I ask that You let this time, where they are facing the most difficult challenge of their life, be the time that they learn what faith is all about. Let them grow closer to You.

Let them use one another for strength.

Have Your way God,

And let anger be released."

Something shifted in her that night. Those words awoke something in her that she had been trying to hold back. And now here, in her bedroom—as she tried to lift her head—she let spite, anger, and rage win. *She* had been released.

Dexter yanked the quilt off the bed, throwing it in a corner. "Look now, I done worked too hard for dis moment. Now come on, River, the people want to see you, so get up!"

Charlette's head throbbed with intensity, each pulse a reminder of the tumult raging within. Summoning her strength, she rose from the bed and crossed to the vanity, fingers trembling as she gathered her hair. With a determined twist, she fashioned it into a tight bun, seeking Dexter's approval with a shaky voice, she asked if she looked okay.

"Charlie, when we first met you was so pretty, girl," he started.

"So young, so pretty. Hair down ya back, fit in all tha right places. You was a picture." Charlette looked at him longingly, hoping he'd say something nice. "Now you's just thin and old, barren too probably. Gon' on and put on dat white dress we had Bobbie Tolbert make. Gon' on."

Charlette got up and walked into her closet, needing a moment to gather herself. Her head was pounding, and her mind was racing with thoughts. She felt dizzy and lightheaded, struggling with the brightness of the light and the volume of Dexter's voice. After a while, she found the white dress she was looking for and put it on. When she stepped out of the closet, she looked at Dexter as if seeing him for the first time.

He returned her gaze. "Can I help you?" he asked sarcastically, annoyed that his wife was not ready for the day yet. She hurried over and asked him to assist with the buttons on the back of her dress. As she glanced around the room, her eyes locked onto Dexter's reflection in the vanity mirror.

"You think I'm pretty, huh," he said in her ear. "Why don't we show up to the revival late," he asked as he planted a kiss on her neck. "It's been a while since you let me have you, mind, body, and soul." He kissed her between each word. She held her neck to the side and watched him in the mirror as he spoke.

Finally, Dexter's eyes lifted. He jumped from what he saw. He wasn't kissing River. The woman before him was a stranger in his eyes. "It's you," he said as his eyes made their way down to her bleeding abdomen. "You — you da — it's you," he said as he looked at her in astonishment.

A smile stretched across his face. *"Good Job,"* he heard the voice say, *"We'll do it tonight."*

Dexter spoke to the young woman, who had to have only been about sixteen or seventeen years old. She didn't respond with words, but she shook her head in acknowledgement. "You can't look like dat, so find a way to turn back into River—I mean Charlie; Charlette, actually, is her real name. Make yo self look like her."

The girl could do that, but she couldn't change her stomach. Her swollen belly, that bled through her clothes, would not go away. Dexter spent hours trying to figure out how to conceal her baby. How do you get rid of a ghost child in his mother's womb?

Finally, he came up with the idea of dressing her in a white robe and telling everyone that they'd be performing baptisms at the river.

"Here, put dis on," he instructed her. The girl grabbed the robe and dressed in it. "We'll wait until after service is supposed to start, then head dat way—everybody'll be inside tha church, and I'll go get 'em and tell 'em bout da change in plans."

And that's what they did. He snuck the young woman who looked like his wife to the river, unnoticed. She walked into the water, at the south end and kept moving until her stomach was fully covered. He visited the church and brought everyone to the river.

He gave a sermon, he rallied their spirits, and he called them to the water. "I just need one person to be brave enough to get us started," he said. "It only takes one person to be the first person."

To the surprise of everyone, Hop Wilson emerged from the crowd. "My brother," Dexter said. He reached out to Hop and grabbed his hand. He pulled him in closely and gave him a hug.

"This man was the first real friend I made when I showed up to Freedman, years ago," he said to the crowd of people watching. He continued to speak as he helped Hop undress.

"He offered his home to me, he gave me advice, and he helped me find work. I truly believe that without the help of this man, and the love of my wife over there, I would have never made it in Freedman. I'd have just passed by and kept going. But just as God has called him to be baptized today, he called on him to be a blessing unto me."

Hop stood in the water, just in front of Charlette. Dexter beside her, she smiled at both men. Dexter turned to the crowd and asked "Should we baptize this man on today," to which the crowd responded with a thunderous applause. "Charlie, you know what to do."

The young girl, who had made herself appear as River, dunked Hop into the water. She held him there. He started to hit, kick, and swing as she held him.

"Hey dats enough," Henry Stitts yelled from the crowd. "You're killing him, baby," Miss Tolbert shouted. Dexter laughed as Hop's body slowly stopped moving before becoming entirely motionless.

"What the hell is goin' on here," Mr. Brooks asked. Dexter lifted his head and faced the crowd. He began to transform. His skin turned a gray-ish color, with green undertones. His skin started to peel; his flesh started to swell. He laughed and laughed and laughed as people tried to run away in horror.

"You can't escape dis," he said. "Y'all are here now. Sing

yo song for me, Charlie," he instructed.

"Going to lay down my sword and shield,
Down by the riverside,
Down by the riverside,
Down by the riverside,"

Her singing compelled them. It made them mindless, powerless, under her spell. Dexter could only laugh.

"You see, I was sent here to give back to this land. Y'all niggas been living in ignorance too long. My bible believes in an eye for an eye, but my faith believes in taking a hunnid eyes for the cost of one." People all started to form a line at the edge of the river, standing one behind the other.

"Do y'all believe in the power of blood? I do. I know the blood of the innocent can be powerful too. But you niggas ain't the only ones who deserve comfort and safety. Dere's a whole world of Black folk out there being killed, beaten, and abused. Y'all ain't done shit to help em. Dat shit ends today," he said.

"Dat girl back dere, dat ain't yo River. Dat's the spirit of the girl whose baby died so that y'all could live free. Don't dat sound familiar? Yeah dat sound familiar to me. The people were saved by the blood of the son, alright. And his mother died and became a voodoo saint of protection. Y'all been keepin' her hostage, but I'm here to release her to the rest of the world."

The people of Freedman, even those who had never visited the New Hope church, were all lined up now, waiting to face a watery grave. They all were standing, one behind the other, mindless and hypnotized.

"Come on Bobbie," he said to Miss Tolbert. "Won't you come join ol' Hop here in the river. The water's just fine."

Miss Tolbert walked out into the water and the other people followed her. They walked to the center and stood there. River had been singing in the background, looping the words over and over again.

"Gon' now," he said. "Get it over with, Charlie." The young woman who had made herself to look like River turned towards him. She was herself again. Dexter didn't care about her appearance, as long as they finished what they had started.

"Gon' now, gal, kill 'em. You supposed to be doing dat as soon as dey get in tha water."

The young woman stopped singing, but the sound of Charlette's voice continued. From up above, Charlette was levitating towards him. Battling against a surge of conflicting emotions, his anger eclipsed his wonder, driving him to seize control of Charlette's mind.

"Going to meet my dear old father,
Down by the riverside,
Down by the riverside,
Down by the riverside."

Amidst the rippling waters, a chorus of voices rose in unison, enveloping Dexter in an eerie symphony. Hands clasped tightly, the figures formed a circle, their fervent song reverberating with chilling intensity.

"Going to meet my dear old mother,
Down by the riverside,
Down by the riverside,
Down by the riverside."

Dexter's frustration mounted, his attempts to penetrate Charlette's mental fortress were met with stubborn resistance. As his fury intensified, he grappled angrily with her unyielding will, his own resolve waning in the face of her unwavering spirit.

"You don't scare me, Dexter Alexander," she said to him. "You ain't no threat to me." Dexter smirked. He looked down at the girl who had drowned in the river. "What is dis," he asked.

"Y'all two little young gals gon beat me?"

The sky darkened, casting a deep red hue over the tumultuous scene as the waters surged ominously. Deprived of sunlight, the moon's feeble glow offered little solace in the expansive darkness. The young woman began to levitate, reaching out to clasp Charlette's hand in a triumphant embrace.

"You were right Dexter, her spirit is full of rage and anger, but beyond that she was filled with fear and confusion. All that time you spent trying to get me to see her anger, I felt her pain," Charlette began.

"You spent so much time trying to put these vengeful feelings in my head, but Dexter, baby, I can do the same things you do. So, I watched her and I imagined what that moment must have felt like. I thought about what it must have felt like to be in her body. I made it into her mind, and all the time I was praying for my body, my mind was communicating."

"I listened, and I wept, and I loved this woman like she was my sister. And she has a name. It's Polly. Polly Anne, actually, and she don't want to be a symbol of anger and evilness. She wants to be remembered as a martyr for protection, not a weapon for vengeance."

Polly loomed large, her towering figure nearly reaching ten feet, casting a daunting shadow over Dexter's 6'3 frame. Beside her, Charlette matched her formidable stature, the air crackling with their presence. As they stood amidst the water, grounded by the earth beneath and heaven above, the people of Freedman rallied around them, united in song, their voices echoing tales of redemption and rebirth.

Fear gripped Dexter's heart, a primal terror he hadn't known since childhood. Something seized him. Whether the force came from River or Polly, or the both of him, he didn't know, but it rendered him motionless. *Stuck*. Desperately, he struggled against the relentless hold, but his strength was no match for the overpowering grasp.

Faced with the notion of meeting his end, Dexter set his gaze on his wife. His eyes darkened with a mixture of rage and unadulterated fear.

"You think you can just get rid of me? Think you can just kill me and be through? My God sees all. He done seen your evil deeds Charlette Marie. He seen you kill Shelly, he seen you and me in the church dat day," Dexter shouted frantically, unable to hide the sheer panic that he tried to mask with intimidation.

"You's a sinner, Charlie. Some sins is beyond salvation, and I think cummin in a church and killing the innocent is among those things."

Charlette Marie Alexander, formally Montgomery, smiled. She smiled an infectious smile, a glowing smile that radiated from her being into a palpable sense of redemption that hung in the air between them. Dexter didn't know what to make of Charlette's joy but it uneased him. All the false confidence he once had melted away.

Charlette's smile turned into laughter. Triumphant and strong. She shook her head, embarrassed and amused by herself and all she had allowed in the time she'd known Dexter. Where she once felt disgust, she found gratitude. Her memories and Dexter's manipulation tactic filled her with the Spirit.

"Wasn't your daddy a Pastor, Dex? Didn't he tell you 'bout the fountain filled with blood..."

His eyes had been fixed on River the whole time, but suddenly all he heard was a voice in his ear. Dexter's slow, half dead heart skipped a beat.

"...drawn from Immanuel's vein? And sinner's, plunged beneath the flood..."

Dexter could hardly hear River speak over the sound of his loud, preserving heart. His eyes moved frenziedly around the air, looking for the woman he had come to love, and he truly loved her, in his own disturbed way.

His breath was staggered and short, quick and uneven. The hums of the people of Freedman reached his stunned ears. Their melody was unchanged, still crooning about laying down the heaviness and armory they carry in the presence of tranquil water. Dexter didn't want to hear it. He still had burdens to bear, he wasn't ready to drop his sword and shield. He closed his eyes in an attempt to silence the voices of the people around him.

His eyes shot open. Polly was eye-level with him. Terror took hold of his heart just as she did. Locking eyes, they stared at one another. His heart, apathetic and cold, beat slowly in her hands. His half dead body was cold to the touch, a stark contrast from the eliminating heat that shone in a crimson hue from Polly's body.

She drew her hand back quickly, separating his heart from his body. Dexter's face contorted into a desperate expression of anguish.

"You will pay for the lives you have taken and the souls you have corrupted!" Charlette's voice rang out, imbued with both sorrow and righteous anger. "From the man in Eatonville to Eddie, and even Shelly's blood is on your hands. You will pay!"

Polly's eyes blazed with determination as she reached out, wrapping her fingers around the ribs she could grasp. With all her might, she forced them as far apart as she could, ripping his chest open.

In that moment, a surge of divine energy coursed through

her, piercing Dexter's very essence with the truth he had long denied. The dominance and strength he had possessed left him as he shrieked in agony as memories of his past sins flooded his mind, overwhelming him.

Charlette placed a hand on Polly's shoulder, reining in her rage. The two women both breathed in through their noses and exhaled peacefully.

Polly's eyes watered. She felt it all around her: vindication. And though Dexter wasn't Chester Johnson, he represented him--the twisted interpretation of what it meant to be a believer, the delusion of how to obtain protection; they were one in the same in her eyes.

Dexter, suspended in the air, kept alive only by anguish, cried out in pain. In a final act of defiance, Dexter attempted to get a plea with River, begging her to release him. But Charlette held him down under the water. Her voice, filled with compassion and unwavering faith, called out after him.

"You already died once," Charlette said, her voice cutting through the chaos, her words carrying an otherworldly weight. "Go back, and may you be forgiven, finding God's peace this time."

With solemn resolve, she and Polly laid their hands upon him, invoking prayers for his deliverance. Dexter's body bore the marks of their touch, a testament to the battle raging within him, yet his essence radiated with an unearthly glow.

In an instant, Dexter vanished into the depths of the river, his spell broken, and the people of Freedman liberated from his dark influence.

"What the hell just happened," Hop asked as he rose from the water. "And who the hell are you," he asked Polly. She blushed before turning to Charlette, giving her a hug.

"Be Blessed," Charlette said to her. "And rest well, sister."

Polly smiled, shedding a single tear as she looked into Charlette's eyes.

"If I ever need you, I know where to find you. Your legacy of protection will live on." Charlette placed a hand over her heart and over Polly's.

Everyone emerged from the river confused and exhausted.

"I'm sorry Dex had us all jump in the river for nothin'," Charlette said to the disoriented crowd.

"Who," Hop asked.

Charlette looked back and saw that the bridge was gone. She looked ahead and saw that the dirt road at he the other side of the river had vanished.

"Hop, when was the last time you seen Eddie," she asked.

"Hell, Ion think dat boy been back even once since he went up to Atlanta; why you ask?" Hop replied.

Charlette shook her head and said that she was just missing him. Her mother and father emerged from the water, wet and shivering. She wrapped them both in her arms and asked if they could go home.

"I don't see why not, 'specially since we live der," her mother said. Cleo laughed at his wife and daughter and hugged them both. They walked home as a family, joking and teasing one another like they used to.

Charlette's faith had been renewed and Freedman, Georgia was back to what it once was—a small town and safe haven for the folks who lived there; Blessed and protected by the power of faith and sacrifice.

EPILOGUE

The sunrise was beautiful. The colors were breathtakingly vivid that morning. Charlette, who less and less people remembered as "River," leaned in her doorway. One shoulder on the frame, with the rest of her body angled to her right, her legs crossed daintily at the ankles. She sighed. "Not even Solomon in all his glory," was the thought that brought tears to her eyes. Taking in the brisk morning air through her nostrils, she stood up straight.

"How much more will he clothe you," she said silently and somberly to herself.

Charlette turned to walk back into her home when she heard her name being called from the street. "Miss Monty, Miss Monty," she heard the young familiar voice call.

"Miss Monty, my mama told me to come get you quick. It's a man in the sto' say he know you. I ain't neva seen him befo' though," the little boy said. He was a handsome little thing. Smooth, even, Black skin, that looked as if God bathed him in the finest chocolate before sending him down to earth. He had big, round eyes, the kindest you'd ever seen. And his smile was as infectious as his mother's. Shelly had done a wonderful job raising him these last eight years.

No one remembered her ever leaving Freedman, they all just assumed she up and ran because the pressure of tending to her mother proved to be too hard of a job than what she was willing to do, but of course, Charlette knew the truth, even if she only understood part of it. When the rest of the people of Freedman emerged from the water, baptized and confused, Shelly remained dead. Or at least that's what Charlette thought. It wasn't until she received a letter from Shelly the next year did she learn that Shelly had woken up in Galveston, Texas just hours after her death.

"I don't understand it myself," she wrote. *"You killing me was the best thing you could have done for me, River. Death ain't nothing like what Pastor Johnson preaches about. Ain't no fiery furnace, ain't no pearly gates with streets paved in gold either. There's nothin. Just nothin. And the worst part is that you're awake for all of it. Just awake with your own mind and your own thoughts hauntin' you while you float around in darkness."*

"But maybe I wasn't ever really dead because at some point I saw Him. Not His face, we don't get to see that, but I saw a figure, a man I think, taller than a height any of us can imagine, taller than the clouds and air itself. His robe was so white that He may as well have been dressed in clear, bright light. And the air and sky around Him was a shade of blue that I can't even describe. He stretched His hand out to me. Just one of His fingers was bigger and taller than any building they have in New York city. I felt smaller than a ant. I knew He wanted me to grab hold of Him, but He was too big. I was scared. Then I heard Him, not with my ears, but in my heart, tellin me to come near. So, I walked up, and before I could even touch Him, I was awake. I was on a beach in Texas. A man, a lil short man, found me and took me home. We married now, and I love him, River. Take care of my Ma. Write me if anything happens, but I have a feelin' that nothin' will hurt her. Not for a while. I don't know what's happened with you, but when I wrote Eliza about you and Dex, she said she never heard of a Dexter Alexander. Can't say if you remember everything, but I do. Be careful, River gal. If He's real, then so is the devil."

As Charlette walked from the home, she had built next to the house she had grown up in, she thought of Shelly's words. She remembered how overcome she was when she read the letter. As did most things that connected to those years, it brought a swell of tears to the ducts of her eyes. Almost in the same instance that the first tear fell, Shelly's son Marshall, grabbed her hand. "He not scary lookin' or anything, Miss Monty," he said. "He look real smart. He say y'all used to be good friends."

A lot of people had outgrown Freedman, leaving it behind and regarding it as their humble beginning. With the world growing and expanding around them, most of the townsfolk had found new places to get in where they fit in. Langston Hughes had called all of their creatives to Harlem, the threat of the klan pushed others to anywhere else but the South. So, Charlette genuinely wasn't sure who she was waiting for her.

Mr. Jenkins had long passed, and Hop Wilson was still around. Henry Stitts up and left after meeting a woman from Savannah. They moved to North Carolina and birthed twin boys who were as Gullah/Geechee as they come.

It had been nearly ten years since Charlette last saw anyone else who mattered to her. Shelly was the only familiar face from her past that was still around, and even she was gone for six of those ten years. Shelly returned to Freedman when Marshall was just learning to walk, her husband had taken a job in Fort Worth, Texas, and had bought a house in the Como neighborhood. He promised to send for Shelly and their son after he saved enough money for them to make the journey from Galveston, but sadly he died at work before ever being able to bring them there. Shelly and Eliza both returned home that year because their mother had just died the month before. Shelly said she wanted to be home in Freedman rather than be stuck in Texas with folks she didn't know. She wanted Marshall to know his roots. Mr. Brooks had no children to leave the general store to, so he wrote Shelly into his will, leaving it to her, saying she was "the only person in Freedman who ever really gave a damn" about him and his store.

But the small town they had known in their youth had gotten street signs and lampposts. Not everyone had cars, but enough people did that a trip to Savannah only meant about an hour in a motor car to people looking to travel that way, rather than a four-hour walk. She truly had no idea who could have called on her from the Brooks' store, rather than just walking to her home. As Marshall escorted Charlette up the steps and into the store, Charlette found herself struck with disbelief. She couldn't see him yet, but she knew the sound of that laughter anywhere. Her heart sank, her stomach dropped, breath hinged in her throat. "Miss Monty," Marshall called to her in concern. She looked down at the boy and gave him a nervous grin.

Marshall ran through the threshold of the open doors and wrapped his arms around his mother. "I went and got Miss Monty, mama, but she won't come in." Shelly looked up at Charlette nervously, flashing her the same uneasy smile that Charlette had just given her son. Her gaze went from *River* to the man. He stood up from leaning over the counter and straightened his vest. He turned slowly, taking in deep, audible, breaths before looking her way. A smile, a beautiful smile, stretched across his face. Charlette all but fell to her knees.

"It's been a while ain't it, Letty?" Edwin-Hendricks Delroy Johnson, doctor and scholar, had returned to Freedman for the first time in twelve years. River couldn't believe her eyes. The last time she saw him, he was…let's just say she hadn't let herself remember the last time she had seen him in nearly ten years.

"You got old on me," Charlette said weakly through a voice laced with her soon-coming tears. She walked towards her friend with arms outstretched. Eddie didn't hesitate to scoop her up in his arms, engulfing her in a warm embrace. He hadn't realized how much he truly missed her. Shelly covered her mouth, silencing the sob that was caught in her chest, gnawing at her throat to come out.

The soft sound of their breathing and the occasional sniffle could be heard as they held each other, both lost in their own thoughts and emotions. The warmth of their hug was punctuated by the gentle sound of heartbeats in sync. Their quiet sobs and murmured words were the only sounds in the room, a symphony of shared emotions and unspoken apologies. The rustling of their clothes as they held on tighter, never wanting to let go again.

"C'mon Marshall Linn, let's give Miss Montgomery and her friend some privacy," Shelly said as she gently pushed her son into the back office.

Charlette and Eddie stood in a warm embrace, their bodies fitting together like puzzle pieces. Their eyes keenly focused on the details of each other's face. They smiled and laughed at each new laugh line and the skin that stretched into wrinkles around their eyes.

There, in one another's arms, it was like they were thirteen again, and love was still pure. And just like when they were thirteen, her heart ached for the friendship, while his pained for the romance they never got to explore. They were so young when they had to part, so new to life and adulthood. And while twelve years doesn't seem like too much time passed, the gap seems more significant when it starts at eighteen and ends at thirty; the amount of knowledge and experience gained in that time is immeasurable. Although at eighteen, they both were wise and intelligent young people, at thirty they both could appreciate how little either of them knew about life and love back then.

"I shouldn't have left you here, Letty. I should have run off that train and got you," Eddie said to her. His voice dripped with regret and self-pity. Charlette shook her head.

"You did exactly what you were supposed to do, exactly what God wanted you to do. Your time in school, away from here, was the best thing that could have happened to you," she replied honestly. Her eyes full of content and sincerity.

Pastor Johnson told her all the time about Eddie's success and well-being. He offered to take her up to Atlanta with him when Eddie graduated from undergrad; he all but begged her to come with him to his med-school commencement ceremony. But Charlette couldn't bring herself to see him, not after what she had put him through. She knew he, like everyone else, wouldn't remember it, but there was a part of her that figured he'd be like Shelly and could recall it all. It was a risk that she wasn't willing to take.

"I love you Charlette Marie Montgomery. I always have," Eddie said candidly. For some reason, the admission came as a surprise to Charlette. She didn't know what to make of it. Her eyes widened with surprise as she looked at Eddie, her brows furrowed in confusion. She couldn't decipher the expression on his face. His lips were curled into a bittersweet smile, his eyes filled with sincerity and longing.

It was like a sudden gust of wind that blew all of her carefully constructed defenses away, leaving her vulnerable and unsure. She had guarded her heart with such intention since the end of that summer and the year that followed it, yet here he was stirring something new within her. Charlette laid her head on his chest and closed her eyes. Her mind raced as she searched for the next thing to say, though the words "I love you too" fell out before she could decide on anything else to say at the moment. Perhaps this version of Eddie, who had broken free from his father's constant need for validation and instilled sense of entitlement, was an improved version from the one she knew in the past.

"I love you too, Eddie," she said, giving into the feelings she had been trying to ignore for so long.

The couple sat on the porch at the back of the store for what felt to them like hours. They caught up on everything. Eddie told her about his studies and travels, he told her about the women he dated and the friends he made. He told her that he got offered a teaching position at a famous Black school, that he affectionately referred to as "the Mecca."

Charlette told him that life for her was almost identical to her life when he last saw her. She still devoted most of her time to church and studying the Bible. She still prayed for people and made them Blessed oil and Holy water, all for free. "Freely you have received; freely you give," she quoted (Matthew 10:5-8).

After a full evening of filling one another in on what they had missed in each other's lives over the last twelve years, Eddie offered to walk Charlette to her home. "So, you mean to tell me that some man built you a house and fenced in some land just because you went on a few dates with him," Eddie asked.

"That's exactly, what I'm saying," Charlette replied. She never kissed the man, certainly never slept with him, but they dated a few months when Charlette was twenty-two. He proposed to her, and when she said she wasn't ready, he spent the next three years building a house for her, in hopes of winning her affection. But then he met another woman at a toe party in the next county over, and Charlette never heard from him again. The two of them laughed about it as they walked into Shelly's general store.

"I'ma go speak to Shelly real quick, say my goodbyes, then I'll walk you home," Eddie said. He walked around the glass counter and knocked twice on the office door before entering.

As Chalette stepped out of the store, the autumn breeze tousled her hair gently. She was lost in her thoughts, contemplating the mysteries of life, when suddenly she collided with someone. Startled, she looked up and found herself locked in a gaze with the most beautiful man she had ever seen. His eyes held a depth that seemed to transcend time, and a faint smile played on his lips.

"Dexter?" she whispered, the name escaping her lips before she could stop it. The man's smile widened, favored to the left, at the recognition.

"Hey Charlie…"